THE KILLING HOUSE

CLAIRE MCGOWAN

Headline

First published in 2018 by
HEADLINE PUBLISHING GROUP

First published in paperback in 2018 by
HEADLINE PUBLISHING GROUP

1

Cataloguing in Publication Data is available from the British Library

ISBN 978 1 4722 2827 7

Typeset in Sabon by Avon DataSet Ltd, Bidford-on-Avon, Warwickshire

Printed and bound in Great Britain by CPI (UK) Ltd, Croydon, CR0 4YY

HEADLINE PUBLISHING GROUP
An Hachette UK Company
Carmelite House
50 Victoria Embankment
London EC4Y 0DZ

www.headline.co.uk
www.hachette.co.uk

To all my Oxford friends

Margaret

1993

They'd told her, back when she'd first started doing their dirty work, how it was likely to happen. There'd be a knock at the door, hard and demanding, and when you opened it there'd be a bag over your head. That was for two reasons – to stop you seeing them, and to stop them seeing you. So you'd be less human, somehow. Not an ordinary woman in her kitchen, a mother with a daughter due home from school any minute, but a tout, a traitor.

Then you'd feel rough hands on you, pushing you into a car. They wouldn't speak to you. They wouldn't have to: you'd know who they were. And you'd know there was no point in arguing or fighting, because they had no say in what happened to you next. They were just the delivery men.

Then the car would drive for a while, and if you could see the light under the rough sacking you'd be able to tell you were heading to the country, from the low green shade to the darkening air and the sound of cows and birds, and then the car would bump over a rough track and a cattle grid or two and it would stop. You'd be dragged out, in the same rough way, and you'd be marched and sat down on a hard chair and your hands would be tied with rope, and you'd know from the noises and smells you were in some kind of farmhouse, way out in the country, where no one could hear what they did to you next. And that was when they'd take off the bag and then you would really start to panic because you'd know that if they showed you their faces it was all over for you. You'd pray they had a balaclava on. A balaclava meant there was a chance.

So far, it had all gone exactly as they'd told her, except that they'd left the bag on for a long time after she'd been pushed into the chair, while she'd watched their feet in heavy boots move about and listened to their low voices rumble. Snatches of words here and there were all she'd caught. *What – fecking woman – Paddy.* The floor of this place was bare earth, cold and dirty. It made everything echo. For a moment she allowed herself to imagine today had been different. That she hadn't found the word in the dirt on her car two days back – TOUT – and she hadn't stayed in the kitchen writing that note to her daughter, and they hadn't come for her, she'd made it away in time. That Edward had got her away like he'd promised. Or that she could just turn things back to how they were before. Then she'd have been there when Paula came in, standing at the sink asking the usual questions about school, doling out the usual warnings not to eat too many biscuits, not to forget her homework. And later, when PJ trailed back in, stamped with exhaustion from whatever terrible things he'd seen today, she'd maybe have pulled herself together enough to smile and act normal. Her hands might have shaken when she drained the potatoes and she might have switched over from the news to something American with fake recorded laughter, and she might have lain awake beside him until the weary winter dawn crept in, but he wouldn't have noticed a change in her. Because it had been going on for years now.

It had been so small at first. She'd glance at confidential papers she was copying in the law office where she worked, the one where they defended so many Republicans. Maybe make another copy and slide it into her handbag; sure no one would notice, and what harm would it do? Slip the copy to Edward, the names and addresses of suspects, people to keep an eye on. They were bad men, even if they were her own side. Murderers. She told herself these small acts – a name here, a nod there – might lead to a better future, where her daughter could grow up safe. Her husband not get killed on the job. When she lay awake at night she saw wee Aidan's face, at the hospital after they'd shot his father right in front of him. The blankness. Like he'd never be right again. She hadn't wanted that for Paula, her father dead, her childhood gone, but how was this any better? Her mother taken and bundled up in a car with a sack over her head?

She began to tremble, from cold and shock. Thinking of her daughter, who would by now have come home and found the house empty and dark, the curtains open. Who'd have read the note left on the worktop. Called the police maybe, called her father. Maybe they were looking for her already. Maybe they were almost here to save her. Of course, even if they did, everything would change – they'd have to run and hide and change their names and leave the country and she'd have to tell PJ what she'd been up to. All of it. Her arms contracted; she'd gone to touch her stomach automatically, but her hands were tied behind her. She was so vulnerable. These men were used to dragging in young fellas, hard and rangy, not middle-aged mothers taken from their kitchens. Maybe they'd go easy on her. She tried to remember had they ever killed women. A few times. Not many. And surely not one who was—

There were footsteps coming towards her, and a hand on her head, tugging on strands of her hair as the bag came off. She stifled a cry, blinking in the cold light. It was all so stupid. Tied to a chair, of all things. They'd been watching too many gangster films. Someone stood in front of her, blotting out the light from the bare bulb so she couldn't see their face. A man, of course. A big man, tattoos on his hands, a bomber jacket. Smell of tobacco and bubble gum. Paula always wanted to buy it with her pocket money but Margaret wouldn't let her, said it looked vulgar to be chewing like a cow. As if that mattered now.

'Margaret,' the man said. Surprisingly musical. The accent from over the border. 'I hope they didn't hurt you.'

She shook her head, wrong-footed. Maybe this was going to be OK? 'My daughter . . .' She could feel the cold of it around her neck, Paula's cheap little necklace that she'd grabbed off the kitchen counter as they took her. It was all she'd had time for, and for once she was glad her untidy daughter always left everything lying in a trail behind her.

'No one's going to touch your daughter, come on now. We don't hurt weans in this organisation.'

She could have asked did they hurt women but she knew the answer: if they really deserved it, then yes. And she deserved it, no doubt about that.

He pulled up a stool and moved closer, and she could see his face now her eyes had adjusted to the gloom. He was a good-looking man. A full head of black hair, fine soft lips like a woman, sharp blue eyes. Not what she'd expected; a thug maybe, with a broken nose and shaved head.

That was when Margaret realised *she could see his face*, and that meant he wasn't wearing a balaclava, and that meant she was in much, much more trouble than she'd even been afraid of. That meant she probably wasn't going to make it out of this alive.

4

Chapter One

London, 2014

Eight million, five hundred and thirty-nine thousand. That was the number of people in the city she was staring down at from her tenth-floor window, give or take a few thousand. So many people she couldn't even absorb it, the sheer number. Among those millions, what were the chances she could find one in particular? Was her mother here – had she been here in London all along? Not dead for twenty years in an unmarked grave, but alive and walking the same city streets her daughter had crossed a hundred times?

Paula spun her wheely chair away from the distracting view and back to her desk. She was typing unenthusiastically at a document about procedures in missing persons' cases, which was making her both bored and disgruntled. None of these procedures had been followed when her mother went missing from their kitchen on a cold October afternoon in 1993. A report from a neighbour about seeing masked men approach the house hadn't even made it into the file. Basic searches hadn't been done. Her medical records had disappeared. It was days before they'd even dusted the place for prints, and Paula and her father were still living in the house and present at the scene when they'd finally searched it. They'd just given up on her, despite the fact her husband was a police officer. Paula was doing her best not to imagine what might have happened if they'd done things properly, because she knew that was the surest route to crazy, but it was hard.

A knock at the door made her look up. 'Oh, hi.'

'How's the report coming?' said DI Guy Brooking.

She wrinkled her nose. The Missing Persons' unit had official oversight of all the missper cases in the London area. Surely Guy could find her something more interesting to work on. 'It's a bit dry. Have you anything good for me?'

He shook his head. 'Not since those girls got on the plane to Syria. We had to hand it over to Interpol. And the one from this morning turned up at her boyfriend's house.'

The missing girl who'd been logged in earlier that day was fifteen. 'And how old's he?'

Guy winced. 'Thirty-seven. So maybe we can charge him with something there.'

Paula sighed. It was good, of course, when a missing girl was found safe, but she needed something juicier. She'd taken the job with her old boss's new team knowing it would be largely research-based, looking at strategies to prevent teenage girls from being radicalised or groomed, joining gangs, being sucked into abusive relationships. She was sure they were doing important work, but still. A bit of mystery would pep her day right up. She wasn't asking for much. Just something where the girl hadn't had a fight with her parents and run off with an unsuitable older man. Because ninety-eight times out of a hundred, that was what had happened.

Guy came in and perched on her desk, the smell of his citrus aftershave filling the room. His sleeves were rolled up and his skin lightly tanned from the week of warm weather they'd had. You actually got summer in London – sometimes, anyway. Back home in Ireland it was ten degrees and raining, despite being June. Paula still checked the weather every day, even though she officially lived here now.

She moved her chair away a little. It was never safe to be too close to Guy, despite the gallons of water under the bridge between them. His aftershave triggered all sorts of complicated sensations in her, and she couldn't have that. There was too much at stake – her job, her daughter. Aidan. But she wasn't thinking about him. 'How's Maggie settling in?' Guy asked, performing his annoying trick of reading her thoughts. 'It must be strange, moving to London from Ballyterrin.'

'Oh, she's fine. Kids are adaptable, I suppose. And the day care's great – I can pop down and see her in my lunch break.' She did feel bad about taking Maggie away from her grandparents. Paula's father had remarried, and his wife Pat was technically Paula's stepmother, but almost also her mother-in-law. Pat's son, Aidan, who Maggie thought was her father, was currently in prison back in Northern Ireland. Part of Paula knew that by taking Maggie away, she was giving her daughter the chance to forget. She was only three. Maybe she wouldn't even remember those two years when she'd had a father. Not that he was actually her father.

She wasn't thinking about that either. 'How's Tess?' she offered in return, with forced brightness. After a wobbly year or two, Guy and his wife were trying to make another go of it. She was pregnant. A Band-Aid baby, as they called it. Paula was happy for them, of course she was.

'She's fine. You know what it's like, the final stretches. And this heat doesn't help.'

She nodded. She knew more than he realised. She pushed her chair a little further away from him and that distracting waft of lemon. 'Sure.'

Guy got up, his chat and check-in done, time to move on to another staff member who needed a pep talk. He was such a good boss. It was annoying. 'Good. Well, if anything interesting comes in you'll be the first person I call. Promise.'

'Thanks.' She forced a smile. It was good, working with him. The environment was supportive – it always was around Guy – and she could make a difference here, and work on a range of cases that weren't all steeped in the horrors of the Troubles. That didn't remind her every day of her mother. But still. She was *bored*.

Guy went, leaving a cloud of citrus behind him, and Paula wrenched the office window open, letting in the stale summer air of London, the hoots of traffic far below. It was hard to breathe here. The air didn't seem to make it down between the high buildings. Not like at home, the cold pure wind blowing off the wet mountains. On impulse she got her phone from her bag and dialled a number. A man with a slack Belfast accent answered, coughing the words. 'Davey . . . *hem, hem* . . . Corcoran.'

'Davey, hi. Paula here.'

'Oh.' She knew what that 'oh' meant. She'd been badgering him non-stop, ever since the private eye had found out her mother might have fled to London in the nineties. It was a very slim 'might' – the man who'd been her mother's contact in Army Intelligence, and also probably her lover, had moved there in November 1993, just weeks after her mother went missing. Given up his post running informants,

8

retired from sight. Maybe he'd got her mother out too. Maybe she'd been safe in England all this time. 'I've nothing more for you. Sorry, love.'

She bristled at the 'love'. 'What about the house in Hampstead?' The last known address for this 'Edward', if that was even his name, had been there.

'Neighbour said he moved on not long after. Dunno where to.'

The neighbour had also said there was a child. That the man, her mother's possible lover, had lived there with a woman, and a baby. It was all so slight. It barely held up. Paula sighed. 'Thanks, Davey. If you find anything . . .'

'Aye, aye, I'll let you know.' He was staying in a Premier Inn near Heathrow while he did his digging, she knew, and she wondered how much all this would end up costing her. It didn't matter. She had to find out, no matter what. Had to keep moving forward, doing something instead of nothing. Hiring a PI. Moving back to London herself. Destroying the fragile peace her family had found.

She spun in her seat again. What was wrong with her? She had a great job, back in the city she'd loved for years, before a brief secondment to her home town had stretched into three years and an unexpected baby. She was working with Guy, who understood her and inspired her more than any colleague she'd ever had, she was away from Ballyterrin with its sadness and secrets tearing her apart like wet cardboard. She should be happy. Instead she was . . . restless. Maybe it was the blast of summer heat that had swept into the city, pushing groups of office workers out onto the pavements every evening, pints in hand, sweat patches under the arms of their shirts. It was too clammy to sleep in Paula's little flat, and she didn't have many friends left here now, so there she was, stuck in limbo while the rest of the city seemed to open in the heat like an exotic flower.

A ring from the desk phone disturbed her, and she answered in her best work voice. 'Dr Paula Maguire, MP Task Force.'

A familiar voice said, 'Would Dr Maguire have a wee minute for an old colleague?' The Northern Irish accent was a cold breath across the sea, fresh and bracing.

'Helen! Always got time for you. How's everyone in Ballyterrin?'

'Grand, grand. You'll be back for the wedding of the year, I take it?'

'Wouldn't miss it.' Her former colleagues Avril and Gerard were getting married the following week, so a trip back to Ballyterrin was inevitable. She wondered if Guy was going too. He'd had an invite, she knew, but had been non-committal about whether he was actually attending, and she'd been avoiding asking him. She avoided discussion of Ballyterrin with him wherever possible, hoping to pretend that the time they'd worked together there, and its explosive consequences, could simply be forgotten. Turn their backs on it and move forward. Which was stupid. If anyone knew that you couldn't turn your back on the past, it was Paula.

'How'd you like to do a wee consult for us while you're here?'

Paula felt a watch-tick of interest in her stomach. 'What is it?'

'Well, you know how normally in missing persons we've got someone we can't find and we're looking for them, or more accurately, their body?'

'Yeah.' That was the sad truth – any longer than a few hours gone and there was rarely a happy ending to the story.

'Well, this is different. We've got a body and we don't know who it is.'

'You've got a body?'

'Sure do. Two, in fact.'

'Two bodies?' Ballyterrin had seen more murders over the years than you'd expect in such a small town – its troubled history and location on the Irish border made sure of that – but two at once was excessive.

She heard Corry settle down, imagined her perched on the edge of a desk, the sound of the incident room around her. The local accents, the smell of Cup a Soup from the kitchen. For a moment she felt something strange – home-sickness, maybe. Which was weird when she'd run from her home as fast as she could, as soon as she was old enough.

'So there's this old farmhouse way out the Killeany Road,' Corry went on. 'Red Road, they call it. Abandoned since the nineties. You know the place?'

She missed that, the way people gave directions back home. *Out the road, turn left at the big tree, go on till you pass the boulder.* 'Think so.' It was called Red Road because the richness of the soil gave a coppery tinge to the ground.

'Well, it's been sold to some grand-designs eejits and they're digging the whole place up, and what do they turn up but a nasty surprise under the barn floor.'

Paula hitched the phone under her ear. 'Who were the previous owners?'

'Well, that's the thing. The family, they were bollocks-deep in the IRA. One of the brothers is in jail here in Ballyterrin, the other's been on the run for years.'

Suddenly, it hit her, and she understood why Corry was using her special gentle voice. Shit. SHIT. 'Oh. The bodies, are they . . .'

'One's female.'

'Oh.'

'It's not her, Paula. I mean, we don't have the forensics yet – but this girl is much younger. Black hair. OK?'

'OK.' She was glad she was sitting down. Of course it had happened before, several times over the years. An unidentified female body would surface in a bog or drain or yes, the foundations of a house, and Paula and her father would troop up to the morgue and take a look. The first time she'd been thirteen, dragged out of a Maths lesson in her school uniform, and she'd thrown up into a bin right there in the sterile white corridor. 'Is Dad . . . ?'

'We'll inform him, of course. But it's highly unlikely to be her, Paula.'

'I know.' The lift-drop in her stomach told her she'd allowed herself to hope, after promising herself she wouldn't give in to it again. Over here in London, ostensibly for the job, when she knew very well it was for the one in eight million chance of one day passing her mother on the street. Not that they could even be certain she was here. She might have never left Ireland. She might easily be dead and buried beneath the ground of this farmhouse, or some other forgotten patch of soil. 'So what's happening now?'

'We'll speak to the family who used to own it, the Wallaces, if we can track them down. Then search the missper data-bases.'

'So where do I come in?'

'Once the forensics have been done – and it won't be her, I really believe it – I'd like you to work on the case. What do you say? Find a name for a body, rather than a body for a name?'

'I'm working here.'

'I know, but you'll be back for the wedding anyway. I'd just like you to take a look. There's a few strange things about the way they're buried.'

Paula breathed out hard through her nose. It was impossible to say no to DI Helen Corry. 'Um . . .'

'Paula, pet, just save both our time. You know you want a peek. Get an earlier flight and give me a hand for a while. It's the least Brooking can do, since he's after stealing you away from me.'

'OK, OK. I do have some holiday saved up.'

'Brilliant. And Maggie'll love to see her grandparents. I saw Pat the other day in Dunnes. How is she these days?'

'She's not too bad.' The guilt at leaving was always there, even though Pat was not actually Maggie's grandmother, and even though Paula had already left at eighteen and only intended to go back for a few months the last time. There was also Aidan, of course, rotting in his prison cell. He wouldn't let her visit, or contact him, but it still felt like a betrayal to be over the water, far away from him. At least when they were in the same country she felt close to him, somehow. She'd look out her window over the dark town, trying to pick out the lights of the prison where he was. 'I better go,' she said to Corry. 'Work to do here. I'll come, though.'

'How's the work there, something exciting?'

'Um. Sure. Send me the details once you get them.' She was talking as if she already knew it wasn't her mother under that barn – and it wasn't, of course it wasn't – but she felt the anxiety claw at her all the same. Two dead bodies. She imagined it – the digger turning over the cold ground, the noise and churn of it, and suddenly the glimpse of white bone and rotted flesh, the nasty secret the house had been hiding all this time. It would hit the news soon, surely. Grisly mysteries always did. She'd better call her dad. Even if it wasn't her mother – and it wasn't, surely it wasn't – the idea of a long-dead woman was never fun, and it was sure to stir up unwanted memories for him too, squirming with beetles as they were brought reluctantly to light.

'Look, Mummy, a bird!'

'That's right, pet.'

'Look, Mummy, a dog!'

'That's right,' Paula said distractedly. They were heading for the bus stop, Maggie trotting beside her pointing out everything she saw. As she'd spent the first three years of her life in a small Irish town, London was endlessly fascinating to her, even the crammed red buses and the tiny one-and-a-half-bed flat they were renting on the Isle of Dogs. Paula's skin felt coated in dust and sweat. In her head she was turning over the case. She'd have to start prepping Maggie that they were going back home for a visit but not staying. Yes, they'd be seeing Granny and Grandpa and Auntie Saoirse. And hopefully Maggie wouldn't remember or ask about anyone else.

'Look Mummy, Daddy!'

Paula's heart stopped. They were boarding the bus now, struggling on through crowds of people with bags and pushchairs and walking sticks, and Maggie was pointing out the window. The bus was drawing off. She squeezed through to the side and looked out, stupidly, heart pounding. A hipster man slouched at the bus stop, tapping at his phone. Scruffy dark beard, band T-shirt. Not Aidan, of course. Stupid. Aidan was in prison. 'It's not Daddy, pet. Just another man.'

It was the first time Maggie had mentioned Daddy since they'd left Ireland. She'd hoped the child might have forgotten. It was possible, wasn't it, to forget the people you knew when you were two? No matter how much you'd loved them or they'd loved you? And there was Guy, asking so casually after Maggie, unaware that she was, in fact, his daughter. Paula had resolved to tell him so many times, and still hadn't. They worked together so well. He respected her. He was back with his wife and she was pregnant. Paula knew she would not tell him. Not any time soon.

She pulled Maggie onto her knee as the bus juddered off. 'Look, a doggie! See his waggy tail!'

Oh God. Why did she ever think she could get away? Ballyterrin would never leave her. It was cold dark ground pulling her down, crushing her arms and legs, closing up her eyes. She would have to go back.

Chapter Two

Rain. There was a saying in Ballyterrin, that if the cows in the fields were lying down it was about to rain. If they were standing up, it was already raining. Amazing how she'd managed to forget that already, in the heat of a London summer. Paula stood now and lifted her face up to it, that soft Irish rain that misted you all over, soaking you to the skin. Her hands were shoved in the pocket of the North Face jacket she'd hastily bought on the way from the airport. Beside her Helen Corry was turned out in a navy trench coat, slick and tailored, and a minion in uniform and a DayGlo jacket was holding a brolly over her head. They were staring into the dark pit that had once been a barn floor. It had been half-demolished when the builders made the discovery, and the remaining ceiling and walls stood crumbling in the rain, their insides exposed. Some twisted metal bars stuck up from the churned ground; places where animals had been tethered, she imagined.

'So this was it?'

'Aye. The couple's builders were breaking ground when they turned them up. Making an "annexe", whatever that is. Two bodies.' Corry gestured with an elegant hand. 'The man is older – mid-twenties, maybe. They were buried at the same time, we think, based on soil disturbance. He was in a classic execution pose. Arms bound behind him, knees folded, gunshot to the head. Thirty quid in cash shoved in his jeans pocket, no other identifying documents. The clothes, and the cash in the man's pocket – it all suggests they were put down there around the early nineties.'

'And the female . . .' Even though it wasn't her mother the resonance was there, and Paula felt desperately sad for the girl, whoever she was, buried in this heavy earth.

'Pathologist thinks she was somewhere between twelve and eighteen. She'd never had a child or been pregnant. That's how we knew for sure. That it wasn't your mother.'

Margaret Maguire had obviously had a child. And what Corry didn't know was she'd also been pregnant when she'd gone missing. Paula still didn't know what to do with that nugget of information, which she'd been turning over like a stone in her pocket for months now. 'Anything else?'

'Black hair. She was in her nightie, with a sweatshirt on top, socks but no underwear – and a pendant. It's quite distinctive. And she had her arms crossed over her chest, like this.' Corry demonstrated; her minion moved the umbrella, panicked lest a drop would fall on the boss's shiny fair head. 'I've not seen something like that before. The way she was placed.'

'The man. That suggests we're looking at an IRA killing.'

'Most likely. It's how they executed informers. But the girl . . . We don't know. They hardly ever killed women. And they never arranged people like that. It shows . . . I don't know.'

'Respect,' said Paula, who was thinking of Egyptian burials, young princesses laid out with such care. 'Not an execution, then. Her at least.'

'Doesn't look like it. We think she was strangled – the bones in her neck are snapped.'

Paula looked up from the dark pit. The farmhouse stood on the other side of the field; the couple who'd bought the place were halfway through renovating it, with big glass walls and grey slate tiles. She could see the wife in the window, a toddler held in her arms. Poor woman. She could just imagine how she'd feel with Maggie running round near a pit like this, that held such grisly discoveries. 'Reckon they know anything?' She nodded to the house.

'Nah. They only bought the place a few months back. Must have thought they were after getting a lovely bargain. No, it's the Wallace family we need to look at. And if you know anything about that shower, they're not the type who like to be looked at. Not the type at all.'

Later, in the dry of the station, Paula walked in slightly abashed, casting awkward smiles at her former colleagues. Back already. It was even more awkward when DCI Willis Campbell, the head of Serious Crime and never her biggest fan, clocked her. 'Dr Maguire! Over so soon?'

'Just a consult.'

'I thought your specialty was finding the missing. Nobody's missing here.'

Corry shepherded her past. 'We've bodies and no names for them. I thought Dr Maguire's experience would be useful.'

His handsome face twisted. Paula wondered, not for the first time, did he highlight his hair. 'And I suppose we'll be inundated with press. That Commission lot have already been on the phone nosing around. Make sure we get the credit for finding the bodies, OK?'

The Independent Commission for the Location of Victims' Remains had been set up as part of the peace process, to try and find the bodies of long-missing people the IRA had killed and buried back in the darkest days of the Troubles. They had clout. And money. And they weren't without controversy, because if a body was found as a result of information they received, no one could be prosecuted for it. But these bodies had been dug up accidentally, so Paula wasn't sure why they would be involved. And the girl, that was not an IRA killing, unless something had gone very wrong.

'It was the builders found them,' Corry muttered, but Campbell was already gone, striding across the room to upbraid some other unfortunate member of staff. 'Right, so, we need to go through all those missing persons' files you had back at the unit. They're still in storage. See if a man or a girl was reported missing at any point back then.'

Paula was already mentally scanning her memory of out-standing cases, which had been part of their remit in the now-axed Missing Persons' Unit she'd come back to work in three years ago. A young woman in her teens, missing for perhaps twenty years. 'You said the girl was strangled?' She closed the door of Corry's office behind her, noting the new photos pinned to the wall. Corry's teenage children, growing up at what seemed an impossible rate. Life going on.

Corry shoved over a picture. Paula saw the white flash of bone against the rich soil – crime scene pictures. 'Pathologist reckons so. There isn't much left of her, as you can see.'

Strangling was often the method of killing in intimate murders. Family, loved ones. You held them close as you squeezed the life from them. Paula looked at the pictures of the girl's clothes. Sad, skimpy things, partly rotted and clogged with soil. A cheap towelling nightshirt with a cartoon dog on the front, an Adidas sweatshirt with white stripes on the arms, photographed on a shiny steel surface in the morgue. 'What shoes had she on?'

'Shoes?' Corry frowned, leafing through her pictures. 'Don't think we found any of those. She was just in socks.'

'So, she'd not have got far walking without shoes. And the farm is pretty out of the way.'

Corry was nodding along. 'Right, so someone took her out there in a car.'

'Or she lived there to start with. She was in her night-clothes, obviously. Getting ready for bed. Or asleep already. What do we know about the Wallace family?'

'We've a file on them a foot thick. Vocal Republicans. One of the sons, Ciaran Wallace, is serving a life sentence here in town. The other, Paddy Wallace, disappeared some-time in the nineties, never been heard of since. He was the head of an IRA punishment squad back then, fanatical about tracking down informers – any whiff of betrayal and he'd kill you as soon as look at you. A dangerous man.'

'So the body under the barn could be him?'

Corry shook her head. 'We discounted that. Too short – he's a big fella, Paddy Wallace. We think he's on the run – you've been following all the hoo-ha with the on-the-runs?'

'Sort of.' She tried to keep up with the news from home, but had forgotten the chasm of perspective that opened up when you stepped on a plane and crossed the narrow sea, the way so much of local politics took on the character of a storm in a very small teacup. She thought the scandal was something to do with IRA suspects, still on the run for various crimes in the past, being secretly told by the British Government in the late nineties that they would never be tried. A part of the peace process that had been kept under wraps. The scandal over it had caused a major court case to collapse back in February. 'The Wallaces. Was there a sister, or a daughter?' she asked.

'We can't be sure, based on what's in the files. We need to find someone who knew them. Apart from Ciaran, they all seem to be scattered – that's why the farm came up for sale. Old Mrs Wallace is in a nursing home and the place had to go to pay for her care. I suppose it makes sense none of the family wanted to claim it, if they knew what was under the barn.'

'A family tree would be really helpful. I'll ask Dad, he'll probably remember them.' Paula's father had an encyclopaedic knowledge of the criminals he'd pursued as an RUC officer, especially those he'd never been able to nail. Most of them would have seen Catholic PJ as a traitor to his own side, a legitimate target, deserving of a bomb under his car or a bullet in the head. As a child she'd always been scared that he wouldn't come home one day. She'd never thought to worry about her mother, who was always just there in the kitchen when she came in from school. Stupid. If she'd known she would have asked so many questions. Maybe then she wouldn't have been left hanging for twenty years, nothing answered, nothing explained. 'You mentioned a pendant?' she said.

'Oh yes. Here, I have it.' Corry took a plastic bag from her locked drawer and held it up to the light. 'Needs to be logged in to evidence. Look, there's strands of her hair caught in it. Must have hurt.'

Paula's blood stopped. Corry frowned. 'What is it?'

'I . . . Can I see?' She took the bag, her fingers clammy against it, and held it up to the light. A thin chain, cheap and mass-produced, and on the end a silver dolphin leaping through the air. Black hairs caught in the clasp. The kind of thing a teenage girl would wear. Had worn.

Corry was watching her. 'Mean anything to you?'

'Oh – no. It's just, everyone had those in the nineties, didn't they?' She realised she was clenching the wrapped pendant in her fist, and it was digging in. She put it down on Corry's desk, rubbing at the indentations on her palm. 'So if we can find out who this girl is, who they both are – someone must know why they're there. Who put them there.'

Corry nodded. 'Right. Are you fit to work on this? By rights I shouldn't ask you – the possible connection to your mother . . .'

Paula just raised an eyebrow.

Corry sighed. 'Fine, yes, I know, if none of us worked on cases we had a connection to we'd never get a stroke done in this town. And with Wright and Monaghan off choosing wedding chair covers or what have you, I need your help. I was hoping the pendant would be more of a lead, but maybe you're right. I'm sure there were loads like that in the nineties. My Rosie has one like it now, sure.'

'Right.' And Paula, she'd had one too, hadn't she? Exactly like this, a dolphin on a cheap chain. When had she lost it? She couldn't remember. Had she seen hers since 1993, after her mother went? Was it possible this was her actual pendant, something real, a clue, a breadcrumb in the trail she'd been blindly following?

And if by some chance it was . . . did it mean her mother had been at that farm, the place where two dead bodies had just surfaced?

Chapter Three

Tonight she wasn't staying at her old house, the one she'd been born in and which her mother had gone missing from. It had been sold when she left town, so she was at Pat and her father's place. The house Aidan had grown up in. All the same she made a small detour down her old street, the narrow terraced houses and parked cars leaving little room for two vehicles to pass. She loitered outside for a moment. The new people had painted the door and window frames green, and spruced up the untidy gravel at the front of the house, which she and Aidan had let choke with weeds in the two years they'd lived there. She wondered had they sorted the back garden too, the one that had never recovered from the police digging it up in 1993, in a vain search for her mother's body.

A curtain twitched in an upstairs room, Maggie's old room, and before that Paula's. A hand pulling them over, so she caught a glimpse of a child in a bed, cosy in the glow of a lamp. Paula pressed her foot down on the pedal and pulled away.

Pat's house would never feel like home. Something about the washing powder she used, or the smell of lemon cleaning products that permeated the place. Paula and Maggie were sleeping in what had been Aidan's room as a teenager, and even though it had been redecorated in neutral cream and blue stripes, there was a ghost of teenage boy about the place, as if the football posters were still there under the wallpaper, and piles of sweaty football kit lingered in the corners. She'd only been in there once as a teenager, when Pat was out – they weren't supposed to go in each other's rooms, even though they were eighteen and seventeen at the time. Catholic Northern Ireland had different rules.

She ran her hand gently over the new wallpaper, feeling the silkiness. Papering over the past. Maggie was already asleep, splayed out like a starfish in the middle of the bed, small palms turned up. Paula eased her over and climbed in. From downstairs came the sound of her father settling the house down for the night, locking doors, turning off plug sockets, checking windows. Habits learned from many years in the RUC. She wriggled, trying to get comfortable. Being back here was so strange. A guest in her father's house, while he was downstairs with Pat. Stepmother, mother-in-law, who knew what to call her. The only mother she'd known for twenty years.

Restless, Paula kicked back the covers. She'd never sleep like this. It was too hot, and the lights of cars kept moving over her window, and whatever Pat washed the sheets in made her skin itch. After a while she got up and padded downstairs in her pyjamas, noticing a faint blue light from the living room. 'Hiya, Dad.' His bad leg kept him up a lot, and it wasn't unusual for him to be awake till the early hours as well. On the TV some shiny young politician was being interviewed, articulate and moderate, the kind that gave Paula hope for the future. No one she'd heard of, but the surname, Dunne, stuck in her head for some reason. A past case, maybe. Everyone in Ballyterrin was connected, roots beneath the surface.

'There you are,' said PJ observationally. 'The wee one down?'

'Like a light. She doesn't take after me.' Stupid, to say that, and remind him that Maggie's biological father was an English police officer who didn't even know that's what he was. Who thought the little girl's father was Aidan, whose involvement was only to have slept with Paula once.

She sat down, yawning. In the old days, it had been just her and her father in the house, often meeting in the kitchen when insomnia drove them both from bed, and she'd pick his brains about her cases. 'So, I'm working on this Red Road thing.'

'Oh aye. The Provos by the sounds of it. Some daft young fella who got himself mixed up with them, like as not.'

'The farmhouse belonged to the Wallace family. You remember them?'

PJ paused for a second, combing his memory banks. 'Paddy and, what was the younger fella called?'

'Ciaran.'

'Aye, that was it. We never managed to pin anything on them back then, though Paddy Wallace for one was up to his eyes in it. You know what they used to call him? The Ghost. Cos he never left a trace at any of his crime scenes. Not a print, not a hair, and him always nowhere to be found when we wanted to question him. Still haven't caught up to him. He's that good.'

'What about the brother?'

'Aye, well, we lifted him a few times but he walked. Always denied all involvement, but they got him on something all the same in the end.' A grim satisfaction in PJ's voice, and she wondered not for the first time how it must feel as a former policeman, to see the men you knew had done murder walking around free in your home town. Knowing they'd shot or blown up your colleagues. Even those who had gone to prison were out already under the terms of the Good Friday Agreement. The doors opened and murderers set loose.

'Yeah, in 2003.' Ciaran Wallace had been convicted of a murder in London that year, she'd learned, some former Army officer. He'd been brought back to Ballyterrin to serve his time, so they knew where he was, at least.

'It's not one of the Wallace brothers then, your dead fella?'

'We don't think so, no. Someone else.'

'There's a lot of families'll be watching the news with interest,' PJ said. 'Waiting all this time to hear what happened to their son. Hope it brings them some comfort.'

That probably explained why the Commission were calling. They wanted to check if it was anyone from their list of the Disappeared. A trawl through the missing persons' archives, now thankfully digitised, had revealed no promising links. There were missing teenage girls, of course – there always were – but none exactly matching the description of the one in the morgue. None that had not turned up again, as happened in ninety-nine per cent of cases. This girl had been one of the one per cent that stayed stubbornly missing, a sentence with no full stop, a question with no answer. Those were the cases that Paula could not let go. So why had no one reported her gone? 'The girl too. We don't know who she is. Had the Wallaces any sisters?'

'Don't know, pet. If they had we never arrested them.'

She kept looking carefully ahead at the TV, which was showing some kind of late-night news programme. Politicians arguing about on-the-runs or whatever the issue of the week was. 'What did you think when they – when the bodies were dug up? The female?'

A short silence. 'They knew it wasn't her, so they did. Too young, poor wee girl.' Paula's father had given up on finding his wife. She'd known that when he remarried. He'd not have done that if he thought there was the slightest chance Margaret was still alive, and neither would Pat, staunch Catholic that she was. So what happened if Paula found what she was looking for, and her mother *was* still alive? What would that do to PJ and Pat and this life they'd made?

'Daddy . . . did you always think they got her? The Provos?' This was dangerous territory. They didn't talk much about her mother, groping past the high walls they'd put around her disappearance. You had to, just to survive.

He paused. 'I hoped they didn't. But she was . . . well. People said she was up to something. Getting names from her work, passing them on to some Army Intelligence fella.'

'Did you believe it?'

'No. But she was gone. And we never found her, so . . .' He shrugged. Paula understood. Her mother had either been taken by someone or she'd gone of her own accord, leaving them both and never sending back a word to say she was all right. And which was worse?

Paula looked around her at the framed photos on the walls. Pat and PJ's wedding, a pregnant Paula avoiding a stony-faced Aidan, before they'd worked things out between them. Maggie at every age from baby to now. Friends, relatives. PJ had built this, left behind the past and grabbed the happiness in front of him, even if it meant raising eyebrows, which for a stoical Catholic man in his sixties was no mean feat. Why couldn't Paula do the same?

Tell him, her mind urged. *Tell him about the note in the kitchen. Tell him you've got a private detective searching for her in London. Tell him she might have been there, still be there even now.* But how could she shatter all this, this comfortable over-warm house, Maggie's grandparents, their happiness, settled so late in the day? She couldn't. Not when she knew nothing for sure. She stirred herself. 'I'll make us some tea, Daddy. Are there any biscuits?'

Margaret

It started with the sound of a chair scraping over the floor.
He was back. Her breath quickened like a dog's, the fear
coursing through her veins and the sack over her head
already damp with sweat. She hated that. They hadn't even
hurt her yet, so why was she so scared?

'Margaret. Good morning.'

The sack was lifted off, gently this time, and he was
sitting in front of her with his blue eyes and charming smile.
A face you could trust. He reminded her of Edward in a
way, which was a terrible thing to think. Somehow you
wanted to tell him things. And she had told Edward many
things, secret things that could get a lot of people in trouble,
and he'd promised he'd look after her, but she'd been here
for how long – a day? two days? – and he hadn't come for
her. So what did that mean?

'Now, where did we get to?' Pleasant. As if it was an
interview.

'I took the documents.' Edward had told her there was no
point lying. Men like this could spot it a mile off, and anyway
they'd have proof. The best way to save yourself was admit
you'd done wrong and tell them nothing else. You were
insignificant, a tiny cog in the wheel. You didn't know who
you reported to.

'You copied the files of the Republican prisoners your
boss represented.'

'Yes.'

'And why would you do a thing like that, Margaret?'

'I . . . I wanted to stop it. All the dying. I have a wee girl,
she was scared all the time, crying. And my friend John . . .'

'John O'Hara, oh yes. I remember.'

She sucked in breath. They'd shot him, gentle, clever John, murdered him in his office and left him with his blood leaking out over the floor and his son, only seven, hiding under the desk in mute horror. It was the thought of wee Aidan that had spurred her on to do what she did. Imagining that same look on Paula's face. It was years ago now. Had this man been involved? He looked too young, only in his twenties surely. And here she was helpless in front of him.

'So you wanted to stop it. And you thought the best way to do that was to hand over information about your own side – men fighting for our freedom?'

She said nothing. They weren't freedom fighters, they were killers. She and PJ had always been united on that. And he, a Catholic RUC officer, had been a dead man walking since the moment he put the uniform on when he was eighteen. His own family had never spoken to him again. Had she made it worse for him? Please God they'd only go after her.

'Tell me, Margaret – who did you give the documents to? The ones you stole from your work.'

'I don't know.'

'Ah, come on now.'

'I didn't know his name. A man. English.'

'This man?' He flicked a picture up between his fingers, like a magician with a card. She was so shocked to see Edward's photo here in this place, that for a moment she couldn't even hide it. It had been taken without him knowing – he was opening his car boot. They knew what his car looked like. Did they know where to find him? She was cold, suddenly, her skin goose-bumped. 'Edward, aye? That's his name? Your Brit boyfriend. Does your husband know, Margaret?'

Margaret closed her eyes. How stupid she'd been, to

think she could outwit these men. 'Please don't hurt him.'
Her voice sounded dry. It was a long time since they'd given
her any water. The slats of the chair bit into her back and
arms; she knew her skin would start to break soon.

'Who? Your husband or your boyfriend? The peeler or
the Brit spy? You can really pick 'em, Margaret, can't you?'

'Please. My daughter. Please don't hurt her, she's only
thirteen and—' A horrific scene came to her mind, Paula
orphaned at thirteen if they went after PJ too. She'd have to
live with her auntie Philomena and they didn't get on at all.
Her cousin Cassie would drive Paula mad with her make-up
and her ballet lessons. Maybe Pat instead. Pat O'Hara would
look after her family, she knew it, cook for them, mind them.
Thank God for Pat.

She almost laughed. Here she was, a killer sitting opposite,
and she was already making plans for Paula's dinner. As if
there was anything she could do now.

'We won't touch your wee girl, who do you think we are?
But we're fighting a war here, Margaret, and you're handing
over the names of our soldiers. Now, do you think that's
fair? You leaping into bed with the same fella that's spying
on your countrymen, having our men shot dead in the street?
What kind of woman does a thing like that?'

She knew what kind of woman she was. A tout. A slut. A
betrayer, of everyone and everything. Once again she
wondered how on earth she'd ever ended up here. And how
she would ever get out, when everything they were saying
about her was true.

'What do you want?' she said. 'What is it you want from
me?'

He smiled. It was the worst thing Margaret Maguire had
ever seen.

Chapter Four

She could never pinpoint what it was about prison that got to her. The smell, maybe, of bleach and cooped-up men, stale coffee spilled on the cheap plywood tables of the visiting room. The sound, that echoed like a swimming pool, a barely suppressed fury. The way she felt naked, stripped of her phone and cash and make-up compact and headphones and other random contraband. It was in a prison that she'd experienced one of the worst moments of her life – Aidan telling her he wasn't Maggie's father, that he'd known it for two years, after Pat had secretly done a DNA test on the child. That he'd been lying to her all that time, pretending their agreement to not find out still stood. That he wasn't going to fight his arrest for killing Sean Conlon, because it was highly likely he had done it. That it was over between them, despite the fact they'd been about to get married when the police came for him. Her mind still shied away from that. Aidan might have punched and kicked Conlon, the man who'd shot his father right in front of him when he was a child, but someone else had finished the job. Surely they must have. Aidan was no killer. She had to believe that.

Corry was striding ahead into the visitors' room, confident in her trouser suit. Paula skulked behind, scanning the rows of men to see if Aidan was one of them. Her palms felt sweaty. How could she see him now, after all this time? He'd almost been her husband. He'd slept beside her every night for two years. How could they be strangers? Since his trial back in March, which she hadn't come back for – he hadn't wanted her to, and a craven part of her was relieved – Aidan was now part of the general prison population. A convict. Doing eight years for voluntary manslaughter. He'd been lucky, in many ways. He could be out in half that, if he kept his head down. It wasn't so very long for killing a man.

She tried to focus on the job. A dark-haired man slouched at a table. Thin, nervous, forty but looking older. Corry took her seat briskly. 'Mr Wallace, hello.'

His voice was croaky. 'Ciaran.'

'Ciaran, all right. I'm DI Corry and this is Dr Maguire, a forensic psychologist who works with us. You know what this is about?'

He just nodded. He'd been handsome once, maybe, but prison had made him old and grey, his fingers gnarled with too much smoking, the nails dry and cracked. Would Aidan look like this soon? Ciaran Wallace was in for murder, had been in for more than ten years, and wouldn't be out any time soon. Paula tried not to think about the things he'd done. It was easier to focus on the person in front of you, in these situations. She sat down, scraping her chair over the bare floor.

'The farm,' he said.

'That's right. We've found some bodies at your old family house, buried under the barn floor.'

He didn't react as you'd expect to such grisly news. He just tapped the edge of his plastic coffee cup, his nails making a percussive sound. 'Aye, well. Our Paddy used the barn for all sorts back then. Touts, informers. Interrogations, you know.'

Her mother had been a tout. The worst word you could call someone back then. Paula kept her voice calm, professional. 'Can you help us identify them, Ciaran? So their families can maybe find some peace?'

He shrugged. 'Dunno who they are. I never had nothing to do with that side of things, that was our Paddy.' He caught Corry's sceptical look. 'It's true. I never done that murder neither – never shot a gun in my life, even.'

'You didn't do it.'

'No. I'm innocent.' He looked around the room. 'Suppose it hardly matters when I've been in here ten years, but for what it's worth, yeah, I didn't do it.'

Paula could see Corry's small head-shake: they always said they were innocent. 'So it was only your brother who brought people to the farm for interrogation,' Corry said. 'Where is he?'

Another shrug. 'Haven't seen him these years and years. He's hiding out down south somewhere, far as I know.' Paddy Wallace, the Ghost. Infamous even in IRA circles for his violence, his lack of mercy. It was men like him who'd killed Aidan's father, and who may well have taken her mother from the house that day. To interrogate, and maybe afterwards to murder. 'It's probably some informers who had a run-in with him.'

'And the girl?' said Corry impatiently, as if expecting an answer. It was one of her tricks, to ask something as if she already knew what you'd say. 'Who's she, then? She's a bit young to be an informer.'

Ciaran looked blank. 'Girl?'

'We found the body of a young woman laid in with the

man's. We can't be sure of her age, but she was likely under twenty and had dark hair.'

The change that came over Ciaran Wallace was astonishing. His laconic, seen-it-all demeanour had gone and he was trembling. 'Who is it? Who is she?'

'That's what we don't know. She was put there in the early to mid-nineties, we think. Any ideas?'

He was still shaking. 'No. No. I told you, I don't know anything about no bodies.'

Corry said casually, 'Have you sisters, Ciaran, by any chance?'

His hands clenched on the coffee cup. 'The girls never had nothing to do with it.'

Girls. More than one sister then. 'Can you tell us their names and ages?' Paula asked. Taking notes gave her some semblance of control, though her eyes kept darting round the noisy room. Was Aidan there?

Ciaran didn't answer for a long time, as if trying to get himself under control. 'Mairead, she's the second oldest. Aisling was the youngest. Mairead, she'd be . . . Jesus, she'd be in her forties now. Our Paddy was the year above her, then a gap till me, then Aisling. Mammy, she lost some weans in between, I think.'

Corry asked, 'So where are they then, the girls? How come the farm had to go up for sale?'

He cleared his throat. 'I dunno. We're hardly close. Mairead's in England, probably. Ran off soon as she was able, don't blame her. Did the same myself.'

'Where did you go?'

He looked irritated by this question. 'London, all right. Everyone went across the water in those days. I was no different.'

'Can you remember when?'

'Would have been, I dunno, ninety-three or ninety-four. Can't remember.'

Paula made a careful note; 1993 was the year her mother had gone missing.

'The City of London bombing was in ninety-three, wasn't it?' said Corry conversationally. 'One person killed. That was the IRA.'

'I wasn't there then.' Ciaran was scowling. 'I told you, I wasn't involved in all that. It was our Paddy.'

That was the kind of thing they could easily check, so Corry let it go for now.

'And your sister Aisling? What happened to her?'

His face tightened. 'Dunno. We lost touch too.'

'Aisling would be, what, in her late thirties now?'

'She was only a wean. She didn't know nothing. She probably left too. Why'd she want to stay in this bloody town? Nothing for her here.'

Aisling had not been that much older than Paula, then, when Ciaran left. What must it have been like, living in a home that had become a slaughterhouse?

Corry had slid some photos across the table. Not of the bodies, nothing gruesome, but the piles of dirt-stained clothes in plastic bags were sad enough on their own. 'Recognise any of these items?'

He glanced quickly at the pictures then pushed them away. 'I wasn't here, I don't know. Can you not get DNA testing or that?'

'We can if we have names, of course, but we've no idea who this girl might be. If we'd a sample from you we could tell if it was one of your sisters.'

He frowned. 'Me?'

36

'It would really help us out. They might be fine and well, of course. But if you haven't heard from them in years, and now we've found a girl's body at the house, well, don't you want to know? If someone killed your sister?'

He jerked, his hand balling into a fist, and then he stood up, scraping back his chair, and walked off towards the cells without a word. Paula flinched at the sudden movement, but Corry was immovable, calm. 'We'll be in touch about that sample, Ciaran,' she called after him. She turned to Paula, her groomed eyebrows raised. 'He knows something.'

'Not talking, though.'

'No. He doesn't know much, does he, our Ciaran? Not about the murder he's in here for, not about his brother's IRA activities, and not about these dead bodies.' Corry sighed. 'Come on, let's go back and try to track down Mairead Wallace.'

Paula got up. She'd almost forgotten where she was, her brain pulling at the puzzle, trying to get at it from every angle. Ciaran had reacted in such a strange way. Was the dead girl one of the Wallace sisters? And if so, which one? What was Ciaran hiding and why would he refuse to help them?

But that was when she saw him out of the corner of her eye. Aidan. Her almost-husband, across the room, in a queue of men waiting to be processed back into the locked part of the prison. 'Aidan!' She was shouting before she realised. 'Aidan! It's me!'

He turned, reflexively, and she saw his surprise. He'd have thought her far away in London. His face was in shadow under the high window but she could see he looked unhealthy, scrawny and defeated, like the rest of the men in here. Would he speak to her? Last time they'd seen each other he'd told her to leave town, make a life for herself, and try to forget him. Leave him to rot, and accept his punishment. He'd barely even spoken at the trial, she knew. There was little defence to offer – he'd been in the pub that night, he'd fought with Conlon, he'd come home with blood on his T-shirt. There were witnesses, a motive, forensic evidence. His lawyers – with no help from Aidan – had successfully argued for a voluntary manslaughter verdict. No weapon, no premeditation. Loss of control. He'd pleaded guilty, buying himself a lower sentence, and then there was parole. It wasn't so very long, she told herself again. But there was Maggie. Even four years was a long time at that age.

For a moment, she thought he would speak to her. But as she watched, Aidan's face closed up again, and he set his shoulder to her and walked away. Paula was left standing like an idiot, her heart pounding and people looking at her curiously. She felt Corry's hand on her arm. 'Come on. Leave him.'

Outside, back through the metal detectors and the locked doors, the fresh air hit her face and she began to shake. Was it always going to be this way? Were she and Aidan . . . over? She'd always thought of this time as a sad interlude, a terrible misunderstanding that would end some day, and they could pick up where they'd left off, get married maybe, buy another house, look after Maggie. But if he still wouldn't see her – perhaps there was no hope. 'I thought, maybe . . . now there's a verdict, you know. He might come round . . .'

Corry was sympathetic but frank. 'You have to let him be, Maguire. No sense in chasing a man, not ever. Even one that can't get away. He's got a lot to work through. Leave him be.'

But Maggie, she wanted to say. It was one thing to push me away, but how could he leave that little girl he put to bed every night, read her endless stories about princesses and ponies and goblins, tucked her back in when she woke up demanding to know was it morning yet? How could he do that, even if she wasn't his daughter?

Her mouth felt full of unshed tears as she followed Corry shakily to the car park. It was then it occurred to her: if Aidan was in the visiting room, who was visiting him? Not Pat, she was looking after Maggie. Not Saoirse or Dave, they'd have reported back to Paula. A lawyer maybe – he could be considering an appeal. But then she saw the car in the other part of the parking area, the old run-down Volvo, and she saw from a distance who was unlocking its door and getting in. 'Is that . . .'

Corry followed her gaze, squinting. She was too vain to wear glasses while out and about. 'Yeah. Hmm. What's he doing here?'

'Visiting, maybe.'

'Does he know Aidan?'

'Not as far as I know. Just through me.'

'Well. Maybe he's up seeing someone else. Now come on, let's get out of here. I've had enough of prisons for one day.'

As they drove away Paula was thinking: why was Bob Hamilton, her father's former partner in the RUC, her former colleague at the missing persons' unit, visiting the prison? Was he seeing Aidan, and if so, what was going on that she didn't know about?

Chapter Five

'We've found Mairead Wallace in Liverpool. Alive and well, so it's not her in that grave. She's forty-seven now.'

'Already? How did you manage that?' It was later in the day, and Paula was back in the office preparing her initial report on the crime scene. Noting the contrast in the modes of death and burial. One executed, tumbled into the grave. The other strangled, and laid out so carefully with her arms crossed. She'd had to refer back to the crime scene photos and autopsy reports, even though something about seeing bone in soil made her recoil. As Corry had said, there wasn't much left of the bodies to help with identification. She noted the report on the dead man: estimated mid-twenties to mid-thirties, gunshot wound to the head. Arms tied behind him with rope, likely kneeling when killed. In the pocket of his jeans was thirty pounds in cash – no wallet, no ID. The notes dated the death to the early nineties. The coincidence of the date, the nearness to when her mother went, made Paula's neck twitch. They were going through their missing persons' archives trying to find out who the male body might be, but as quite a few young men had died during those last bloody years of the Troubles, it was taking a while. She put her work aside for a moment and listened to Corry.

Corry rolled her eyes. 'How else, bloody Facebook. She's not on it, of course, that would sort of defeat the object of running away. Although it wouldn't be the first time I've seen it. No, it was her daughter. Carly Jones is her name, and a few months ago she put out a call to find her family. One of those stupid viral things.'

'Did it work?' asked Paula, thinking of course of her mother. Facebook had not been imaginable when she'd gone, or even having a computer at home.

Corry gave her a withering look. 'Don't you be even thinking about it. I'd tan my Rosie's hide if she ever did such a thing. It's an open invitation to every creep in the world to make contact.'

'It works, though. A lot of the time.'

'That's the worst thing. Well, it seems the Wallace siblings have something in common, and that's not wanting to be found by each other. Wee Carly only got weirdos contacting her, as I could have told her in advance. But it meant we were able to find her too. Look.' She spun her laptop and Paula was looking at a Facebook entry, the poster a girl in her late teens pouting into the camera, all lips and eyes. I AM LOOKIN FOR THE FAMILY OF MY MUM, HER NAME IS MAIREAD JONES WAS WALLACE, CAME FROM A PLACE CALLED BALLEYTERIN ('She's spelled that wrong. What do they teach them in schools nowadays?'). SHE HAD 1 SISTER AND 2 BROTHRES AND I WANT TO FIND THEM. PLS LIKE AND SHARE SO THIS CAN GO VIRAL AND I CAN FIND MY FAMILY.

Below were dozens of comments, some from other unrelated Wallaces, some from internet sleazebags or well-wishers or bossyboots. Paula hated Facebook. Even if her mother by some chance was alive, and on it, she'd hardly be using the same name. She pushed the thought aside for now. 'So nothing from the rest of the family?'

'Nope. Like I say, the rest of the siblings must want to stay off-grid. But that's two of them we've tracked down. I also found this.'

Corry clicked further onto Carly's page and revealed a scanned photo, of five people standing on the steps of a house. It was the Red Road farmhouse, and Paula felt a chill down her spine. In the picture was an older woman, eyes narrowed at the camera as if she distrusted it. Two young men, round about their twenties, both smiling and strapping, in striped-leg tracksuits. It was the nineties, after all. Paddy and Ciaran. Two girls, one also in her twenties, with shiny dark hair and hoop earrings, ample breasts in a peasant top. 'Mairead,' said Corry. The other girl was a teenager, pretty, in jeans and a sports sweatshirt, the kind of clothes kids wore back then. Shy, dimpled smile. Aisling, this must be. The Wallace family. They were a good-looking bunch. They even looked happy, back then. Paula wondered who'd taken the photo. She peered closer. 'That jumper. Could that be the one our dead girl's wearing?'

'It's very similar, certainly.'

'Everyone had those back then, of course.' Paula's mother had refused to buy her one, thinking them over-priced and ugly.

Corry tapped the screen. 'Aisling Wallace. That's who we need to find. Unless we can find her, I'd lay bets that our dead girl is her. And that someone in her family knows exactly who put her there.'

'So what's the next move?'

'What I said. We'll have to try and track the rest of the family down. But there's another complication we haven't discussed yet. Ah, bollocks.'

'What?' Corry had stopped talking. A man in a blue

jumper and slacks had appeared in the doorway of the interview room, a visitor's pass round his neck. He had glasses and floppy brown hair, and was looking around as if trying to spot someone. 'Who's that?'

Corry hissed, 'They're bloody here already. Well. This is going to throw a massive great spanner in the works and no mistake.'

She pasted on a smile and moved towards him, Paula trotting after her, whispering, 'What's going on? Who is that?' No answer.

'Mr Tozier, is it?' Corry's hand was extended.

'It is. Declan.' He held out his hand to Corry's and they shook, with no warmth.

'DI Helen Corry. Dr Maguire, who's in to consult. I wasn't expecting you so soon.'

'I'm afraid you should have been, DI Corry. Usual procedure would be to inform us right away when such remains are found.'

'We've no evidence so far to suggest these are relevant remains. They were found during building works, as I'm sure you're aware, and there's no proof of paramilitary involvement.'

'We've received some information that suggests otherwise.'

Corry stopped dead. 'Oh.'

'Yes. As you probably know, DI Corry, there's a set protocol to follow and we're already behind. I need to brief you immediately.'

Corry's tone was still pleasant but her eyes were pure steel. 'Now? As in, take me away from the ongoing investigation?'

Paula had no idea what was going on.

'That's what I mean, yes. This is very important. We need

to get a media strategy in place, bring in Victim Support, inform the relevant families before they see anything on the news. It's probably too late for that, though. That's what the media strategy is for and we've missed our window.'

Corry's mouth narrowed. Those were two of her least favourite words, Paula knew. *Media strategy*. And to top it off, here was her least favourite person hurrying towards them, buttoning his expensive suit. 'Hello, hello, DCI Campbell, head of Serious Crime. You must be Declan?'

A hearty handshake. Paula caught Corry's minuscule eye-roll. The new man said, 'I was just saying we need to get DI Corry briefed right away.'

'Of course, of course. We can use my office.' Campbell bustled off with the newcomer, shooting Corry a look that clearly said: *hurry up and follow.*

'Who is that?' said Paula, who'd never seen Willis Campbell move so fast when there wasn't a TV camera in the vicinity.

'The thorn in our sides,' said Corry bleakly. 'That fella there is from the bloody Commission. We can kiss goodbye to any actual progress now, Maguire. Feck it.'

'Maguire. Your man from the Commission wants us all in the meeting room.' DS Gerard Monaghan, Paula's ex-colleague at the missing persons' unit, was leaning over the partition wall by her borrowed desk. She was using it with distaste; it was dusty, and someone else's crisp crumbs were stuck in the computer keys.

Paula looked up from her report. 'Does he? Making himself very much at home, isn't he?' She followed Gerard, letting him open the heavy internal doors as they went through. Gerard was in the gym every morning before work, and prayed each day for a chance to give chase and wrestle a suspect to the ground.

'And how. Corry's gonna blow her top soon. I've got my money on today before lunch.'

'There's money on it?' Paula lowered her voice as they neared the meeting room.

'Oh aye. Up to a hundred quid. Avril's keeping the records in a wee spreadsheet.' He held the door for her and she ducked in. Declan Tozier was standing at the head of the table, lanyard swinging, a PowerPoint ready to go. He was so clearly not police; something in his calm manner, his neat clothes. He knew exactly what he was supposed to be doing, and how it would help people. Paula envied that. There'd been a lot of controversy around the setting up of the Commission – over the very idea that you'd appease terrorists, allow them immunity so they might tell you where they dumped the bodies of their victims – but on the whole it had been a success, with many of the Disappeared already found, bodies returned to their families for burial. Part of the whole process of healing, forgetting, moving on. Though not everyone liked it.

Corry sat beside Tozier with a stiff expression on her face. 'Come on, come on,' she said irritably. 'We don't have all day. Shut the door, Monaghan, were you born in a barn?'

They found seats. There were several people in the room Paula didn't recognise, someone from the CSIs, maybe, and other agencies. Finding IRA victims was a total headache. 'Thanks, everyone.' Tozier had a professional little smile. 'So. As you probably know, the legislation around the ICLVR is a complicated beast.' Paula saw Gerard writing down the acronym on his notepad, mouthing it to himself. *Independent Commission for the Location of Victims'*

Remains. 'The laws were made so information could be given without fear of prosecution – to find the bodies of long-missing victims and give the families some measure of peace. However, this doesn't necessarily mean no one can be prosecuted if we do find something. Do you see?'

Paula didn't. The law seemed a Mobius strip, and she understood why Corry was so cross about it.

'But these remains weren't located from a tip-off,' Corry said, arms folded. 'What does the law say about stumbling over bodies when you're trying to put in a new conservatory?'

'Well, it's a different situation, but we still move cautiously. What we usually do in this situation is open a confidential hotline for information, while also proceeding with normal enquiries. The crime scene needs to be carefully preserved and the media handled with the utmost discretion.'

'So what we'd do anyway, then.' Corry was frosty. Gerard nudged Paula: top-blowing was imminent. 'What about the girl? What if she wasn't an IRA victim – what if there was a murder back then and she was buried in with the man? Do we ignore her, let her killers walk free too?'

'Absolutely not. We just tread carefully.' Tozier clicked his screen on. 'Now, we've received some information that our dead man could be a Fintan McCabe. He isn't included on the list of the official Disappeared, as the IRA never admitted responsibility, but he's been missing since the nineties, which seems to fit the timeline we're looking at.' *We. Our* dead man. Corry wouldn't like that one bit.

'What information is this?' she said, narrowing her eyes. 'Are we getting access to it?'

'Confidential, I'm afraid. We're not allowed to ask for details. This is Fintan.'

He pulled up a picture of a sandy-haired man, probably

in his twenties, in one of those terrible blurry photos that were typical before the advent of megapixel camera phones. 'His mother reported him missing in November 1993. He was a member of the IRA and active in a so-called "punishment squad" based around Ballyterrin. Police seem to have assumed he was killed in some internal feud, but his body was never found. If it's him, that will help tie down a timeline.'

'But the Commission doesn't officially cover him?' Corry interrupted.

'Our remit is the uncovering of any remains pertaining to terrorist activity during the period of the Troubles.'

'But this was the nineties. It was more or less all over by 1993 – most of the Disappeared are from the seventies.'

Paula's stomach lurched again as Corry repeated the year. Was the date just another coincidence, like the pendant that looked exactly the same as one she'd had? These dead bodies had gone in the ground around the same time her mother had disappeared. Her fingers curled on her pen.

'Just a few months away from the ceasefires,' said Tozier, nodding. 'We believe paramilitary behaviour actually changed slightly in the last few months of the Troubles. They were once again more likely to hide the bodies of their victims than leave them out to be found. They wanted to show they were still strong, coming down hard on informers, but while not getting caught or knocking the peace process off course. It was a confusing time.'

That's what she'd always thought, that her mother had been caught up in some end-stage war, quietly disposed of. Had she been there at this farm – was that pendant Paula's? Did she know this dead girl and man? Corry caught Paula's eye over the table. She knew the significance of that year too.

Paula looked down at her pad, where she'd scrawled mean-ingless scribbles, like Maggie would do if left alone with pen and paper (or a wall and an eye pencil, as Paula had once found out).

Gerard said, 'So how do we proceed then, Mr Tozier? Can we try to identify the bodies at least? We've still no idea who the girl is.'

'Certainly, you can proceed with that, Sergeant. Fintan McCabe's family will need to know if it's him. His mother is still alive – we'll contact her right away and try to arrange an ID. But as to prosecuting anyone for his murder . . . that may be a different matter.'

Corry heaved a huge sigh. 'One day, we'll live in a country where if you murder people you go to prison for it. You don't get let out after five years and you don't get immunity.'

Tozier smiled thinly. 'I know it can be hard to accept. But the main thing is for the families—'

She cut him off. 'Yes, the families. If it was my family I'd want to know their killers weren't going to get off with a slap on the wrist. Excuse me, I have work to do.'

As she swept out, Gerard curled his wrist in a mini fist-pump, muttering under his breath. 'Get in. Hundred quid to me, that'll help with the bloody wedding.'

Paula watched her go, knowing that now they had a year, Corry would ask her if her mother had any connection to that place. And that she would lie about the pendant, lie to her friend and colleague, because she didn't know what else to do. And there was no way she was giving this case up.

Chapter Six

Bob Hamilton and his wife Linda had lived in the same drab cul-de-sac for forty years. It wasn't advised, when you were in the RUC. You were supposed to move around frequently, hoping to evade a shot to the head or bomb under your car, but Bob never had. Paula wondered why. Stubbornness, maybe. Even she had sold the house she'd grown up in, finally, after keeping it for so many years in case her mother walked back in one day. Paula had nightmares still about it. *Why did you sell the house? I only went out for a minute. Did you forget me?*

She rang Bob's doorbell, eyeing the arrangement of garden gnomes fishing round a small dry pond. If she'd timed it right Linda would be out. She'd volunteered at a centre for disabled children since the death of their son Ian a few months back. He'd been Paula's age but had severe health problems. It was sad, so unbearably sad. Poor Bob. She'd spent a lot of her life hating him, sure he'd messed up the search for her mother – he'd been the lead investigator – and that it was his fault her father had been injured and left the police. She was positive he'd taken a promotion meant for PJ, his former partner, and she knew for a fact he'd suppressed the report from their neighbour, about seeing men at the house the day Margaret went missing. But she'd found out in recent years that Bob was in fact a mystery to her. For a start, he'd known something about her mother's disappearance. More than he'd ever said, Paula was sure. The cover-up seemed to be to protect her, and hide her mother's secrets. And now there was something else – Bob was maybe visiting Aidan in prison.

He came to the door, shuffling in his slippers. Like an old man. Hard to imagine him and PJ as young officers, in their green RUC uniforms. All that was gone now and Bob and PJ had been swept out too. New brooms. No place for them. 'Paula,' he said, surprised. 'You're back?'

'Yeah. For the wedding, you know. Got a minute?'

'Come on in. Did you bring the wee one?'

'She's at Dad's.' Bob loved seeing Maggie, she knew, and Linda did too – they'd never have a grandchild of their own, after all – but selfishly, she wanted to talk to him without the distraction of her daughter's endless chatter.

Paula declined tea, wanting to get down to it. 'I'm sorry to barge in, Bob. Thing is, I saw you earlier. At the prison. I wondered if you were . . . if it was Aidan you were seeing.'

'Oh.' He sat down carefully on a striped armchair, moving the antimacassar back into place. The sitting room was stifling, kept pin-neat for visitors that never came. 'I visit him the odd time, aye. The young fella.'

That was Aidan, who at thirty-four was hardly that young. Old enough to know better, for sure. 'Why?'

Bob thought about the answer for a long time. 'I knew it was causing you grief, that he wouldn't even try to fight the conviction. I thought maybe I could convince him. I know those fellas. The Republicans. There were plenty would have liked nothing better than to wipe Conlon off the map.' Sean Conlon, the man Aidan had supposedly killed. Just out of jail, he had been a marked man when he died. He'd known too much. Bob thought his death was an old Republican score being settled. It had given Paula hope, to hear that. Just to know there was a chance Aidan hadn't killed a man. That another person might have come along to the dank car park while Conlon was still alive. That someone else finished the job, after Aidan had left and gone staggering home. 'I was first on scene, you know. The night Aidan's da died. 1986.'

'Were you? I didn't know that.'

'I don't think he remembers. But I'll never forget, that wee white face staring out at me from under the desk. His da on the floor, blood all over the place. We thought he was dead too, the wean. But not a mark on him. That was the same night I met her, too.'

'Who?' She was distracted by the image of Aidan as a small child, which never failed to squeeze her heart in a fist.

'Your mother. I met her that night. The RUC Christmas do.'

'Oh. Were you . . .' She didn't know what to ask. For a long time now, she'd been getting the feeling Bob Hamilton was haunted by her mother. She'd thought it was because he'd failed her, bungled the search for her. But maybe it was more than that. 'You were friends?'

'Ah, no now. Not friends. PJ and myself were partners then, that was all. But she came to me for help the year after, when the soldier got shot in her arms – you know about that?'

'Yeah.' Paula would have been seven or so, and she didn't really remember. Her mother had been stopped at a checkpoint, waiting in her car, when a sniper had shot the soldier checking her licence. She'd got out and tried to help him, cradled him as he died. A young private, no more than

51

twenty. The kind of thing that happened all the time in the eighties. But it must have made a terrible impression on her mother, because not long afterwards she'd started stealing information from her job in a solicitor's office and passing it to Army Intelligence. Touting. Betraying. 'What did she want, when she came to you?'

'I think just someone to talk to. Your da, he's – well, you know what he's like. Couldn't leave a thing be. Obsessed with the job. And she was angry, Margaret. Very angry. That someone would shoot a young fella dead in the street like that.'

He'd said *Margaret*, not *your mammy*. As if he forgot, sometimes, who he was talking to. Paula asked cautiously, 'Did you know what she was doing? Passing the information?'

He hesitated, then nodded. 'I had an idea.' And he'd never said. He'd directed the search for her as best he could, turned it away from the truth, thrown suspicion on PJ, even though if she'd been touting, the most likely thing was she'd been taken away to be shot. All to cover up her mother's betrayals. 'I know you must blame me,' said Bob hoarsely. 'But there were reasons. I promise you that. I swore to her I wouldn't tell you.'

'She knew she was going away?'

'I . . .' He swallowed hard.

'Please, Bob. I don't blame you. Not if you promised her. But I need to know. I'm close. I think maybe she got away. Please, tell me what you know.'

He looked at his hands. Dry and chapped from gardening, the nails thick and square. 'She knew she was in danger. They were onto her, the Provos. She thought she might have to run.'

That made sense. She'd left a note, not knowing teenage Paula would carelessly knock it down behind the worktop and not find it for twenty years. 'But why did she not come back? Or send word?'

'Because. She didn't get away. That's what I think, anyway. They came for her before she could run.'

'Oh.' The tick of the clock was very loud. 'She's dead? Is that what you're telling me?'

'I don't know. How could I? None of us does.'

So Bob had stayed quiet, just in case her mother had made it away, wondering all the time was she dead and he'd done the wrong thing keeping her secrets. And now he was visiting Aidan, trying to help him too. 'This thing with Sean Conlon. You have names, for the people who were after him?' Bob was silent. There was more that he knew, she was sure of it. 'You're not going to tell me.'

'Ach, Paula. I can't. It's dangerous. These fellas, they don't mess around, even now. It's being looked into. That's all you need to know. I just thought, maybe if the lad knew there was some hope . . .'

She knew there was no use arguing. Bob, in his quiet way, was implacable. Doing his best to protect her family, as he had for twenty years.

She thought of Bob and Linda in this neat, empty house, taking care of Ian for so many years, following the rules, living quiet lives. What if all this brought danger to their door? Was it worth it to find out the truth? She'd already lost so much. What if when she found it, it was more than she could handle?

On her way out to the car, she saw she had a missed call from Corry and buzzed into the office. She'd left while they were all still working, hoping to chat to Bob before Linda came home. 'Yep?'

'Good news. We've spoken to Mairead Wallace and she's agreed to travel over to try and identify the bodies. Asked a lot of questions about the girl.'

'So . . . she must think it's her sister?'

'Maybe. Couldn't get much from her, though. She says she left home years back, got out as fast as she could, lost touch. I'd say she feels sore guilty about that now.'

Paula knew that feeling. She too had left Ballyterrin as soon as she was able, hiding herself in a big London university, running away from the sadness that threatened to sink her like a leaking boat. 'What about the dead man? Is it definitely this McCabe?'

Corry made a noise of annoyance in her throat. 'Not confirmed. Things would be a hell of a lot easier if we knew who rang in the tip-off. We're up to our eyes in missing IRA members and that Tozier fella's commandeered the place. Kitchen stinks of green tea. Can you get in early tomorrow? Mairead's flying over tonight.'

'I'll be there.' She cast a last look back at Bob's house, shuttered up as if no one lived there, and pulled off, heading for Pat's, thanking some vague sense of God that she had a place to go to, with Maggie, with her dad, with Pat. Grateful for the family she had left.

Margaret

She couldn't tell how long she'd been there now. Three days, maybe? She'd been slipping in and out of consciousness, tied to that chair. They hadn't been cruel, exactly. They'd offered her food, freed her hands while she ate it, taken her to an old toilet in the corner of the barn, no lid or seat on it. It stank but she was glad to have it. The whole place stank, in fact, of boggy soil and septic tanks and the unmistakable smell of the cows that had lived in here until fairly recently. Bits of old straw still littered the cold floor, and she could see the remnants of cattle troughs. She'd had a lot of time to look around her prison, the broken skylight in the roof, the padlocked metal doors. She should be trying to think of how to escape. If she could get the ropes off it wouldn't be that hard. But they were tight, and her legs had gone numb on the first day. She wasn't sure she'd be able to stand now.

On what might have been the third day the food was brought by a girl. She couldn't have been much more than seventeen, pretty and dark, her hair long and straight down the sides of her face. She was wearing those tracksuit bottoms Paula always begged for, the ones with poppers on the side, and a white vest top. Margaret had never understood why the girls nowadays wanted to look like boys, hiding away in sports clothes. Maybe that was the point. To hide. The girl looked surprised as she came into the pale light, saw Margaret there. Likely they didn't bring many women here. 'Oh.' Awkwardly, she held out the plate of spaghetti hoops and toast. 'How do you . . . eh?'

'They usually untie me.' Her voice sounded hoarse and unfamiliar. They'd not been giving her much to drink. When she fell asleep she dreamed of water, of bathrooms and rivers and the vast sea, before waking herself up with a jerk, her mouth dry and neck stiff.

The girl looked unsure, but she did it anyway, setting the plate of food down on the ground so she could undo the tight knots. It chinked against the concrete. Untying her was a struggle and it took a while, Margaret helping, thinking how strange it was, how totally ridiculous that anyone would tie her up, respectable mother and wife that she was. As the girl bent to help, she knew she could have kicked and run. Bashed the girl's head against the ground and gone. Over the fields, away and home to her life, her daughter.

What kind of person was she, to have these thoughts about a young girl? Anyway they'd catch her, hunt her down. She rubbed some feeling back into her arms, waiting for the pain to rush back along with the blood. 'Thank you. What's your name?'

'I'm not meant to talk to you.'

'Can't do any harm now, can it? I'm not going anywhere.'

The girl said nothing, hiding her face with her long dark hair, but her hands were gentle as she helped Margaret hold the plate.

The food smelled good, cheap and unhealthy as it was, the kind of thing she'd only let Paula have now and again for a late tea on a weekend. Her hands were sore and she struggled to pick up the fork, spilling tomato sauce on the jeans and sweatshirt she'd been wearing for days now. She'd been trying to dress for going on the run, as if she knew how to do a thing like that. They stank, no doubt. She stank. 'Do you live here?'

'In the house.' The girl jerked her head, as if Margaret knew the layout of where she was.

'And are you . . .' She took a guess, based on the family

resemblance she'd spotted. 'That's your brother, maybe, who's in charge?'

The girl flinched.

'He is?'

'I'm not— I can't talk to you.'

'Do you know why they have me here? It was a bit of a shock. I was in my kitchen, just getting ready to put the dinner on.' A lie, but a small one. It was what she would have been doing on any other day. 'My wee girl comes in from school about then. You'll have left school yourself, I'm sure.'

The girl nodded reluctantly, and Margaret knew she'd judged the age right. Seventeen, eighteen or thereabouts. A child who'd been told she was now a grown-up. That might be useful. 'I . . . They bring people here to ask questions. Our Paddy and his mates. Oh . . . shite.' She bit her lip, realising she'd said the name, then angrily picked the plate up, her hair swishing.

Margaret had a name, finally. Something to anchor herself on. *Paddy*. The terrifying man was Paddy.

'I see. But I answered their questions, I told them everything. So will they let me go?'

'I dunno. I'll get in trouble if I talk to you.' She sounded unsure, though. She wouldn't have expected a mother to be in this situation. Just sharp, streetwise lads who'd played the wrong hand in a deadly poker game. That might be useful too. Margaret would use everything she could get.

She had eaten all the food now, cramming it in so fast she'd burned her mouth. 'Thank you. I needed that. It feels like days I've been in here. Any idea when I might get out?' As if she'd been kept waiting at the doctor's office.

'I dunno. I dunno anything about it. He's busy today so

he said give you something to eat. I've to go back now.' So Paddy was away. Were there other men outside, guarding the place? Margaret wondered where she was. Were these people her neighbours? Colleagues, schoolmates? That was the trouble with small towns. You couldn't avoid anyone. 'Is your brother nice?'

The girl's eyes shifted, as if someone might be listening. 'Um . . . yeah.'

'Right. He seems nice.' A lie. He seemed like the kind of man who'd smile at you as he snapped your neck. 'Thing is, I'm just someone's mammy, and I'm so worried about my wee girl. Is your mammy here?' What kind of woman would raise a killer? A man who'd tie an innocent person up to a chair in a barn?

But then again, she wasn't innocent, was she? Margaret pushed the thought away. She looked innocent. That was why they chose her in the first place, Edward said. She had to play on that as much as she could.

The girl was putting the ropes back now, fumbling with them. 'Aye, course. She's in the house.' In the house! What mother would let this happen in her own back garden? Maybe she didn't know. Maybe Margaret could speak to her, and woman to woman they'd sort this whole mess out. *Don't be so stupid, Paddy*, she'd tell her son, giving him a clip round the ear. *Whatever are you playing at with this carry-on? Clean that barn out right now*. Maybe they'd even say sorry for keeping her like this. But where was Edward? Why hadn't he come for her, or the police, or anyone? Was this a test, to see what she could cope with on her own? She'd thought she was so smart, laying plans so the police couldn't trace her when she ran, but now it just meant they might not even be looking. Or looking in the wrong place.

'Could you tell her what's going on, maybe? Tell her they've got a woman in here, someone's mum? I'm sure it's never normally women they bring, is it?'

'No, but . . .' The girl's head turned at the sound of voices outside and she jumped, taking the plate and scurrying out. The door was locked behind her. But they'd made contact. Margaret had some hope. Surely she wouldn't die out here, in this cold stinking barn, with a family living just metres away. Surely no decent person would let that happen. The whole idea was absurd.

Chapter Seven

Mairead Wallace, now Jones, had done her best to reinvent herself. A Liverpool accent overlaid the Ballyterrin one like the thick make-up on her face. She wore hoop earrings, pink tracksuit bottoms tucked into Uggs. But otherwise she hadn't changed at all from the girl in the picture, and bore a strong resemblance to her brother Ciaran. The watchful blue eyes and thick black hair, glossy in spite of her forty-seven years, the still watchful face, the impression of much more going on behind it. She was sitting in the Family Room, on the edge of the sofa. The place they took the bereaved and the shocked. Nicer than the interview rooms with their bald lighting and scratched tables. Corry eased in the door. 'Mrs Jones, thank you so much for coming over. You'd an OK flight?'

'Not too bad.' She was sizing them up, Corry in her crisp suit and Paula with her messy plait. No threat there, she'd be deducing, and then Corry would do most of the talking while Paula observed her, noticing the things she tried to hide. That was kind of their MO. Paula realised she'd missed it. It was months since she'd even interviewed anyone, interrogated anything other than a spreadsheet.

'They've told you what's happened?' said Corry.

'They said yis found bodies at the farm.' Flat, straight-forward. It didn't seem like a shock to her.

'That's right. Two bodies. Did you know about them, Mairead?'

'I'd nothing to do with it. But our Paddy and that lot – they used the barn out there. We knew that. After Daddy died he just ran wild.'

'They used it to interrogate suspected informers, is that right?'

'Aye. We paid them no heed. I didn't want no part of it but . . . I knew why they did it.'

Paula understood. Many people in Northern Ireland would have had that mentality. You didn't like what was going on, and you certainly didn't want blood on your own hands, but you didn't exactly disapprove of killing those who'd betrayed your cause, and you weren't about to stick your nose in it and maybe get shot for your troubles. Her mother had been unusual there. Willing to risk her life, and her family's life, to try and end the war. Paula hadn't worked out how she felt about that yet.

'We were hoping you might be able to help us ID them. A young man, in his twenties most likely.' They'd decided not to mention the name Fintan McCabe until it was confirmed, wanting to get Mairead's unbiased response. 'There's also the body of a young girl or woman.'

Her face stayed impassive, but Paula noticed her hands clench into fists. 'You said.'

'We're not sure who she is. We think she was in her teens, dark hair . . .' Corry paused, then said gently, 'Mairead. We know you have a younger sister. Where is she?'

'I . . . I haven't seen any of them in years. We're not in touch.'

'So the place was just abandoned? Did you know your mother had gone into a home? The farm had to be sold to pay for her care.'

Mairead swung her head away. 'I didn't want it anyway. It was only full of bad memories, rotten things. I went as soon as I could. The way our Paddy was . . . I was getting scared.'

'And you never went home, never called or anything?'

She shook her head. 'Mammy said I was dead to her, as soon as I got on that ferry.'

'But now your daughter Carly's been looking for them, your family.'

'Aye. Well, she should have known better. Too late now.' There was bitterness there. Mairead had really not wanted to be found.

'Who's your daughter's father, Mairead?' said Corry easily. 'You were married?'

Mairead bit her lip. 'Just some fella in Liverpool. We took up together for a time, but it didn't work out.'

'How old is Carly?' Paula had caught a glimpse of the daughter in the waiting room, and she looked to be in her late teens, also wearing lots of make-up and jewellery.

'Eh, she's . . . nineteen.' Mairead seemed reluctant to say it. 'Can we leave her out of this, though? She doesn't need to know what happened back then.'

Paula wondered why Mairead had brought her daughter with her, if she wanted to keep her away from the investigation. Perhaps for moral support. Coming back could not have been easy, after all this time. It would have taken courage, for a young woman to leave on the ferry in the nineties, never to see her family again, and start a new life in a strange city. Paula knew a little bit about how that felt, and could only admire Mairead for it.

Corry went on. 'So let me get this straight. You left Ireland in 1993, yes? Sometime after that, the rest of the family scattered too. Your brother Ciaran went to jail ten years ago. He's still there by the way, if you want to see him. Your other brother . . . where's he?'

'God knows. Slippery bastard's probably hiding out somewhere. Our Paddy was always the wild one.'

'And your sister?'

Her face shut down again. 'She was only young. I didn't want to leave her there, with all Paddy's mates around, but Mammy was – well, I had to go. Aisling was seventeen and Ciaran was nineteen. I haven't heard a word from any of them since the day I left.' So it could be Aisling Wallace in that grave. Paula wondered what was going on in Mairead's head. The unspoken question seemed to hover in the air.

'You never tried to find them on Facebook or anything like that?'

'I hate that stuff. Raking up the past. It's not safe. But try telling a wean that nowadays.' The accent had slipped back just a little on the *wean*. Paula always found that too, when she'd been home a while. There was no way around it, she'd warmed to Mairead Wallace. She leaned forward, sympathetically.

'We're sorry to have to ask this, but we have two unidentified bodies in the morgue. The clothes . . . is there any way you could take a look and say if you recognise them? I know it must be hard for you.' Paula had identified bodies herself more than once, knew too well the strange mixture of hope and dread.

'You think the girl is my sister.'

'We don't know. But we have to look at that possibility.'

Mairead visibly pulled herself together. 'Aye, well, I owe her that much, at least. Where are . . . they?'

'Just up at the hospital. We'll take you there now.'

Carly Jones was waiting outside the room when they came out, texting furiously on a phone with a pink cover. She had matching hoop earrings and the same long, shiny dark hair, just like her mother and aunt in that picture. She saw her mother's face and frowned. 'Mam! What's wrong? What did they say to you?' She glowered at Paula and Corry.

Mairead hugged her tight and fierce, whispering something in her ear, and Paula felt it all the way down in her stomach. If she found her mother again – if she was alive – would they embrace like that? Or would they be strangers?

'Take your time. No need to rush.' The morgue attendants were always so respectful, even though to them, this must be an everyday occurrence. Stripping the dead, cleaning them, packing them away; that was simply their job. But for most people, standing on the other side of the glass, looking at a corpse that might be your loved one, was something you'd only have to do once. Except for Paula, who'd done it three times already. If her mother was alive, she wasn't sure she could forgive her for that. Three corpses that she didn't need to see. Three times expecting to see that well-loved face shrivelled and dead, the bones showing through. Three times hoping for answers, finding none, and not being sure if that was even a good thing or not.

Mairead was only looking at the clothes, which was some small blessing, biting her lower lip again. It was dry, the lipstick flaking off. You always got dried-out on planes. 'The jumper, that was our Aisling's, I think. But the rest . . .' The pendant. Socks with pig faces on, threadbare pink nightie from Dunnes. Everything plain, cheap. Nothing at all unusual or unique.

'Yes?' prompted Corry gently.

'I don't think Aisling would have worn stuff like that. She had sort of plain tastes, you know. Tomboyish.' She kept staring, puzzled. 'What's that necklace thing?'

Corry tapped on the glass and pointed, and the gloved and masked attendant lifted the item closer. 'It's a dolphin pendant. You don't recognise it?'

Paula kept her head down, heart thudding, asking herself again: could it be her own? If so, how did it end up round the neck of a dead girl? Much more likely it was just one like it.

'No. But I was gone a few months or so by that point . . . she could have bought it.' Mairead's fingers curled on the glass, leaving finger-marks. 'How old did you say she was, this girl?'

'We can't be sure. Early to mid-teens, most likely.'

For a long moment she just looked. 'I don't know. I'm sorry. I don't know if it's her or not.' Her voice thickened. Corry nodded to the attendant, who wheeled the tray away. Mairead had already looked at the man's clothes and come up blank. Paula believed her – she hadn't known those bodies were down there.

'That's OK, Mairead. We do appreciate you looking.'

'What'll happen now? To . . . whoever she is. The girl.'

'We'll go back to the missing persons' databases, see if anyone contacts us now it's been on the news. Someone must know who she is, after all. Will you be staying in town for a few days?'

'I . . . I don't know. I haven't been back in years.' She cast a look towards the waiting room, to where her daughter was. 'Carly wants to see where I'm from. The farm, even.'

'That's a crime scene now, I'm afraid, but you're welcome to go and look from the edges. It would be good if you could stay in town. We can arrange accommodation if needed.'

Mairead nodded, her face a strange mixture of fear and openness. She said again, 'I just haven't been back in so long, you see.'

Paula knew what she meant. If she could have, she would have warned her to be careful. However far you ran, and however long for, Ballyterrin had a way of sucking you back in.

Chapter Eight

'Yes, Mammy. I spoke to the woman about the flowers. I told her Auntie Samantha's allergic to lilies. Yes, Mammy. YES.'

Across the desk, Avril was rolling her eyes and miming strangling her mother on the phone. Paula smiled sympathetically. She'd had no mother breathing down her neck when her wedding was imminent, only her best friend Saoirse nagging her to get on and organise things. It still hurt to think of the dress, the crumpled ivory silk, in the back of the wardrobe. All of it such a stupid waste and humiliation.

She was back at her desk now, having dispatched Mairead and a hostile Carly with a Family Liaison Officer to the secure flat they'd be using. There was not the same urgency there'd be for a high-priority missing person, and that made Paula sad in a way. This dead girl, whoever she was, had been killed and buried and no one was even looking for her.

To flesh out her report, Paula had been researching Mairead's brother, Paddy. The Ghost. What she'd found made her blink at her screen. The couple shot in their home, killed in front of their three small children, bullets landing in the baby's cot. The victims of his 'interrogations', dumped with their fingernails pulled out, cigarette burns, brands all over their skin. The tapes made of 'confessions', dying screams sent to family members. Grim reading.

'Dear God,' Avril exhaled, hanging up the phone. She'd come a long way from the prim girl who'd started as a civilian analyst in the now defunct MPRU. Back then, when she'd never had a drink in her life and wouldn't have dreamed of taking the Lord's name in vain, she was engaged to an insipid youth pastor called Alan. Now she was a DC, she was marrying Gerard Monaghan despite his dodgy Republican family, and Paula counted her as a friend.

'Mammy giving you grief?'

'It's going to be the end of me. I swear, there was less negotiation about the Good Friday Agreement than there is about this ecumenical wedding service.'

Paula grimaced in solidarity. This was a long-running saga. Gerard's priest cousin, Father Eamonn, was to celebrate the wedding, but in Avril's father's church, and many concessions had to be made so that the Reverend John Wright could be happy with such Popish ways. Avril was also Bob Hamilton's niece on her mother's side, so he'd be there. And of course Guy Brooking had been invited too. If he brought his pregnant wife along Paula was planning to get very drunk. 'It'll be OK. Afterwards everyone will just say how lovely it was.'

Avril's face darkened. 'Paula, I'm an eejit, moaning away here to you when you're . . .'

She shrugged. If she didn't let anyone see how much it hurt, her own aborted wedding, she could manage. Rewrite history. If she never thought about it, it never happened. She'd never agreed to get engaged and she'd never put on a stupid white dress or pinned flowers into her hair or seen Aidan dragged away as she waited in the church porch. It was hard to keep this up, however. For one thing, Maggie still sometimes slept with the headband she'd been bought to

68

wear as flower girl, now mangled, its silk blossoms wilted.
'It's fine, honestly. It's not like no one else is allowed to get
married now, is it? Did Mairead and Carly settle into the
flat?'

'We've got someone down there. Keeping a wee eye on
them, like. Mairead made three phone calls from the
payphone in the lobby as soon as the FLO left. Not from
her mobile.'

So, she was trying to cover it up maybe. Paula gathered
that Mairead was not supposed to know someone was
keeping a wee eye on her. 'Any idea who the calls were to?'

'Nah, she one-four-one'd them, but our guy said she
was crying afterwards. Then she went and sat outside the
building for a while, smoking. I checked and the prison
Ciaran Wallace is in got a phone call last night about the
same time.'

Mairead was trying to contact her brother. Interesting.

'Oh, and our guy says he also saw her punching in the
code for the South.'

The South, where her other brother Paddy was rumoured
to be hiding. 'I see. And on that note – I've been away, can
you explain to me the whole thing with the on-the-runs?'

Avril still had data at her fingertips, as in her old job, but
she was also tough now. The previous year she'd been
attacked while undercover, drugged and almost assaulted,
and Paula thought again how fond she'd become of the
younger woman. She had no friends like that in London.
Just nodding acquaintances, people to drink with after work,
old university friends she kept saying she had to meet up
with but never quite managed to. They'd all moved to South
London now and bought houses, which they were slowly
filling with retro furniture and babies. Avril said, 'They're

terrorists hiding out from police, usually in the South. They got secret letters during the Good Friday Agreement to say they wouldn't be prosecuted, but now it's come out, people are saying the scheme wasn't legal. So it's all a bit up in the air.'

'And Paddy Wallace, the brother, he was one of them?'

'He was certainly wanted. A list of murders as long as my arm.' Avril's mouth compressed. Paula knew she had strong views on the 'let's forget all that nastiness' spirit which had prevailed in Northern Ireland for the last twenty years. As did Aidan. It was one of the reasons she'd not been surprised to hear he'd beaten up Sean Conlon, the man who'd shot his father. Horrified and sickened, yes, but not entirely surprised. 'He disappeared in the nineties, and I think we thought he was dead, to be honest.'

Three out of four Wallaces gone away, two still missing. How could a whole family vanish into the air? It was highly out of character for an Irish person to leave their village, their homestead, and fall out of touch with their family. It just didn't happen. It was a country where, if you didn't take care, you'd put down roots as soon as you stopped moving.

'And old Mrs Wallace, the mother? We'll have to visit her, I take it?'

'Yeah, but we might not get much from her. The farm came up for sale because she went into a nursing home a few years back, and her fees weren't getting paid. The staff there said she's never had a visitor in all that time.'

Paula found that shocking. To have four children and still rot alone in a home. 'Not a one of them visited? Not Paddy, if he's at large?'

'No. Might have been worried we have the place under

surveillance or something. Someone'll go out to her this afternoon, if there's time.' Avril nodded to her partition, over which Gerard Monaghan had stuck his excessively gelled head. 'Mammy's on the warpath again,' she told him darkly.

Paula smiled at Gerard. 'Well, there's the groom. How's it going your end?'

He rolled his eyes in an exact copy of Avril's expression. 'This better work out, Maguire, because I'd rather wax my balls than do it again. If you have the number for Senator George Mitchell maybe you could send it our way?'

'That bad?'

'My mammy won't stop crying every time we talk about the ceremony. It won't be in God's eyes! You won't be properly married if it's not in a Catholic church! Auntie Siobhan was going to sing Ave Maria and now she can't! What is it about weddings that send people crazy?'

'Dunno. Family. Emotion. All mixed up in a big expensive pot. Did you want me?'

'Just to say Fintan McCabe's mammy's down at the morgue. Should have an ID soon, if it's him.'

'Poor woman,' murmured Avril. 'Must be awful, whatever her son did.'

'You live by the gun, you die by the gun,' said Gerard. 'Anyway, he's not the only murder I have on my desk. Another scumbag just got shot last night, so I'll be working late again.'

'Drugs?' said Avril, with world-weary distaste.

'Like as not. Still, you know what that means? Overtime pay.' He made a gesture like someone firing two pistols, and loped off back to his own desk, making the partition wall shake behind him. Paula smiled after him, until the thought of the morgue made her frown again. Looking through glass, not knowing if you wanted to see the person you'd lost there or not. Something she might find herself doing again, if her mother's body turned up at last.

Chapter Nine

'Ooof! Take it easy, pet!' Maggie had flung herself at Paula with full speed when she went to pick her up from 'Auntie Saoirse's' house after work. Strange to think of her little baby as a sturdy child, one who could almost knock her mother off her feet.

'Mummy, Mummy, Auntie Saoirse has my Little Pony Canterlot Castle, come and see, come and see!' The pink turreted monstrosity, a present from Saoirse and her husband Dave, had stayed behind in Ireland in the move. It was far too big to bring over to London and Paula had concocted an elaborate lie about how it had to stay here so Maggie could always come back and visit.

'OK, pet, in a minute. I need to say hi to Auntie Saoirse first.' Paula's best friend from school, a doctor in Ballyterrin Hospital's A&E, wore a loose white top and glasses. Paula hugged her briefly. It still felt stupid. She and Saoirse had been joined at the hip from ages five to eighteen, and back then they wouldn't have dreamed of hugging or kissing cheeks or anything like that. Why would they, when they saw each other every day? 'You're looking well.'

'Thanks! You too. The big city must agree with you?'

'Oh, I don't know. It isn't home.' It was a sore subject, the way Paula had fled when she was eighteen, dragged reluctantly back home three years ago. She hadn't even gone to Saoirse's wedding, unable to face a trip to Ballyterrin. 'Thanks for minding her. Pat isn't up to a full day any more, I don't think.'

'I saw her down the town the other day. She's not too bad, a bit failed, maybe.'

'I know.' Another sore subject. She'd abandoned her father and stepmother right after Pat's heart failed during chemo treatment. Taken away their adored only grandchild, fled to London for a new job. Trying to save herself, once again, by running as fast as she could from the past. 'The place looks great. Puts me to shame.' Saoirse's house was always so neat, even after a day of Hurricane Maggie. Candles on side tables, framed pictures, tasteful cushions on the grey hessian sofa. She was good at life, unlike Paula. 'Dave at work?'

'Aye. Wait a second. I wanted to show you something.' Saoirse had a secretive, pleased look on her face, and Paula's heart lurched. It couldn't be. Could it? Saoirse produced her phone from her pocket. 'Look.'

Paula squinted at the picture. 'Is that . . . What is it?'

Saoirse beamed. 'Lines, Maguire. Two massive fat ones. On a pregnancy test.'

'Oh my God!'

'I know!' Suddenly Saoirse had tears in her eyes. 'Six bloody years I've been waiting to see those lines.'

'I know! Wow! God, it's amazing. How long?'

'Not long. Four weeks maybe.' She slipped a protective hand over her stomach. Paula remembered that – except when it happened to her she couldn't tell anyone for ages, since she didn't know who the father was. She hadn't even been sure she was going to keep Maggie to start with – no father, not the right time, etc. – which was something she tried not to think about on sleepless nights, the child asleep in the next room. But God, if anyone deserved it Saoirse did. The latest round of IVF must have worked, finally.

'That's brilliant, Glocko. I'm so happy for you.'

'Early days. I don't want everyone to know.'

'Maggie will be delighted. She's obsessed with babies at the minute. I keep getting her these gender-neutral toys and all she wants is baby dolls with frilly pink dresses.' She gave her friend another quick, hard hug. 'I'm thrilled for you.'

Saoirse's face turned sombre. 'If it holds. Christ, I'm terrified.'

'Pat would tell you to say a novena. Does she know?'

'Well, yeah. I thought she'd be a good person to tell, you know?' Paula understood that. Her stepmother was kindness itself, and adored babies. She'd lost so many of her own, only her precious Aidan making it to birth, and now he was sitting in prison, his sentence stretching ahead of him. If her own pain was bad, what must Pat's be? Saoirse put the phone away, snapping the screen off decisively. 'Anyway. Let's not talk about it any more. It's bad luck. What is it has you back in town this time? The wedding?'

'That and the Red Road case.'

'No missing people there, though?' Saoirse frowned.

'Other way round. We've got bodies and no names. And worse, the Commission are involved. Corry's raging.'

'Poor people. Imagine being dead and no one knowing where you were.' But despite Saoirse's sombre words, there was a rare lightness to Paula's friend, who spent most of her time, as she put it, up to her elbows in blood and guts. A giddiness that made Paula's heart both glad for her and sad for herself, in a small selfish way. Could she ever feel that way again, after everything that had happened? She'd been right not to tell her friend what she'd learned about her mother. It was too much of a burden to place on anyone.

'Tell Dave congrats from me. Maggie, come on, pet, we need to get home for tea.'

Saoirse watched the child fondly. 'Any time you need her minded, just shout. It's good practice! We can even feed her here. Dave loves potato waffles and beans. He's like a big wean himself. Otherwise, see you at the wedding?'

'Avril and Gerard's? Oh, yeah, see you there.' She hadn't even realised Saoirse was going. They only knew each other through Paula, surely. She forgot, sometimes, how small Ballyterrin was.

Paula bundled Maggie out under extreme protest and bribing promises about coming back tomorrow, thinking how happy Saoirse looked. Please God it would last. Not that she even believed in God, but something about being in Ireland meant she found herself praying all the same, in a vague, scared way. Today had made her ache with home-sickness, somehow, after the months she'd spent in London, anonymous. Everyone in Ballyterrin was tied together like the trees in a forest, an unbreakable tangle. She'd run away from that once before, from being 'that wee Maguire girl', the one whose mother was a tout. Could it be that she'd actually missed it?

'Mummy, can we have a new baby too?'

'What?' Startled, she peered back at Maggie in the car mirror.

'Like Auntie Saoirse's baby you were talking about. Can we have one too?'

'You weren't supposed to be listening in, Miss Big Ears. Now come on. Back home for tea.'

Another baby, she thought, pulling away from the kerb.

How and when would a thing like that even happen? Her life seemed to have frozen the day Aidan was arrested, and yet now it was a year later, and Maggie would be at school soon, and life was moving on whether she liked it or not.

On her way home she drove past the block of flats they'd put Mairead and Carly in, and Paula wondered about the strange mysteries this case was throwing up. Where the remaining Wallace siblings had got to. Why both brother and sister had at first appeared unsurprised by the discovery of bodies, but been upset all the same when told one was female. As she took her child home to bed in a house where she'd be safe, and loved, and cosseted, Paula made a silent promise to the dead girl, unnamed and forgotten in the ground, that she would do her best to find out what had happened. Not that it would make any difference to her now.

Margaret

What she hated most, apart from the cold and the smell and the welts in her arms and back from sitting, was the way she'd become like a lab rat. Whenever the door rattled up, she tensed. Fear flooding her. What would it be today? Yesterday – or another day, maybe, she was losing track – he'd held a lighter to her face. The heat singeing her nose, making her struggle backwards, panicking while he laughed, dancing the flame around her. 'Same colour as your hair,' he'd said, fondling it. Her red hair that was now so dirty and matted it looked brown.

Today, it was one of the other men. Sean, she thought he was called. He was carrying a bucket of water and he set it down beside her. Caught her eye quickly with a guilty look. As if to say *I'm sorry*. Then there was the sound of whistling and Paddy strolled in, slamming the door down behind him. 'Margaret. Good morning.'

Sean stood aside, fixing his eyes to the floor, as if he wanted to pretend he wasn't part of this. An innocent bystander.

She looked at the water. A red shiny bucket, like the kind PJ used to wash the car. Water sloshing in it. Were they going to help her wash? She was very dirty, after all. She looked up at Paddy, to see the smile curving his lips. He knew what she was thinking. It wasn't for washing.

Suddenly, he'd seized her by the hair and forced her face down into it. She hadn't time to take a breath. She clamped her mouth shut but it was filling up her nose already, burning, freezing. She struggled under his hand. He wouldn't. He wouldn't. Just a warning just to scare her just to – Christ! She was drowning! Margaret's eyes opened in panic, filled

78

with fractured light. Water in her nose, her eyes, her mouth. One clear thought in her panicked mind.

I'm going to die.

Then she was out, gasping in the air of the dank barn. She was crying, spitting out water, snottering down her face. Her hands not even free to wipe it. 'Please . . . please . . . why are you doing this?'

'You know why, Margaret. You've betrayed us, and you won't tell me anything. You leave me no choice.'

'I've a family . . . a family . . .' Her voice was drowned in tears. A storm of coughing.

'You should have thought of your family when you were opening your legs for that Brit bastard.' He leaned towards her, reached out his hand to grab her hair again. She screamed. He sat back, as if satisfied. 'Now we're getting somewhere. You don't want the bucket again?'

'Please, no. No. I'll talk.'

'You'll tell us what you know about lover boy. Who else he's using as his wee spies. I want names, Margaret.'

'Yes. I'll talk. I'll talk!' She didn't know any names. Her mind was trying to work, think of something she could tell them that sounded true. But inside her head she was screaming, in terror and panic. It was all she could think about. *Not the bucket again. Please, not the bucket.* And under that was another thought, a lurking shameful one she didn't want to look at. If Edward had not come for her, had given her up, why should she not give him up too?

Chapter Ten

'Thanks for coming in again, Mairead.' Corry's soothing tone was back, her irritation with Tozier from the previous day all packed away. 'So it's looking like we have an ID for the other body we found and I just wanted to update you. We think it's someone called Fintan McCabe. He's been missing since the nineties and was thought to be involved with the IRA.' There was a clearer picture of him on the table in the Family Room, supplied by his mother. An average-looking short young man, twenty-five years old, in a sweatshirt and jeans, with a nineties curtains haircut.

Mairead was frowning. 'Fintan?'

'That's right. Maybe you've heard of him? He wasn't officially Disappeared – the IRA never claimed him – but that's what his family always thought, that he got killed by them. His mother's fairly certain it's him.' Paula imagined how that would feel, to finally get some answers, even if it meant your loved one was dead. The Commission must see that all the time. At least someone was looking for the victims on their list, refusing to forget them. No one was looking for her mother except her.

'But . . . they were friends. Paddy and Fintan. They were always around our house, mucking about. Ciaran too. They were all about the same age.' She was biting her lip again, as if picturing them back then, those murderous young men.

'I see. So you're surprised he would be found dead at your farm?'

'Aye. Well, you see, it was where they took . . .'

'Informers,' Corry supplied. Paula kept silent.

'Aye. People they thought were up to something. Fintan helped Paddy collect them.'

It sounded so benign. Collect them. Kidnapping them at gunpoint more like, a sack over their head and bundled into a car. She shivered. The aircon was up much too high in this place. It was Ireland, for God's sake, how hot could it get?

Corry said, 'Fintan was shot in the head from the back. I'm sorry, this must be upsetting if you knew him.'

Mairead was staring at the diagrams of the bodies Corry showed her, the way the two had been packed into that space, Fintan jumbled up like an old rag doll, the girl laid so gently down. 'No, no, it's just . . . that's how they did it. The informers. They had a sort of code. They'd tie their hands, make them walk a few steps.' Her eyes were faraway, as if she was watching it happen again. 'Then they'd get them to kneel. Facing away. They'd put the gun, you know, to the ear.' She raised her finger to her own head.

'You've seen this happen.' Corry was gentle, but it wasn't a question.

Mairead nodded. Her hands were pushed up into the sleeves of her baggy jumper, far too big for her. 'But Fintan . . . he was one of them. Paddy trusted him. I can't think why he'd have been shot. You know, he was Paddy's friend.'

'Mairead . . . tell me what it was like, living there. Before you left. You were twenty-six when you went?'

'Aye. I lived at home before that all my life. Daddy died when I was twelve. The Army shot him on patrol, thought he was someone else. He was sitting in his tractor and they just shot him. So it was just us and Mammy, and she went . . . she really turned against the government. Wanted us all to join the fight, even me and Aisling. But I never had any interest in that. Paddy, though . . .' She trailed off. 'I don't know how to explain it to you. Living there, on the farm, it was like . . . an army camp. There were people tramping through it day and night, fellas in balaclavas, guns under the beds . . . and I was expected to cook and clean, wait on them hand and foot. It was no life, always expecting soldiers to come and kick the door in any minute, or someone to get shot. And the farm, it was dying. The boys had stopped looking after the animals, so they got sick. They just let it go to rack and ruin.'

'So you left earlier this same year Fintan went missing, is that correct – 1993?'

'Aye. It was bad again here. I just needed to get away.'

'And you had no contact with your family since.'

'None. They wouldn't have had me back. And they're all gone now, aren't they? All of them.' She spoke sadly, but there was an undercurrent of something else there, which Paula couldn't quite identify.

'So when you left there was Ciaran and Paddy at home?'

'Aye. And our Aisling.' She sounded impatient. 'I told you this.'

'I know. Just let me get this straight, Mairead. When you left, all your siblings and your mother were still at home, and Fintan McCabe was a regular visitor.'

'Practically lived there.' Something else in her voice again, a jagged edge sticking out. Paula couldn't read her at all.

'And now we have two dead bodies, and your brother Paddy and sister are missing. Correct?'

'Suppose. If you say so.'

'But you maintain the female body is not your sister.'

'I don't think so. She wouldn't dress like that.' Present tense. It was often a good indicator that someone knew a person was dead, if they used a different tense when talking about them.

Corry went in for the kill, asking it so casually it was barely a question. 'If we had a DNA sample from you, we could know for sure.'

Mairead jerked in surprise. 'From me?'

'Yes. Just for comparison. It's only a little swab, it—'

'I don't want to. I don't have to, do I?'

Corry blinked. 'Well, of course not, but it would really help us to know if your sister is still alive or not. You know, so we can put all this to rest.'

Mairead kept staring at the open file, the picture of the smiling boy. Likely chosen to make him look innocent and happy, not the gun-toting terrorist he had been. So much black and white back then. So many shades of grey. 'I don't know anything. I've told you everything. Can I go now? I need to be with my daughter.'

The nursing home looked like they always did. Drab, squat, mobility equipment on the steps and vans parked outside. It was the same one Paula's grandmother had been in. She'd died there without ever knowing what happened to her daughter Margaret. They weren't a demonstrative family, on either side – Paula barely knew her paternal family, who hadn't taken it well when their son joined the RUC – and she'd never really known how her mother's lot felt about the disappearance either. Had they suspected Margaret was up to something? Everyone had heard the rumours. *Tout*. Or had they picked up that there was another reason for her to run? Paula's Auntie Philomena, a confirmed busybody who never stopped talking, was unlikely to know anything. She wasn't the kind you'd trust with your secrets.

'Did Mairead not want to come with us?' said Paula, as they got out of the car.

'They had a row, back then. I think it's too painful for her,' said Corry. 'Sad, isn't it? Raising four weans and not a one of them to visit her. Makes me wonder if my Connor and Rosie'll bugger off and leave me in my old age.'

'The Wallaces had their reasons, maybe,' said Paula, who had also buggered off and left her grieving father. It was deeply frowned upon in Northern Ireland, but sometimes you had to run to save yourself, as if from a burning building. 'The mother was quite harsh, by the sounds of it.'

'They thought you had to be strict in those days, or your weans would run wild. You're too young to remember.'

And she'd had no mother, of course, to chide her about boys and decorum. No one to spot how hard she was falling for damaged Aidan O'Hara, and the harm it was going to do her. Was still doing her. 'Let's go in.'

Inside, the familiar fug of disinfectant and boiled food. The carers wore pink uniforms, and the TV blared out the lunchtime news. 'Fidelma Wallace, please,' said Corry to a girl who was scurrying past with a tray of cups.

The girl blinked. 'Fidelma, is it? She doesn't get many visitors, now.'

'Yes, well, that's why we want to talk to her. Where is she?'

They were directed to a tiny, hunched woman in the corner of the room, her spine compressed on itself. The shocking thing was she wasn't that old. Paddy, her eldest, wasn't even fifty, and Fidelma was close to seventy. But bent over, grey and wizened, she could have been ninety. Paula wondered was that the effect of losing touch with all four of her children.

Corry pulled out a stool, pausing to brush it off before she sat down in her good Louise Kennedy trousers. 'Mrs Wallace, hello. I'm DI Helen Corry, this is my colleague Dr Paula Maguire. Do you know why we're here?'

Her eyes didn't move from the spot they'd been fixed on, somewhere north of the TV screen, on the blank cream wall. Corry ploughed on. 'Maybe you saw it on the news, but the people who bought your farm when you had to sell it, they dug up the barn. And they found bodies there.'

Paula watched but there wasn't a flicker. Had she known? Could you live somewhere all your life and not know you were walking around on top of bones?

'There's one male body, who we believe we've identified as an associate of your son. There's also the body of a young girl, aged somewhere between twelve and eighteen, and that's why we're here, Fidelma. We know you had two daughters and we've located Mairead.' If they might have expected a reaction to the name of her estranged daughter, there was none. 'I need to ask you if you know where Aisling is. Her whereabouts.'

Nothing. Paula met Corry's eyes – could the old woman even take in what they were telling her? That they were saying her daughter might be dead? Corry leaned in. 'Mrs Wallace? Fidelma? When did you last see your daughter?'

Now Paula could hear a low noise, like a dog growling. It was coming from Fidelma Wallace's throat. 'Ungrateful shower,' she muttered. So she could understand. She was saying something else. Paula leaned in, catching the stifling smell of old food and decay. '*Traitors.*'

Corry went on. 'You understand what I'm saying, Fidelma? I need your help to work out if it's Aisling there. You realise I'm saying she might be dead?'

'*Good riddance.*' The old woman's voice creaked. Paula blinked. Had she really said that? Even unflappable Corry looked taken aback. 'Good bloody riddance. Not a one of them worth a damn except my Paddy. *Traitors.*'

Corry kept going, as if this was all normal. 'Well, that's another thing we wanted to know. Paddy hasn't been seen for years and we believe he's on the run. We'd like to talk to him, off the record, about what he knows. We just want to identify the girl. Is there anything you can tell us about where he might be?'

'It's what she deserved. What she deserved.'

'Who, Mrs Wallace? Are you talking about Aisling?' Corry leaned forward.

'Ungrateful shower,' she muttered again. Then she sank back in her chair. Paula's heart sank too.

'I don't think she's going to tell us any more,' she said quietly to Corry. 'Come on, we should go.' The place was beginning to press down on her, the idea of ending up here all alone, no husband, her child gone to live her own life.

Corry stood up reluctantly. 'She knows something, I'm sure.'

'Maybe she can't remember.'

'Can't or won't? Why is it, Maguire, that no one in this family seems to give a damn about the rest? Neither Ciaran or Mairead wants to give a simple DNA sample to help us find out if that's their sister dead in the morgue. What kind of things would you have to go through to end up like that?'

And what kind of mother would you have to be not to care when someone came and told you one of your daughters was likely dead? 'What else can we do?'

'We'll have to keep looking. If we find Aisling Wallace alive, that'll be our answer, I suppose.'

And the girl in the ground. Buried without a name or grave. Paula understood now the work of the Commission. How, even when you'd lost everything that mattered, there were still things that could be taken away from you. At least they might be able to find out who this girl was, and give her a proper resting place. She thought of what Mrs Wallace had said – *it's what she deserved* – and wondered again about Aisling Wallace in that picture, so young, so innocent. And no one could say where she was.

Chapter Eleven

Press conferences. Paula had been to so many over the years, hiding in the crowd if she could, sometimes reluctantly dragged on stage to blink in the lights and try not to show on her face what she and everyone else was thinking – how small the chances were of finding the missing person alive. As a psychologist she could run the odds in her sleep, calculate the risk factors. An older man, with alcohol or drug problems, no family? Likely wandered off, maybe dead, certainly unmourned. A three-year-old child gone from a holiday beach? If there were no parental abduction factors at play, then they were dead. Drowned or snatched, gone for good even as their parents sat in front of the cameras and begged for the child's return. Perhaps even dead at their hands – statistically, that was the most likely thing. A teenage girl, gone missing on her way to school? Was there a boyfriend? Mental health problems, eating disorders? Was suicide a factor? If she hadn't run away she was dead too. Dead, dead, and still they had to go through the motions of looking for them. It had begun to weary her, after so many years.

But this was different. Now they had bodies and no answers as to why they were there. The man, that was easy. Fintan McCabe. His mother had been interviewed on the news earlier, a stooped woman with white hair who'd wept silently. 'He was only a wean,' she kept saying. 'Only a wean.' But this wean, this victim – he could have been one of the men who took her mother. And he'd ended up dead in that pit, while her mother was who knew where. Could she really mourn his loss, search for his killer?

No, it was the girl she was thinking of, even as she sat in the crowd with her face carefully composed while Corry talked about bringing Fintan's killers to justice. He'd lived by the gun and died by it too, as Gerard said. Occupational hazard. But the girl, to be buried in that pit without a name or grave marker – it wasn't right. It stirred Paula, the need to track and find.

'Yes.' Corry pointed at a reporter in the crowd. Paula recognised the middle-aged woman as Aidan's replacement at the *Ballyterrin Gazette*. He'd have been all over a case like this, asking if the police were holding back information because the Commission were involved. He was violently opposed to the Commission anyway, but Paula, who had no body and no grave where she could go to visit her mother, could privately see the point of it. Not that she'd say as much to her police colleagues.

The reporter was asking something about Tozier's presence. He'd insisted on sitting on the panel to field questions, his pale-blue shirt rolled up at the sleeves and the light reflecting off his glasses. He looked like he should be working at NASA.

'The remains found do not fall under the remit of the Commission,' said Corry crisply. 'They were not found as a result of any information received. However, we're working with the Commission in an advisory capacity, to minimise potential upset to the families of the long-missing.'

Tozier nodded, as if he'd authorised her to say that. He

leaned too close to his mic. 'If anyone has any further information about the remains found, they can contact the confidential tip-line we've set up. Anything they have to say will be treated in full confidence.'

Another thing Aidan hated. Provos getting fits of conscience, or more likely looking for a quiet life after years on the run, offering up titbits of information in exchange for letting it all be swept under a giant carpet of forgetting. He could not forget that men just like Fintan McCabe had killed his father, and he could not forgive.

She pulled her attention back to the room. No sense in thinking about Aidan. He was gone, time was unspooling without him, and this was her job now. Find out who that dead girl was, and lay her to rest. Someone else had asked a question about her.

Corry said, 'At the moment we don't have an ID for this young woman, and we'd ask anyone with information to come forward, so she can be identified. We have here a digital reconstruction of what she'd have looked like at the time.' Paula sat up; she hadn't seen this yet. A picture was flashed onto the screen, a mock-up of the face over the skull. She'd been pretty, even with her features set in the strange Picasso-like shapes the computer programmes threw up. Surely someone, somewhere, must miss this young girl. 'We think she was aged between twelve and eighteen, though it's hard to be sure. When found she was wearing nightclothes and a jumper – I think we have an image of those now.'

Paula ducked her head as the picture came up, those soil-stained clothes, the pendant that gave her an uncomfortable jolt every time. Again, the questions. Could it be hers? What was it doing there if so?

Another reporter raised his hand, some kid in his first

suit, reminding her again of Aidan, that scrappiness, the arrogance. 'DI Corry. Are you saying there won't be any prosecutions as a result of these finds? Even the girl, if she's found with Disappeared victims? Isn't that how the legislation reads?'

Tozier opened his mouth but Corry cut right over him. 'I'm not saying that at all, Matt. It's Matt, yes? As far as I'm concerned this is a murder scene, with two dead bodies in it, and we'll be using every resource we have to bring the killers to justice, no matter who they were or how long ago it was. That's how the law reads, to my mind. Thank you. No more questions.'

She pushed back her chair and was gone. Tozier was media-trained but not well enough to hide the annoyance that crossed his face.

In the audience, Paula caught sight of Mairead Wallace, her face in darkness beneath the blue of the screens. It was the first time she'd seen her without her daughter. Paula pictured the lines of Carly's pretty, petulant face, caked in make-up, hooped earrings tangled in her thick dark hair. And then she realised, with a jolt down her spine: Carly and the dead girl could have been sisters.

'. . . unacceptable to announce you'll be pressing charges. It completely undermines the trust we've built up within the community, the chance of further tip-offs coming in—'

'And what community would that be, Mr Tozier? The terrorist community? How am I expected to lead an inquiry if you have information you won't share?'

Paula couldn't help but listen in to the heated discussion going on inside Corry's office, between Tozier, Willis Campbell, and herself.

'Wish I'd had some money on him losing it too,' remarked Gerard, who was Googling shoes to spend his previous winnings on. 'He didn't seem the type.'

'Everyone has a breaking point,' Paula said, hunched over her computer pretending she wasn't watching through the shuttered glass window. 'It's just a matter of finding it, is all.'

'I'd say they'd found each other's, right enough.' Gerard pushed his seat back suddenly. 'Avril, what do you say we start another pot? Likelihood of love blossoming between the boss and the new fella?'

Avril frowned. 'Don't be daft. She can't stand the sight of him.'

'You couldn't stand the sight of me at first.'

'Still can't, sometimes.' She smiled at him.

He turned to Paula. 'Maguire, you agree with me? Banter, sniping, blow-ups . . . it's all foreplay, right, even if they don't know it?'

'You want to throw your money away, it's no skin off my nose,' she remarked, but she was thinking of herself and Aidan, how things had always combusted between them, and she knew he was probably right.

'I'll do it if I can keep the usual house fee,' said Avril, calling up a new spreadsheet.

'Listen to her, Maguire, she thinks she's running a Vegas casino. What would your daddy the reverend say to that?'

Avril tossed her hair. 'Oh, he knows I'm long past salvation, now I'm marrying a Taig.'

Paula tuned out their banter. The door of Corry's office had opened, and a cross-looking Tozier had come out, being placated by Campbell. 'You two tear away. I need to speak to Corry.'

* * *

'There's something Mairead's not telling us.' Paula paced in Corry's office, frustrated. It was a small, functional space looking out on the concrete box of the car park, where in the eighties nine officers had died in an IRA mortar attack. Children's drawings were pinned to the noticeboard, though Corry's kids had long grown out of that and would have been mortified if they'd known such relics were here.

Corry sat calmly at her desk, answering emails. She was taking a Zen approach to Tozier from now on, she'd announced. *If I pretend he's not there, he can't annoy me.* Now she said, 'There's a fair few somethings she's not telling us, I'd say.'

'She won't give a DNA sample. She rang her brother in prison the other night, which she never mentioned. And the daughter, Carly. She looks just like the girl we found. Did you notice? Same hair and everything. All the Wallaces are very alike, as we've seen. But Mairead said it wasn't her sister. Did you compare the reconstruction to that picture of Aisling Wallace?'

'Of course we did, Maguire. What do you think this is, amateur hour?'

'And?'

Corry shrugged. 'There are some similarities but nothing conclusive.'

'We need to find Aisling Wallace. If she's even alive. And another thing – I just checked Carly's Facebook again and she's twenty, not nineteen like Mairead said.'

'One year out, it's hardly a big deal.'

'You ever heard of a mother rounding her child's age down? What if she wanted us to think Carly was born later than she was?'

Corry gazed at her. 'Sit down, Maguire, you're wearing a hole in the carpet and we haven't the budget to get it redone. I agree with everything you're saying. But I'm sure Mairead has her reasons for not talking, and for not giving a DNA sample either. She's here, isn't she? Despite what it cost her to get on that plane and come over. That means she wants to talk. Even if she doesn't know it yet. So leave her be, OK? The girl isn't getting any deader, God love her. Let's not push Mairead so hard we drive her away.'

It wasn't good enough. Paula sighed and tried to stop her pacing. Unbidden, her mind turned to Guy in their cosy London office, high above the river. The sun would be setting in it now, turning the dark water blood-red. She'd linger in the office to discuss their cases, before going down a few floors to pick up Maggie from day care. They'd go home, hand in small sticky hand, catching the bus to the flat on the Isle of Dogs. Paula would feed Maggie, and bath her, get her to bed, then sit alone with a single glass of wine. That had been her new life, the one she was making for herself. She'd left it all behind to come back here again, to the town with no answers, only a bottomless hole of questions. 'It's just so frustrating, both Mairead and Ciaran not talking.'

'Tell me about it. And on top of that we've got Tozier breathing down our necks at every turn.' Corry glowered out the door, where the man in question was cosying up to Willis Campbell, another person who knew how to work a TV camera. 'Well, Maguire, you may as well go ho—'

They were interrupted by heavy steps coming up to the door, which was thrown open by a red-faced Gerard Monaghan. He'd put on weight, Paula noticed suddenly. That was what love did to you. Made you comfortable.

Slowed you down. 'Ma'am? There's a phone call. I think you should take it.'

Corry lifted her eyebrows and then her phone, and listened, and her face changed. 'OK, OK, try to calm down and explain. What are you saying? Mairead . . .'

At the name, Paula stared at Gerard, who mouthed: *dunno*. They listened. 'Only an hour . . . OK, I hear you. We'll come. I promise.' She hung up, suddenly grim and in charge again. 'Carly Jones is missing. Mairead got back to find the flat door lying open and no trace of her. Come on.'

Chapter Twelve

The PSNI safe house was a nondescript flat in the new part of town, an anonymous block overlooking the grey basin of the canal. The showroom pictures had been taken on some rare sunny day when the water was shining and ducks and swans swam on it, even some yachts moored up. Canal-side living. But it was still Ballyterrin, and as Paula's father would have said, you couldn't make a silk purse out of a cow's arse.

She followed Corry, clattering through the bare cream-tiled lobby and up the stairs, Gerard in front, adopting a raid stance. 'Stop it, would you?' said Corry, irritated. 'It's not *Miami Vice*, OK?'

'What's *Miami Vice*?'

She shot him a glower and stopped outside the door of number five, rapping softly. 'Mairead, it's us.'

The door flew open. Mairead Wallace was in the same black dress she'd worn to the press conference, her feet shoeless in fraying nylon tights, one false fingernail sticking out as if she'd bashed it on something. Her face was haggard with fear. 'Where's the rest of them? You didn't bring them Forensics people or what have you?' She looked past them into the empty corridor.

'She's only been gone an hour, Mairead; we can't authorise that, I'm afraid. Can you talk us through it?'

She gestured them in, pointing to a plain leather couch. The room was pleasant enough, looking out on the water, but as barren as a cheap hotel. Mairead wrung her hands. 'She wouldn't just go off. She knows I worry. She knows.'

Corry perched on the edge of the sofa. 'So you came back and the door was open? Ajar or just unlocked?'

'Sitting open. She'd never do that. She's a good girl, careful. She's had to let herself in after school from when she was eight.'

'Any disturbances?' Gerard was inspecting the door frame, which looked intact. 'This hasn't been forced.'

'It all looks the same.' Mairead cast her worried eyes to the kitchen. 'Just some cups sitting out, like . . . nothing else. Just like this.' The place was tidy enough, a small purple wheely case pushed to the side, the contents folded away. Corry bent to look.

'She's a tidy girl, your Carly? I wish I could get my daughter to pick up after herself.'

Mairead was distracted, pacing. 'I just keep thinking and thinking what the last thing she said was. Did she say she'd go out for some food, or the shops maybe or . . . but she wouldn't do that. I told her to stay put. I didn't want her at the press thing, she doesn't need to see all that. And the TV was on when I came in. I switched it off before I realised, just habit, you know.'

Corry jerked her head at Gerard, who snapped on gloves and bagged the remote control with efficiency. He loved all this. Mairead watched. 'Is that . . . why did you do that?'

'Just a precaution.' Corry moved to the galley kitchen, where two Ikea mugs sat out on the counter. 'These were like this when you arrived? Is one yours from earlier?'

'No, I didn't . . . we washed them all up after lunch.'

'You found it like this? You didn't make a drink since you came in?'

'No, of course not, I was too worried!'

'Would Carly have used two cups?'

'I . . . Why would she do that?'

Corry was already gesturing to Gerard, who repeated his bagging trick. 'Mairead. Could someone have got in, do you think? Would Carly have let someone into the flat?'

Mairead's face was stricken. 'Who? Nobody even knows she's here. Nobody knows she . . .' She tailed off. 'You will look for her, won't you? On TV it always says you have to wait twenty-four hours, but she wouldn't do this, I'm telling you!'

Corry and Paula exchanged glances. It was worrying, the timing of it, when the girl didn't know anyone in Ballyterrin, and what was also strange was Mairead's extreme reaction to her grown-up daughter being gone for an hour. Her daughter who was one year older than she'd said.

'We'll look,' said Corry soothingly. 'Let me make some calls.'

The station already had a hum that Paula recognised, which matched the thrumming in her own chest. This she could do. A girl was missing, and needed to be brought home. This was in her blood. Corry was already doling out orders, the weeping mother hidden from sight in the relatives' room. 'CCTV on the building?'

Avril, ever efficient, nodded her tidy blond chignon. 'There's one at the front but no sign of Carly on it – she might have gone out through the car park. But it's quiet during the day, so we only saw one black car leave during that time. We're trying to decipher the licence plate.'

'Good. Buses, trains, all that? Could she have got away by herself?'

'Nothing at the bus station or the train,' said Gerard, rolling up his sleeves. 'Uniform have been round with a picture.'

'Paula?' Corry was waiting for a magic answer, expecting her to look at the tangle of clues and pull out a solution like a rabbit from a hat.

'I'd say she went off with someone. Neighbours heard nothing, yes?' They'd struck lucky; the next-door flat was occupied by a newborn baby who never slept and his frazzled parents, who'd been at home all day and heard nothing untoward. 'So, likely no struggle. If she left in a car, that suggests someone came around, she made them tea, and they went off together. But who?'

'She doesn't know anyone here,' said Corry. 'She's never even been to Ireland. Seems to me Mairead made sure of that.'

'That Facebook post – looking for her family. What if someone got in touch?'

Corry was nodding. 'Go on.'

'Can we get into her private messages? Is Trevor still working here?' She'd always been fond of the baby-faced tech officer, despite his low-slung trousers and incomprehensible slang.

'He is, much to my sorrow. Monaghan, get him up here. Wright, keep throwing the net wide. You know the drill. CCTV anywhere in town, buses, trains, taxis – oh, and we better get an alert out.'

'So soon?' Avril had her pen poised but she was right, it was unusual to take action when the girl was only just gone, her tea barely cold. Corry must have a feeling something wasn't right.

A uniformed PC marched up, breathless, weighed down by body armour she hadn't yet taken off. Paula didn't recognise her. She was out of the loop here already, feeling like an awkward visitor. 'Ma'am, we found something in the underground car park of the flats, and traces in the lift. Blood.'

Paula's heart began to pound.

'Is there a camera in the lift?' said Corry, swift and hungry.

'There is, but we can't get anything off it. It's been smashed.'

Corry nodded. 'We'll need that DNA sample from Mairead after all, to see if it's Carly's blood. In the meantime start the alerts and that. Off you go.'

'What can I do?' asked Paula.

'You and me need to have a wee word with Trevor. I think you're right, the Facebook post is the key. Someone answered it, said they were a relative. She arranged for them to come over to the flat and they took her. We need to find out who that was. But first we better talk to her mother again.'

Margaret

When the girl came back she was boking her ring up. It wasn't easy when you were tied upright, and it was going all down her front, a stinking acid smell filling the room. Margaret was too tired to even feel shame. 'Help me,' she croaked, closing her mouth as a fresh wave of nausea swamped her.

The girl's eyes were huge. Today she wore jeans and a GAA shirt, the local county colours. 'Are you sick? Was it the food?'

'No, no.' Although it hadn't helped, cold and congealed as it was. 'I'm having a baby, you see. Morning sickness.'

'Oh.'

'Does he know I'm having a baby? Your brother?' She was sure they'd never had a pregnant woman here before. Some part of her had been afraid to use this bargaining chip. Not at all sure it would make a difference, and of course it left her even more vulnerable. Shying away from telling anyone at all, the secret she'd carried for months now. But surely they'd let her go if they knew, release her on some country lane at dawn. She imagined it, knocking on some random door to use the phone, then calling – who? PJ? How would she then explain this baby? Edward? He'd not come for her so far. Maybe he was already gone, back in England, safe. 'Did you tell your mammy about me like I asked?'

The girl came closer, wrinkling her nose at the smell. 'I better get something to clean you. He doesn't like it, Paddy. Dirt, or mess.'

'Wait! What did she say, your mammy? If she knows I'm here?'

The girl spoke over her shoulder, awkward. 'She said . . . everyone says the same, when they're out here. They're special. They didn't mean it. They didn't do anything. But if they didn't do anything, they wouldn't be here, would they? That's what she said, anyway.'

Margaret's heart plummeted. Who were these people? Aisling went, and was soon back with a steaming bucket of hot water and cleaning fluid. It smelled homely and safe, but all the same Margaret flinched at the sight of it. Just a bucket. The same kind she used to wash her kitchen floor. Which she hadn't done for a week, what with all the running for her life she'd had to do. Would PJ think to do it? She should have mentioned that in her note and . . .

Stop it, woman. What did it matter about the bloody kitchen floor?

The girl had also brought a clean sweatshirt, soft and well washed, far too big. Did it belong to the mysterious mammy maybe? The mother who'd sit in her house, knowing a woman was tied up in the barn outside? The girl hesitated, trying to work out how to get the sweatshirt onto Margaret.

'You can untie me. I won't move, I promise.'

She nodded and pulled at the bonds, helping Margaret out of her stained top and into the clean one. A practical girl, and a kind one. And yet look what she was doing, holding Margaret here, doing nothing to stop them. As she knelt to do the ankle knots, Margaret thought again about lashing out. Fighting for her life, her baby's life, and running. But she couldn't. This girl was not much older than Paula, and she just couldn't. She couldn't believe she'd even had such a thought. Maybe it was true after all, all the things they were saying about her. Maybe she did deserve this.

'Thank you,' she rasped. 'For helping me.'

The girl turned at the door again, Margaret's stinking jumper in her arms. 'Aisling,' she said hesitantly. 'That's my name. I'm Aisling.'

Chapter Thirteen

Mairead sat on the edge of the pale green couch. The room was nice, with toys piled in the corner and carpet on the floor, but there was no hiding the reinforced windows or the smell of industrial cleaner. She balled a tissue between her hands, shredding it to fluffy white pieces. 'She's never done anything like this before. She knows not to let people in if I'm away.'

'We think she asked someone round to the flat, then left with them. Perhaps against her will.' Corry was being tactful. Finding blood was not a good sign.

'But she doesn't know anyone here! How could she?'

'That's what we're trying to work out. Mairead, as I said we found a small bit of blood in the building. We'll need a sample of DNA from you to prove it's Carly's. It's not lots, so don't panic. She might have just cut herself or something.'

'DNA?'

'Yes, but just a cheek swab. It won't hurt, I promise.'

But maybe that wasn't the problem. Paula watched her face, which had suddenly closed up again. 'Do I really have to?'

'We do need to prove the blood came from Carly, so I can put all my resources onto this. Otherwise, you see, we just have a teenage girl going off on her own with no sign of a struggle, and as my colleague here will tell you we get about ten of those a day.'

'But she doesn't know anyone,' Mairead said again. 'I shouldn't have brought her here. Why did I bring her? Oh God.'

Paula said, 'In most cases we find them again, safe and sound, girls her age. She knew whoever this was and let them in, drank tea with them. That's a good sign.' In some ways it was, ruling out random abduction, but Paula also knew what the stats said: a girl Carly's age was much more likely to be injured or killed by someone she knew, someone she'd willingly opened the door to. She'd seen it a thousand times.

Mairead was nodding reluctantly. 'OK. If it'll find her.'

'Thank you,' Corry said. 'I'll arrange for someone to come and do it now.'

Mairead's hands were full of shredded tissue. 'There's something else. Her age . . . she's not nineteen, like I said. She's twenty. That's why I left, you see.'

'You were pregnant?' Corry asked. 'You ran away because of that?'

She nodded. So Mairead had been carrying Carly when she left Northern Ireland. That explained a lot – why she'd run when she did, why her mother wouldn't have had her back. But why had she lied, made them think Carly was conceived in Liverpool? 'I knew Mammy wouldn't let me keep her, see.' It was easy to forget, in this new permissive Northern Ireland which had held the first same-sex wedding in the UK, that even in the nineties this was routine, unplanned pregnancies being adopted away, tidied up. Mairead's mammy had been an unforgiving woman; that was obvious even now. 'So yes, I ran away.' Her voice was defiant. 'I couldn't give my baby up. I just couldn't.'

'I see. Who's Carly's father, then? Not Mr Jones, I take it?' If he even existed.

Mairead just shook her head. She wasn't going to answer that. Maybe she didn't know. 'There's no da. Just me and her. And we're fine that way.'

'I'm sure you are. Just get in the way, don't they, men?' Corry gave her a woman-to-woman smile, but it wasn't returned. Mairead had shut down again, as if a veil had drawn over her. 'Mairead . . . it's good you've told us this. If there's anything else you haven't been honest about, we need to know. The blood tells us Carly likely didn't want to leave, even if she let the person in willingly. They may have hurt her.'

'You said it wasn't much! Why would there be blood? Oh God, if he . . .' She stopped. Corry and Paula exchanged a lightning-quick glance.

Corry spoke in measured tones. 'Mairead. If you have any idea who Carly is with, you need to tell us. We can get DNA off the second cup, maybe. We'll be able to prove they were there, whoever it is.'

'I . . .'

'Mairead. Come on now. We know you made several phone calls to the South the other day. We know you're not telling us everything.'

Mairead's face crumpled like her tissue. 'She asked me all the time about the family. She's no da, so . . . I think she wanted more than just me. To find her da maybe, too. Her real da.' She saw the look they gave her. 'You guessed it. I did marry a fella called Jones, but he was a waster, met him in a bar one night. Just wanted to give Carly another name, not Wallace. He's nothing to her, she's never even met him.'

'So she went looking for more.'

'Yeah. A family. Maybe she contacted one of them.'

'Your sister?' asked Paula. Perhaps this was why Mairead was so sure the dead girl was not Aisling. If they'd been in contact, that proved she was alive.

But she shook her head. 'No. Not her.'

Corry said, 'You called your brother Ciaran the other day too.' Her tone was neutral, non-judgemental. Mairead must have her reasons for not telling them the full story.

'I . . . Yes. First time we've talked in twenty years. He doesn't know a thing. Didn't think he would. He's stuck inside that place. Swore to me he didn't know how . . . the bodies . . . how they ended up in the ground. Said he'd gone by then himself.'

Corry nodded. 'He can't have taken Carly. So you mean it was . . . ?'

'Yes.' She seemed to spit the name up into her mouth. 'Paddy. My brother Patrick. I was ringing around, you see, anyone I could think of that used to know him. Nobody knows a thing. But I think – I think maybe he came for her. I think he has Carly.'

'Mummy, you know Auntie Seer-sha's going to have a baby?' Maggie began conversationally.

'Yes, pet.' Back to this topic. She wondered was Saoirse telling people openly. Paula would have expected her to keep it a secret. They were driving back from Saoirse's house, where she'd been looking after Maggie again while Paula worked late, helping with the search for Carly. You could ask people for favours like that when you lived in Ballyterrin, the town you'd grown up in. Not in London.

Maggie went on. 'Can I play with the baby?'

'I'm sure you can, when it's bigger, but it won't be here for a while, you know.' And please God, if there was a God, it would come.

'Oh.' Maggie stared out the window for a moment, chewing thoughtfully on the end of her red ponytail. 'Mummy? Can you get a baby too? I want one.'

Paula almost drove off the road. Not this again. 'Sorry, pet, we can't have one right now.'

'Because you need a daddy for that.' Maggie sounded sage, and sad.

Paula decided now was not the time to explain you didn't always need a daddy, strictly speaking. 'That's right.'

'And our daddy is away in the bad place.'

Her hands gripped tight on the steering wheel. Except for that once in London, Maggie hadn't mentioned her 'daddy' – Aidan – for months now. Had Pat and PJ been talking in front of her? 'Does Auntie Saoirse have nice toys at her house?' She changed the subject.

That seemed to prompt another worry. 'Mummy, will the baby play with my My Little Pony castle? Because it's mine, Mummy.'

'I think the baby will be too wee for that.'

'Why can't we move it to our house?'

Because their current house was a rented flat in London, overlooking the grey lap of the Thames. Home, though it didn't feel like it. Although she was doing her best to get Maggie away from Ballyterrin and her terrible legacy, being back here just felt right somehow, as if London was a whimsical holiday they'd been on for too long.

'Why, Mummy?' she insisted.

'Just because,' said Paula, taking refuge in that classic phrase of the harassed parent. 'Come on, we're here now.'

She'd pulled up outside Pat's house, now her father's too. Where Aidan had grown up. Would she ever get away from all these tangles?

She'd extricated Maggie from her car seat and helped her down when she saw the figure standing in the shadows by the gate. A man, watching them.

Chapter Fourteen

'Mr Bob!' Maggie ran towards him, her sharp eyes making out what Paula hadn't been able to at first – it was Bob Hamilton standing there in the gloom.

'Oof! Hello, wee pet, how are you?'

'Mr Bob' was what she'd taken to calling him, given that *Uncle Bob* felt wrong and *Mr Hamilton* wasn't something she could pronounce. 'Mr Bob, please can we go to your house and have a biscuit?'

'Maggie!' Scandalised, Paula tugged her back. 'Sorry, Bob. Do you want to come in?'

'Oh no. I just needed a wee word with you.'

Paula patted Maggie gently towards the door. 'Run on in to Granny and Granddad, pet. Tell them Mummy's on the phone.'

'But you're *not* on the phone.' Maggie narrowed her eyes at this obvious lie.

'No, but I will be in a minute. You'll see Mr Bob at the wedding, won't you?' Bob was Avril's uncle, a fact that still seemed wildly improbable to Paula after so many years of knowing them both. She sensed Bob did not want to come in and say hello to her father, his former partner a hundred years ago, or to Pat, whose husband he'd found shot dead back in 1986. Too many connections in this town, pulling you down.

Maggie trotted off, casting dark backward looks that managed to convey her disapproval at this subterfuge. 'She's a lovely wee thing.' Bob was bundled up in an old-man's beige anorak, despite the mildness of the evening.

'Is something the matter?'

'I saw the news. You're looking for Paddy Wallace?'

An alert had gone out after Mairead's confession about her brother, although Paula had misgivings about showing their hand so soon. If he had taken Carly, a man like that, he would have a plan. 'Yeah. It's complicated. His niece has gone missing and her mother thinks she might have been in touch with him. He's been on the run for years, I gather.'

'We never caught up to him, and then everything ended and I suppose no one could be bothered to look any more.'

'Do you know much about him?'

He hesitated. 'Paula . . . it's murky waters, you know. A man like Wallace was of his time. Ruthless. All he cared about was his so-called free Ireland and he didn't care who he murdered to get there. Peace process or no peace process, he won't have changed his mind about that.'

'You knew him, then?'

'Just by reputation. And I heard the name again recently.'

'How?'

Bob sighed, and felt in the pocket of his jacket. Paula switched on her phone light to look at what he held out, which was a white envelope with some names scrawled on the back. *Paddy Wallace. Prontias Ryan. Mark O'Hanlon.*

She looked up at him quickly. 'What is this?'

'It's . . . a list.'

'I can see that. Where did you get it?'

Another silence. The words forced out, reluctantly. 'I got that off Sean Conlon, the day he died.'

Paula stared at him. Bob had spoken to Sean Conlon on the same day he'd been kicked to death in a car park? The day Aidan had come home with bruised hands and blood on his T-shirt? She couldn't make this information fit into her head. 'What?'

'Conlon was just out of prison, remember. He'd a lot of enemies. You remember I told you he was the chief suspect for shooting that fella Dunne.'

Paula nodded. Another Paddy, Paddy Dunne, a man who'd been high up in the IRA until he'd been shot in the eighties. Many thought it was done by his own side, to stop him using his influence to call off the hunger strikes of 1981. Someone had gone to his home and killed him in his doorway, all those years ago. Maybe Sean Conlon, who would have been just a young man then. 'I remember.'

'Well. Conlon, he'd heard his days were numbered and he wanted my help. Those are the names of people he thought might be after him.'

Paula stared down at the paper in her hands, thinking it should be in an evidence bag or something. The man's writing had been awkward and square, as if unused to letters. The person who'd written this had maybe abducted her mother, murdered Aidan's father. In his turn been murdered, possibly by Aidan. Ballyterrin – a circle of pain. Her mind tried to sift through this. 'Wait. He came to you for help?' Under what circumstances would a terrorist like Conlon have had anything in common with Bob, a straight-down-the-line RUC man and a member of the Orange Order to boot? They were as far apart as it was possible to be in this country.

Bob didn't answer. Paula felt the weight of it between them, all the things he didn't want her to know. She sighed.

'Bob. I think it's time to tell me what went on, don't you? Because you know things, and I know things, and I imagine we're both in the same boat here – the missing pieces driving us mad. So let me tell you what I know.' Standing in the puddle of orange light from the streetlamp, she recited the facts she'd painfully dredged up over the past four years. 'Mum was passing information to Army Intelligence. She was approached by someone after a soldier died in her arms at a checkpoint. She was disgusted by the whole thing – the Troubles, John O'Hara dying, everyone always dying. Right?'

She could hardly see Bob's face, or his barely perceptible nod. She went on. 'This man – Edward somebody – she was in love with him too. Or something, at least. And she got pregnant.' It was hard, saying these words to Bob, exposing her mother's secrets. But she was so tired of carrying them around by herself.

Bob flinched. She watched him. Not enough surprise there. 'But you knew that already?'

His voice was rusty. 'She came to me, like I said. For help.'

Even so, it was hard to believe her mother would have chosen Bob to confide in, her husband's former partner. Why him? 'So, she was definitely planning to leave?'

'She knew they were after her. And if she told your daddy what was going on, then he'd have known everything, wouldn't he? About the . . . other fella.'

Paula let that sink in. The confirmation of what she'd suspected, of what had to be the truth. The baby her mother was expecting back then – it was not her father's. It was this other man's. Proof of an affair, of what Margaret had been doing. Enough to make her run.

It felt so wrong, discussing her parents' intimate lives with Bob, Sideshow Bob as Aidan always called him, here outside her dad's house. But she had to plough on. 'So she planned to – what? Run away with him, this man? For ever?'

'She thought it was all nearly over. There was a ceasefire the year after, if you remember. I think she thought if she just got away for a while, if you and your daddy knew nothing, you'd be safe and then it'd be over and she could explain.'

'She left a note. I didn't find it for years, but there was one. In the kitchen of our old house.'

'I went there that day,' said Bob, almost in a whisper. Staring at his feet. 'When the call came in from your neighbour, saying men had been at the door. But she was gone already. Nobody there. I must have missed the note; I was panicking, see, had to get out of there. You must have come in yourself not long after, from school. And for years I never knew nothing. I swear. She'd asked me if I would lead the case when she went, and not look too close into where she was, if you know what I mean. Not say anything to PJ. That's why I hid the neighbour's report. But I never knew was I doing the right thing. Did she get away safe, or did they come for her after all? I didn't know should we be trying to find her or not, was she in danger, had something gone wrong?'

Paula didn't know either. She imagined how it had been for Bob, racked all these years by the secret her mother had left with him. It was too much to ask of someone, she thought. It wasn't fair.

He went on. 'And then when we never heard a word from her again, I thought I must have been wrong to do it that way. But I could hardly say, oh by the way, here's a wee report I forgot to file, now could I? That was all I knew for years, pet. I promise you.'

'But now . . . ?'

He sighed again. 'Are you sure you want to hear all this, Paula?'

'I'm sure.' She had decided long ago. That was her nature, to pursue the truth until it destroyed everything she held dear, burning it up like a white-hot flame.

'Like I said, Sean Conlon came to see me the day he died.'

Her heart lurched up in her mouth, throwing her back to that day. Her stupid hen do. Aidan in the house when she hadn't expected him back so early, blood on the sink in the bathroom. 'Why you?'

'Way back in the day, I did him a favour. So he owed me one. And when your mammy told me they were after her, I tried to call that favour in. Because he'd have known, if anyone was going to lift her. He was tied up in it all. You see?'

Her mind boggled at the idea of Bob and Sean Conlon in some kind of conspiracy. 'And what did he say?'

'Just that we were quits now. He wouldn't tell me anything else, what happened to her, if he helped her or not. After she went, he avoided me, and he'd never tell me if he knew anything. Then he went inside himself and I thought I'd never know. Next thing he's out of prison and on my driveway, wanting a wee favour of his own.'

'Which was?'

'Getting him away from the fellas that were going to kill him. He wanted a deal. Out of the country in exchange for telling me what he knew. But there wasn't time.'

She nodded; the rest of that story she was only too aware of. What she hadn't known before was why Bob seemed to have insider information. And now she did. Because of what her mother had done, trying to bargain for her life. 'He didn't say anything about what happened to her, back then? When he came to you last year?'

Another hesitation. The habit of keeping secrets, long ingrained. She could see him struggle. 'Never knew whether to believe him or not. He was a liar and a murderer, not to speak ill of the dead. But he did say . . . he said they'd come for her all right, that day. In 1993. They took her away in the car, to a farm on the border. They held her there for a few days – interrogation. Figuring out what to do with her. You know, a woman with a family, and the ceasefire coming any day then – they could have let her live. Or hidden the body. There was talk of that, even.'

Paula's heart was drowning out her thoughts. At last, at last, to know the final steps of her mother. And what farm – did this mean the pendant on the dead girl really was hers? 'So what happened?'

'The way Conlon told it, he helped her get away. Let her go, and she ran off over the fields, and he never saw her again. He thought Army Intelligence got her out. He told her if she surfaced again – if he even got wind she'd contacted anyone back home – he'd come after her, and you and your daddy too. See, if those boys knew he'd let her go, they'd have executed Sean instead as a traitor.'

'Did you believe him?' Sean Conlon had lied to her face before, when she'd gone to see him in prison. Told her that when they went to lift her mother from the house, she was already gone. How to know which story to believe?

'Like I say, pet, he was a liar, and looking to save his own skin. But . . . the chance to hope again, to think she might have got away . . . He swore blind to me he'd helped her, but he made her promise to keep her head down. Play dead. A word to anyone, even you or your da, and he'd hunt her down. He'd kill her, and you too. On your way to school. He'd put a bomb under your da's car. And he would have. You see, letting her go, it was a betrayal of the cause. It meant death for him. So that's maybe why she never got in touch, if she did get away. He'd have chased her down if she had.'

Paula let herself imagine it. Her mother had escaped, and been alive all this time, but unable to get in touch. Just like a crazed self-proclaimed psychic had told her, several years ago. Alive. Across the water. Did that mean London, maybe? 'I'm looking for her,' she heard herself say. 'I got wind she might have been in England. That Edward, I found an address for him in London, but he'd moved on years ago. I – I'm working with someone to find her.'

'Davey Corcoran,' said Bob wryly. 'I told him not to tell you about me.'

'You . . .' So that was why Davey seemed to know so much about the case. Bob had been feeding him information on the side. She looked at the man, old and faded in his M&S jumper, and marvelled at how little she had known about him. At the hidden depths everyone seemed to have, and the secrets, buried deep in the dark soil of their hearts.

Paula's head was reeling. Her mother could have been alive all this time. It explained Sean Conlon's cryptic hints when she'd seen him in prison; if he hadn't lied this second time, of course, and that was a huge maybe. It explained why Bob was visiting Aidan in prison, and why he was so sure someone else was behind the killing of Conlon. Her chest burned with hope and pain. 'Sean Conlon. He's the one who helped my mother escape.'

Bob nodded. 'So he claimed.'

'And you never told me?'

'I promised I wouldn't.'

'And . . . Paddy Wallace was involved too?'

'That's what I've been trying to find out,' said Bob. 'If anyone killed her, it would have been him. He ran their "punishment squad".' She could hear the distaste in Bob's voice for their faux-military language. 'He's vicious, Paula. He's still fighting a war that ended twenty years back, and to him your mammy was the worst kind of traitor. And then I hear on the news you're looking for him. It's all connected, pet. That's what I've been trying to work out. All of this – your mother, Conlon, young Aidan – it's connected. And we need to find out how.'

Chapter Fifteen

Back at the station the next day, she could tell something was up. The atmosphere was electric, as if a current had been zapped through it. She found Gerard in the crowd of officers standing round a big TV. 'What's going on?'

'Shhh. Corry's got something to show us. Just came in.'

Corry was fiddling with the AV equipment. She caught Paula's eye and nodded: *just watch*. 'OK, people. Mairead Wallace received a video message an hour ago from Carly's mobile phone. It's been switched off again, but the cell tower it went through was in the border region.' The kind of place where the lines went fuzzy – the phone network switching between the two, the border itself no more than an imaginary line through fields and hedges. 'This is it.' Corry pressed play.

A grainy, shaky image came up. Carly was being held somewhere like a garage, or a barn maybe. Paula could see a stone wall behind her, with an electric light somewhere overhead that cast shadows on her frightened face. Her hands seemed to be tied behind her. Without her make-up she looked very young and scared. 'M-mum? It's me. He says I have to record this. I'm OK. But I'm scared, Mum. I didn't mean this to happen. I'm sorry. I love you—'

The phone was turned around, showing a man in a balaclava, with only slits where his eyes would be. His voice was muffled. It was a similar image to hundreds Paula had seen in the Troubles, but all the same a chill crawled down her back. Was this what her mother had seen, the day they'd come for her?

The man in the mask had a heavy Ballyterrin accent. 'I'll give Carly back if you come to meet me. I won't hurt her. But you give me no choice, darlin', you really don't. You have till tomorrow at five to text me a place. I'll be there. Don't show this to anyone else now – I'll be watching. Just you and me, Mairead. Like old times.'

It ended with the picture shaking, as if the phone had been dropped, rolling towards the ceiling, which was held up with high beams, and the sound of Carly screaming for her mother. Then it went black. A small moment of silence. Corry said, 'It's good that Mairead shared this with us. She's clearly co-operating, at last.'

'Who was it?' said Gerard. 'He talked like she'd know.'

'She thinks it's her brother, Paddy Wallace. The mask, I imagine, was to stymie any future convictions. Not his first brush with the law, of course. We're analysing this video forensically but it looks like it's been taken at a farm somewhere near the border. Of which there are hundreds, of course. But the good news is he doesn't seem to want to hurt Carly.'

Paula was turning it over in her head, the motives, the showmanship. 'No. He wants contact with Mairead, for whatever reason. What's she saying?'

'She says she won't meet him. That's why she gave us this. She wants us to find Carly and take her back.'

That was strange. Mairead had already declared she would do anything to find her daughter safe. But not meet her own brother? 'Maybe we can set something up,' Paula said, thinking aloud. 'If he's gone to meet Mairead, he can't be holding Carly at the same time. It could be we can swoop in and protect them both.'

'Unless he has help,' said Corry grimly. 'The old Republican brotherhood. It hasn't gone away, as Mr Adams once so astutely said.'

'What can he want from Mairead, that he'd risk surfacing like this? The man's been on the run for twenty years.'

'No idea. And she won't tell us, even if she does know. Whatever it is, if he's that determined, he won't be easily duped.'

'Will we put the image out?' Avril was already moving towards her desk, ready to launch their usual arsenal of posters and TV alerts and public bulletins, but Corry held up a hand.

'He said she wasn't to go to us. And she did. If we release this to the press he'll know she went behind his back. We have to be careful here. We have to set some kind of trap for him.'

To catch a man who'd been eluding them for decades. A shadow with a name, who still made people fall silent in fear. 'Where is Mairead?'

'Relatives' room. Distraught, of course, but there's still something she's not telling us. I'm sure of it.'

Paula heard herself say, 'Let me talk to her. I might have an idea.'

Margaret

She was losing track of the days. There was only the walls, the light fading and brightening above her, the stench of terrible things, and then when the door opened every so often, the rush of light and the air with its smell of farm animals. Benign. Blinking and looking to see who it was this time. If it was Aisling, that was good. The other men were OK too – Sean, one was called, the older one, and the other she thought they'd said was Finbar or Fintan or something like that. He hardly looked at her, as if he was embarrassed at what they were doing. So they should be. Maybe she could ask him for help, if she got him alone.

Worst was Paddy, the boss of it all, with the handsome face and the killer's eyes.

Today it was him. 'Margaret! And how are you keeping?' Friendly. As if they'd bumped into each other in the street.

She opened her mouth to say something biting, and instead heard sobs tear out of it, a terrible animal sound. 'I'm afraid. I'm so afraid.'

'That's good. You should be afraid, Margaret. Maybe then you'll realise what you've got yourself into.'

'I do. I have.' Tears dripped off her nose and ran into her mouth, salty. They said blood was salty too.

'Good. So you'll talk.'

The fear rose up in her again, like the beating wings of some terrible black bird. 'I don't know anything! What can I tell you if I don't know anything?'

'You could tell me a name. Who else has been recruited by your fella. The one you've been messing about with, and you a married Catholic lady.' He tutted. 'That's not very nice now, is it, Margaret?'

'I don't know what you mean.' Her voice shook. 'I just passed on the papers. It was a different person every time. I left them in the hedge outside work.' This was what they'd coached her to say if she got caught. At the time she'd thought it was silly. Who would ever look at her, a mother and a wife with a wee office job on the side?

He sounded disappointed. 'Ah now, Margaret. Sure we know that isn't true. We've been watching you for months, love. Meeting up with lover boy in his car. Kisses in the dark. You never left nothing in that hedge. If you don't know names, tell me where I can find him.'

But they knew where his flat was, his car. That meant he must have gone. Back to England, without her? 'I . . .'

'Buggered off, hasn't he? Got wind of something, and left you here all on your owny-oh. So tell me, Margaret. Where would he go? He's a dirty Brit anyway. You'll be better off. Then you can go back to your family and not another word about it.'

She said nothing. She was shaking so hard the ropes were eating into her wrists. It would be so easy. Just say, there's another place, a safe house. A wee flat behind the market. The place it had all happened between them, with its scratched cheap furniture and smell of old cooking. That day she'd wanted to end it all, crying, angry. *I want out. My family. It's not safe.* That time she'd thought someone followed her home, footsteps on the darkening street, fading away. Her breath held. Edward's calm voice, his gentle eyes. *We can't force you, Margaret. But you don't know how many lives you've saved. How many police officers, like your husband, are alive because of you.*

She'd gone to walk out then. How dare he mention PJ! But he'd caught her arm, and something about it, the fear, the anger, and him so close, and it had just . . . happened. She'd broken her wedding vows. A sin. She wondered what her mother, disapproving Kathleen Sheeran, would say if it all came out. If they discovered her body dumped in some ditch with a bullet wound in her head, and they all found out about the baby. What would Paula say, knowing her mother was not only a tout but a sinner too? And this baby. Poor mite, it hadn't done anything wrong, and it was going to die along with her too.

She was crying harder now. *Just say it. Say it! Give him up.* But her mouth was empty, the words gone.

Paddy's face darkened. 'He wouldn't do it for you, I can guarantee. Where is he now, eh? You've been missing for days. Your husband's looking for you, or trying to at least. Not that he's having much luck. So where's lover boy?'

It hurt to think that, of Paula and PJ bewildered and lost, searching for her. As the days went on, going back to her life seemed further and further away.

He stood up. 'That's very disappointing, Margaret.' She felt his hand drop on her hair, matted and dirty now. 'You've lovely hair,' he said, stroking it. 'That red. It's like fire, so it is.' She was trembling. His hand was gentle, until it wasn't. She yelped as he tugged on a handful of her hair. More tears came to her eyes. 'You know what they did to French women, Margaret, in the war? The ones who collaborated with the Nazis?'

She saw where this was going and tried not to feel the blow. It was only hair. It would grow back.

Hadn't she once read that hair kept on growing in the grave, long after the rest of you was bones?

Paddy was taking something out of his pocket, absorbed in the task like PJ when he mended his glasses with the wee screwdriver. He hated wearing the glasses. Thought they made him look weak. It was a knife. Then he had her hair in one hand and the blade in the other, and it was severed, he was hacking away at it. The separation of it felt strangely awful. Just hair, she reminded herself. But she couldn't stop crying. It was pathetic.

It took ten minutes to clear her whole head. She couldn't see it but she could feel it lying in tufts, her neck cold and bare. She'd worn her hair long all her life. Her mother had started to hint it was time to cut it all off. *A woman shouldn't have long hair over forty, Margaret.* Patting her own grey rinse. Margaret saw Paddy frown, and she realised her sobs had turned into demented, cracked laughter. If only he knew he was doing her mammy a favour. None of this made any sense.

Chapter Sixteen

Mairead was in the family room, pacing up and down, twisting her hands together. She looked up as Paula went in. 'Any news?'

'I'm sorry. We're trying to narrow down the search area based on the video. We think it's along the border somewhere.' But how would they find them there, an area full of fields and woods, the actual border just a line on a map with no markers these days? No Man's Land, they'd always called it. In the bad old days, if a suspect could make it there, he could disappear over and hide in the Republic. Something Paddy Wallace had done for twenty years – so why was he back now? Why did he want to kidnap his sister's daughter, who he'd never even met?

Mairead was staring at her. 'Then go there! Get her back!'

'Mairead . . . it's a big area. You haven't given any more thought to his offer?'

She turned away violently. 'You don't know what you're asking. I can't.'

'He won't hurt Carly. He just wants to talk to you.'

Her voice was low. 'You don't get it. There's nobody he wouldn't hurt. He . . . he's not like other people. He doesn't care what he does. Even all the political stuff. Sometimes I used to wonder – did he really care? You know? If you want a United Ireland that much why not get elected to somewhere, do it that way? Not by killing people. I think it's just . . . who he is. It's why I got away. And for years afterwards we moved around, me and Carly, this house, that crappy flat, cash-in-hand jobs. All in case he came after us. Do you understand? He's raging I got away, and he'll do anything to punish me. I never should have come back here.'

Paula knew the feeling. 'That can't have been much of a life, Mairead. Running away, always looking over your shoulder.'

She sat down on the edge of the sofa, put her head in her hands. 'It wasn't. Carly didn't get it – I couldn't explain, could I? She was angry. That Facebook post – I can hardly blame her. She wanted more out of life than just me and her, always running, always leaving jobs and people and towns.'

Paula moved closer, perching on the arm of the sofa. The room was carefully chosen to make people open up – soft pastel fabrics, a carpet your feet sank into, unlike the scratchy thin blue stuff in the rest of the building. 'Maybe this is the chance to stop all that, then.'

Mairead didn't look at her, but her shoulders tensed. 'He won't stop.'

'He will if he's in jail, won't he?'

She seemed to consider this. 'He'd get out in a heartbeat. They all do these days, like we're just meant to forget all about the Troubles, forget all the people they murdered for years and years.'

'The Good Friday Agreement only covers crime up to ninety-eight. Anything he did after that, he can be prosecuted for.'

She thought about it for a moment. 'How long would he get?'

'For abduction? I can't say. Eight years, maybe.' More if

he'd hurt Carly, but Paula didn't say that. 'And if he comes out there's restraining orders, and electronic tagging – we can help you get away again. Start a new life, out of the country maybe. But at least for a while, you'd be free. And you never know. Once we catch him, there might be other charges we can dig up.' Unfortunate choice of words there, but Mairead seemed to get what she meant. The dead bodies at the farm – Paddy Wallace must have had a hand in that, surely.

'I . . .' Mairead's hands were white. 'You must think I'm a terrible mother, not to go and meet him when he has my girl. I'd give anything to get her back, Dr Maguire, I would. But I'm just so scared. I feel like . . . like it's choking me.' A small sob escaped her lips.

'We don't think that at all. But if you can trust us – trust us to follow you with back-up and cameras and officers on standby, I really think this can all be sorted out. Carly back safe, and your brother in prison where he belongs.'

Mairead thought about it, as if letting herself imagine such an outcome. That was more than half the battle, Paula knew. She was getting through to her. 'She's all I have now. My whole family – gone. I had to leave them all behind, cut all the ties. And now he has her.'

Paula settled herself, ready to offer up the last card she had. 'I know what that's like, Mairead. My mother went missing when I was thirteen. We never found out what happened to her.'

'Oh, I—'

'I tried to run from this place too. Start a new life in London. But it kept bringing me back, because I had unfinished business here. It wasn't really living, with all that on my back. Maybe this is your chance, to be free of it.'

'I'm so scared.' The words were whispered.

'I know. But we can get Carly back, Mairead. I wouldn't say that if I didn't believe it.'

'OK,' she said in a small voice.

Paula could hardly believe her ears. 'You mean . . .'

'I'll do it.' She squared her jaw. 'You're right, it's no life, always running with one eye behind you. It's time we ended all this, Paddy and me. It's time we talked.' She looked up fearfully. 'You promise you'll send people with me? I can't do it on my own.'

'I promise. You're doing the right thing.' She wanted to ask more about the dead girl, her resemblance to Carly, but remembered Corry's advice about not pushing, and held off.

Corry was waiting in the corridor when Paula went out, shutting the door gently behind her. 'Well?'

Paula gave a subtle thumbs up.

'You're kidding me.'

'Nope. She'll do it.'

'Maguire, whatever they're paying you in London, I hope it's enough. Let's go and order a helicopter.'

Chapter Seventeen

Since Paula was the one who had persuaded Mairead to go ahead with the meeting, Corry allowed her to go out on the operation. 'But stay with the second team, OK? Willis Campbell would have my hide if he thought I'd put you in the front line. You can observe but you're to stay in the van at all times.' The first team would be shadowing Mairead to her meet-up with her brother, scheduled to take place in a quiet clearing in the woods near the Red Road farm. The second would swoop in once the helicopter, hovering over the border area, had identified Paddy leaving from one of the farmhouses they had under surveillance. They'd found five in the vicinity that seemed promising, and one, abandoned after its elderly owner went into a home, that was the most likely bet.

Mairead was in the incident room, her face like a sacrificial victim's. Paula felt a stab of terrible guilt – how could they make the woman do this? At least she was going along too. That seemed only right, that she wouldn't sit back here and wait in safety while Mairead went out to meet him. And it was the only way to get Carly back. Mairead wore trainers and jeans, a black zip-up hoody, no make-up. As if trying to make herself as small and pale as possible. 'What's going to happen?' She looked round nervously at the Tactical Support team gearing up, the room reeking of machismo and banter. The women on the team were just as bad as the men.

Corry spoke soothingly. 'You'll drive yourself as near as possible to where you said you'd meet.' Mairead had texted Paddy in a carefully worded message the night before. No reply. He'd know they could trace the phone if he used it again. 'We'll be following behind from a safe distance, and officers will also fan out through the woods. Meanwhile, once we get confirmation of which farm he's at, our second team will move in and hopefully get Carly back.'

'And if we don't?'

There was no good answer to that. 'We've planned it as carefully as we can. I'm confident we'll succeed.'

'Do you have guns?' Mairead asked.

'We all have them as a matter of routine here, as you may know. Not like in England.'

She nodded, as if slightly appeased. 'He'll have one, I bet. He was always into guns. Like some kind of gangster, he thought he was.'

'We'll be just nearby. I promise.'

Mairead took a deep breath. Paula knew she was witnessing someone about to go through the most terrifying ordeal of her life. Meeting her own brother. Again she wondered what had happened between the Wallace children. To scatter them like this. To make Mairead run and hide herself, and Aisling too, if she was even alive. She dropped a hand on Mairead's shoulder and the woman flinched. 'You're very brave,' she said quietly. Mairead set her jaw and looked away.

'It's time,' said Corry, who was also dressed in her field clothes, a stab vest and black hat hiding her blond hair. 'Maguire, you stay behind and go with the next convoy.'

Paula watched them walk out, Mairead's slight figure lost in the crowd of officers with their guns.

Not long after, she too was on her way with the second team, driving in an unmarked minivan out of town, through the weekday traffic and quickly out into the wilds, the fields and bogs and forests that surrounded Ballyterrin. A million places to hide a body, bury it so it might never be found again. Gerard was beside her, disgruntled at being sent away from the action, compensating for it by trying to tell the police driver, a huge country fella, the quickest ways out of town. There were also three other officers Paula didn't know, all burly and grim-faced. She felt very out of place.

'You'll want to take the bypass, Market Street does be bunged at this time.'

Paula nudged Gerard. 'Leave it, Monaghan, or you'll be out and walking.'

Gerard scowled. 'This is the crappy assignment. We don't even know if the girl will be there.' They were waiting for the radio to come to life with info from the helicopter team. 'Dunno why Corry put me on this. I've proved myself over and over to her. Cool head, good shot, what more does she want?'

'Relax, would you? If we find Carly you'll get all the glory, saving the missing girl and all that.'

He pouted a bit more. 'Suppose.'

'Anyway, you're getting married soon. Maybe she wanted you safe and sound, you know.'

'She's not my mammy, Maguire.'

'Ah, but you're her wee darling boy all the same,' she teased. The other officers chuckled softly. Gerard slumped, cross. The radio crackled and he sat bolt upright but it was the driver who answered, slow and steady.

'Unit Two. Aye. Aye. Copy.' Then he started the van. They'd been idling in a siding off the motorway, cars whizzing past at way past the speed limit, then slowing down ostentatiously when they saw the van. Everyone knew the police sometimes sat in unmarked vehicles to catch motorists – but today they had another agenda.

'What did they say?' Gerard demanded of the driver.

'It's where we thought. That ould farm out the Dundalk road. Van left there three minutes ago heading towards the forest.'

'Let's go then.'

They were already going, of course. The driver raised his eyebrows at Paula in the mirror, and Paula smiled indulgently to herself. She'd missed Gerard and his *Miami Vice* antics. She'd missed a lot of things about working here, she realised.

The abandoned farm was only a few miles away, down a twisty dirt track and over a cattle grid. There were no other houses anywhere near, just fields and trees sighing uneasily in the breeze. She could see why Wallace had chosen it. 'Careful now,' said Gerard, as the team climbed out. 'He might not be acting alone. Maguire, stay in the van.'

She'd known she'd have to do that, but it still stung, watching them move out in formation across the farmyard, towards a series of dilapidated barns. The farm looked dead and abandoned, but the smell of animals still permeated it. A sad and barren place, the wind blowing right off the mountain. The driver in the front was a solid, silent presence she was glad of. She nodded to the silent radio. 'Anything from the other team?'

He just shook his head, calm, and she sat back, drumming

her fingers on the side of the car. It was hard, to be caught up in the adrenaline of a raid, but not allowed to join in under pain of the worst Corry could come up with.

Jesus! A hand banged against the window, and Paula looked out, startled, to see a white face staring in at her, and a figure shivering in a cheap denim jacket. 'Carly! Can you . . .' The driver unlocked the door and she opened it. 'My God, get in, get in! Where did you come from?'

'Over there. The shed.' Her teeth were chattering. 'He left it open. He didn't lock it this time. I thought, the van – I thought it was him coming back. Then I saw you and I ran. Please, get me out of here!'

'You're safe now. In you get.' The driver was already on the radio as the girl huddled down in the back of the van, murmuring in his unhurried way, while Paula's heart was hammering. Carly looked unhurt, no obvious injuries, no blood on her clothes.

'What do you mean, she's there?' Gerard crackled, over the radio.

Paula shouted, 'She came up to the van! She's fine.' Paula looked at Carly again. 'Are you fine?'

She nodded, still shivering. 'He just locked me up. It was horrible, and freezing at night, but he didn't like, hurt me.'

Gerard's voice, over the crackling radio, sounded almost disappointed. 'There's nobody here. Some food and stuff in the kitchen but otherwise no one's been here in years, by the looks of it.'

'Let's get Carly back home so Forensics can go in. She's freezing, poor girl.'

Carly looked up at Paula, her blue eyes burning. 'Where's my mum?'

Chapter Eighteen

The ride back to the station was tense. The radio remained stubbornly silent, giving out nothing but static. Paula told herself this was normal. Sometimes, in an evolving situation, a team didn't have time to check in. But it should have gone smoothly. The forest had been crawling with cops. They should have been easily able to swoop in and lift Paddy Wallace as soon as he and his sister made contact, bring Mairead back to safety and her daughter.

'Where's my mum?' said Carly again. Paula had given the girl her own jacket to wear but she was still shaking, though it wasn't particularly cold. Shock, probably.

'She went to talk to your uncle. He said he'd give you back if she did.' Paula glanced at Gerard. 'We . . . we're just waiting to hear from the other team who went with her.'

'Why did he even take me?' Carly burst out. 'I just wanted to find my family – she'd never tell me anything about them. He got in touch, he was nice. My uncle. And he came to the house and I made him tea, and next thing he pointed a gun at me.'

Paula gently lifted Carly's sleeve and nodded when she saw the healing gash on the girl's wrist. The blood in the lift had likely come from that. 'You tried to run?'

'Course I did. I saw he was weird. What's the matter with him?'

'Carly, the reason your mum took you away from all this, from Ireland, from this town – well, it's because her family were mixed up in some pretty bad things. Your uncles were both involved in the IRA. One's in prison here in town, and Paddy, he's been on the run for years now. This is the first time he's surfaced since the nineties.'

Carly looked baffled, as well she might. 'So where's my mum now? Did you go with her to meet him? Because he's not right in the head, you know.' Her Liverpool accent rose, panic suffusing her voice.

Paula was aware of the uncertainty in her own tone. 'We shadowed her. He was very clear she had to go alone. We planned to tail them, then monitor the situation and arrest him.'

'And? Did you?'

Paula and Gerard exchanged another glance. 'I . . . we're still waiting to hear, Carly.' She managed not to tell the girl none of this would have happened if she'd stayed put like she was supposed to, accepted her mother's lies as the protection they were, not gone seeking the family Mairead had done everything to run from. She had to try and understand. What if Maggie had questions one day, like Carly had? About who her grandmother had been, and where she'd gone? About exactly who her father was, and what had become of the man who'd been her daddy for two years? 'I'm sure we'll hear something soon. Look, we're almost back at the station. You're safe now. Let's get you some clothes and something hot to eat, how about that?'

Carly was panicking. 'I don't care about that. Where is my mum? What are you not telling me?'

Just then the radio went and the driver spoke, so low Paula could not hear what was said. 'Is that . . .'

'It's the station.'

'And . . .'

He met her eyes in the mirror, glanced at Carly and shook his head. A warning. Whatever had happened to the other team, it was not something they should say in front of the girl.

They just had to wait. The control centre would tell them very little, and gradually rumours filtered in. Something had gone wrong. Someone was shot. The team had gone out of contact. Paula and Gerard paced the floor of the office, clock-watching. An hour had ticked by, and Carly had been despatched to hospital for a check-up, when finally the incident room door opened and Corry limped in. Paula could see from her face things were bad. 'What happened? Oh my God.' Under the body armour, her boss's white shirt was spattered in blood.

'Calm down, it's not mine. Poor Hanrahan. God love him. We had to drop him off at hospital. He's a bullet through his chest.'

'What happened?'

Corry sighed. 'An almighty fuck-up, that's what. I have to go and brief Willis in a minute. A few of the other lads are injured too.'

'He had other people with him?' She couldn't imagine one man doing all this damage, not to a team of six officers.

'That's the worst of it, Maguire. He didn't. Just that one fella. He was waiting for us – he'd guessed what we were planning. Mairead was hardly even out of the car, but as soon as we pulled up there he was. Put a bullet in Hanrahan and before we could track the source he'd got Mairead. Must have dragged her off into the forest, under our noses.

We looked everywhere but they'd vanished. We had no one to stay with the van, Hanrahan was the driver, so we couldn't radio. It was . . . a difficult situation. We had to rush him straight to hospital.'

'Jesus Christ.' She'd done this. She'd convinced the woman to go through with it, and now she was gone. 'But how could Wallace just disappear? We had officers all over the place.'

Corry grimaced. 'The Ghost. That's what they used to call him, aye? Well, I can see why. He knows that land inside out – he'll have spent most of his life hiding from Army patrols out there. We underestimated him, Maguire.'

'This is bad.' Paula shook her head. 'We walked her right into it. Willis will want to see all the risk assessments. We might even be looking at suspensions.' And it had been her persuasion that made it happen.

'I know. The press will crucify us for this too.' Corry heaved a sigh, easing off the straps on her armour. 'I hear Carly's safe and sound, anyway.'

'Well, yes, but she's pretty worried about her mum. She knows something's not right.'

'I don't get it. Why would he let us take Carly back so easily? She wasn't even locked in, I heard?'

'No. He'd been keeping her in one of the outbuildings, giving her food and a mattress, not mistreating her. Then when he went he unlocked her.'

'Why?'

Paula had been thinking this over. 'He was one step ahead of us the whole time. It was Mairead he wanted all along, and he was prepared to give Carly up to get her. Maybe Carly was just the lure in bait and switch – no real interest to him. It was his sister he was after.'

'The question is – why? What is it about that family?'

Paula just shook her head, imagining what she'd say to Mairead, if she ever saw her again. *I'm sorry. I'm so sorry.* She'd thought it would be safe, that he'd be outnumbered, that they could protect Mairead with their firepower and tactics and back-up teams. Stupid. She'd forgotten the number one rule – it was those closest to us who could hurt us the most.

The indignant figure of Willis Campbell appeared in the doorway, bristling from his shiny shoes to his even shinier hair. 'DI Corry. My office, please.'

Corry didn't even roll her eyes. Paula had never seen her so broken down. 'Will you do me a favour and call your wee pal at the hospital? I need to know how Hanrahan's doing.'

Margaret

'Aisling?' She whispered the name as the door opened, the noisy clunk of it making her stomach contract in terror. Light flooded in, letting her see the full squalor of the place she was in. Bare ground, and over in the corner some dark rusty stains she knew in her stomach were blood. People had died in here, many times. Soon it would be her turn. But no. She was still alive, she had to focus on that.

A figure stood in the doorway, silhouetted against the light so she couldn't see who it was. A young girl. 'Aisling, is that you?'

It wasn't, she knew it already. Her spine bristled with fear. The new girl moved forward, pulling the barn door closed behind her, tugging on the string so the bare overhead bulb lit up. It was worse than nothing, these little snippets of the outside she got when someone came in. The smell of grass and cows, sometimes the roar of an agricultural vehicle. Out in the country somewhere, on a farm. She heard the rattle of cattle grids sometimes. She couldn't be that far from town, she kept telling herself; surely they'd find her. Surely any minute now Edward and his lot would come bursting through the door, soldiers in camo coming to rescue her, all guns blazing. Funny how she'd started thinking of the Army as her side. To everyone else round here they were the enemy, the ones who might shoot your kids if they drove or ran too fast past a checkpoint, kill them and then face no consequences. But she'd aligned herself with them. And now here she was.

She could see the girl now. Younger than Aisling, no more than thirteen, but they must be sisters. The same dark, shiny hair, strong nose, ice-blue eyes. Same eyes as the man who asked the questions. A family, then. How many siblings were there? 'Hello,' she tried. 'I'm Margaret.'

The girl just stared, a curious expression on her face, interested and almost excited. 'I wanted to see you. I didn't believe they'd a woman in here.'

'Yes, and I have a wee girl just your age, and I really need to get back to her.' A lie. Wasn't it? She couldn't go back to her old life now, no matter what happened. 'So if you could help me, pet, I'd really appreciate it.'

'Help you?' She wrinkled her nose.

'I know it's your family keeping me here, but honestly I don't know anything. I'm just a mammy, same as your mammy probably. You wouldn't like it if someone took your mammy away, now would you?' Had she judged it right? Maybe the girl was older than she looked. There was a hardness in her eyes that wasn't there in Paula's, who was always crying about something and mooning over boys or that fella off that TV show she loved, the one with the aliens. 'Maybe you could just call someone for me, the police or—'

The girl snorted. 'I'm not a tout, missus. And I know what you did.'

Margaret's heart sank. This whole family was insane for the cause. 'But I didn't—'

'You didn't pass on names to the Army? You didn't copy stuff out of your work?'

All true. She fell silent. 'I thought I was doing good. Stopping people dying.'

'You're a traitor.' The girl walked closer, holding out one finger, the nail bitten. There was red varnish smeared on it, not allowed at Paula's school. She pushed at Margaret's nose. It was gentle but somehow horrific, the idea of this wee girl having power over her. She couldn't move her hands to push back.

'Are you off school today then?' She tried to keep it chatty, in the realm of the normal. Mainly to stop herself losing the head entirely.

'I don't go to school.' She turned, her dark hair swishing and whipping Margaret in the face. 'Has our Aisling been helping you then?'

'No, no, we just . . . she talks to me sometimes. That's all.'

'Silly bitch. She's a traitor too.'

There was the noise again, the squeaking of the metal door, and Margaret felt a stab of relief someone was coming so that it wasn't just this strange girl and herself, even though it was surely someone much worse than a teenager. 'Emer! What the fuck are you doing in here?' A man. The older one, with tattoos up his arms, head shaven. Not good-looking like Paddy. More normal somehow. She recognised his voice – he'd come to the house to lift her, him and some other fella. There were three men in total. Handsome man, this tattooed man, and some other quieter one. Sean, this one was called, she thought.

'I just wanted to see her,' said the girl he'd called Emer.

'Well, you better get out before Paddy catches you. This is no place for weans.'

'I'm not a wean. I want to help.'

The man laughed. 'Aye, well, make us a cup of tea then.'

'Don't laugh. Don't laugh at me, Sean! I know what you're doing. I can help.'

Margaret listened to all this, helpless and passive. Sometimes they talked in front of her like she was an object, or dead already. It didn't matter what the dead heard, after all. That was the thought which chilled her most.

'Feck on out of here now. Come on.' The girl went, reluctantly, and the door squeaked closed, shutting out the sunlight and air. Margaret found she was thinking of something Edward had said to her once, lying in the single bed in that horrible safe house in town, behind the market. Even there she'd been rigid with fear the whole time, sure that someone would see her and ask what she was doing in that end of town, and the market only on Thursdays. You could hide nothing in Ballyterrin. She had her story all planned – she was going to see a physiotherapist. There was one next door and if necessary she'd book and pay for it. Lying was second nature to her now.

Edward had been talking about his training, when he joined the SAS, before the injury that sent him into Intelligence. About this house they used for training soldiers at their HQ, full of pretend people, plastic models. You went in and you had to decide who to shoot and who to leave be, all in a second, like you would on a raid. 'The Killing House', he'd called it, tracing his fingers over her stomach. 'That's what they call it. The Killing House. But it's just pretend killing. It's nothing at all like real life, when it comes down to it.'

Not like here. If she ever spoke to him again, she'd tell him she knew what he was talking about now. That she'd been in the real-life killing house as well, and there was nothing pretend about it.

Chapter Nineteen

Hanrahan, the unfortunate victim of the botched operation, was sitting up in bed by the time they got to hospital, his chest bandaged tight. 'Flesh wound,' he'd said with bravado, though his face was drained of blood. He'd been lucky the bullet had missed his chest cavity, going through his shoulder instead, but he'd need a lot of physio to get movement back in the arm.

'Well, Marty,' Corry greeted him. 'Been in the wars?'

'I'll live. Any news?'

Corry shook her head grimly. 'There's no sign of him. We're combing the area.'

'How?'

'I've no idea. If you're up to it, would you mind looking at the body-cam footage? Might shed some light. You'll have to see yourself get shot, though.'

'Sure I saw it in real time. Show me.'

Corry had brought a laptop with her, which she now placed on his over-the-bed table. The footage was shaky and the audio very poor, given the wind that day, but it showed the rest of the team, plus a terrified Mairead, pull up near a clearing in the forest. The plan had been for Mairead to get out and walk to the meeting with Paddy alone, as if she'd driven herself. But Paddy had clearly been way ahead of them. As soon as the van stopped and Mairead got out, there was the sound of a shot, the camera shaking badly, and then everything was shouting and confusion, people dragging Hanrahan out and tending to him, and random slices of arms, trees, faces, panicked breathing, running feet.

Corry said, 'Then when we looked around Mairead was just . . . gone.'

'Gone?' said Paula, struggling to understand this. They were a highly trained team of six officers, and one lone man had run rings around them.

'She was standing there watching, looking scared, and I was trying to help Marty here, and the rest were fanning out into the trees looking for the shooter, and next thing I know I look back and she's gone. He took her, in the middle of all that.' Corry was shaking her head. Apart from the profess-ional reprimand she'd likely already received from Willis, it was deeply frustrating, and not a little frightening, for armed police to realise they'd been useless when it came down to it.

Paula said, 'Did no one get a look at him, or see anything that might be useful?'

Corry's face was grim. 'No one else had a cam except me, no one saw him. The man's like . . . well, like a ghost.'

And now he had Mairead. 'What can we do?' said Paula, the guilt weighing down on her like a stone. 'We have to get her back – we put her in that situation.' *I put her in that situation.*

'We need to question Carly now, see if she saw anything. Otherwise, I don't know how we're going to find him.'

'I can't let you go in. I really can't. Sorry.' Saoirse was only five foot two, but she barred the way to Carly's hospital room all the same, implacable. 'She isn't well enough to answer questions.'

'But we need to find her mother,' Corry objected. 'Surely she'd be up to pointing at a map, telling us if he mentioned any place names. I thought she wasn't physically hurt?'

'Not now. I'm sorry. She's very distressed – I gave her something so she'd sleep.'

Corry sighed, tapping the toe of her flat shoe. She hadn't changed out of her field uniform yet. 'Well, has she said anything, talked to the nurses? Any information at all would really help us out.'

Saoirse relented. 'You can sit with her for a moment. If she wakes up, you can try a few questions. Don't push her. The poor girl is distraught.'

Corry slipped into the room, and Saoirse put up a hand to stop Paula following. 'Don't crowd her, OK?'

'OK.' Through the window, Paula could see Carly lying in bed, tiny and pale without her make-up. She seemed to be out cold, but Corry settled beside her, giving the girl's hand a tender pat. Her own daughter, Rosie, was not much younger than Carly.

Paula turned to her friend. 'Poor girl. Will she be OK?'

'Physically, yes. But if you don't find her mother . . .'

Paula winced, not wanting to think about the end of that sentence. 'I know. What about you, are you OK?' Saoirse looked well. Glowing, as the cliché went.

'Ah, I'm grand.' Despite the grim place they were in, full of sickness and worry, Saoirse couldn't keep the smile from her face. 'Everyone tells you how awful it is, the boking and the tiredness, but nobody says it's great too. You know that feeling, that you're never on your own? That somebody's always with you? I get these little bubbles sometimes, in my stomach. Excitement. Or maybe it's them, saying hello.' Her hand went over her stomach, protective.

Paula didn't want to ruin it by telling her that the feeling of never being alone was less fun when you hadn't peed by yourself in three years. 'Yeah.'

Saoirse's face hardened. 'I can understand it, you know. Why Carly's mother risked it. You'd do anything for them, wouldn't you? I already would.'

'I know. At least we got Carly back. You really think she'll be fine?'

'I don't see why not. There's nothing medically wrong with her; she wasn't mistreated. She's just worried sick about her mum, poor girl. You'll be able to question her soon and . . .' They both turned as a tapping sound came down the corridor, and a blonde woman with a cane, wearing red Converse, approached them. 'Maeve!' said Saoirse, leaning to hug her. 'God, I haven't seen you this long time.'

'I know, I know, nose to the grindstone. But I hear congratulations are in order?' Maeve nodded to Saoirse's stomach, under her white coat, and Saoirse beamed.

'Early days, but, yeah.'

'Well, that's great. Sinead and me had some good news too.'

Saoirse made a sort of girly squealing sound, which was disconcerting when you knew she'd likely been up to her elbows in someone's chest only minutes ago. 'That's amazing! She's expecting too?'

'Aye, well, I can hardly do it now. Due in Feb.'

'I'm March. We'll have to get together.'

Paula smiled at them, her two friends – though Maeve Cooley, a Dublin-based investigative journalist, had been Aidan's friend to start with. She was happy for them, with their partners and babies and lives, but it just reminded she was spinning her own wheels, waiting for a man who was maybe never coming back, at least not in the same way.

Saoirse's pager went and she departed, promising to email Maeve to compare notes about pregnancies. 'What brings you here?' said Paula, knowing Maeve went where the story was. But surely the news about Mairead wasn't out yet. They'd want to spin that as best they could, not reveal that one man had got around an entire trained team.

'Heard you got Carly Jones back. That's good, is she OK?'

'She's not talked so far. She's in a bit of a state.'

'And it was Paddy Wallace who had her? Did you see him?'

It reminded her of Aidan, this oh-so-casual questioning, which was not casual at all. Paula gave her a wry look. 'Would I tell you if I had?'

Maeve shrugged. 'Worth a try. This on-the-run stuff is getting good coverage right now. Add in the kidnapped girl, the long-lost niece, and well – I might be sticking around Ballyterrin for a bit. How's Aidan?'

The question took her by surprise. 'Well, he's – I don't know. He's been having visitors, though. Seems like a good sign.' She could tell from Maeve's nod she already knew that. 'You saw him too?' He'd see anyone except her, it seemed. She tried not to mind.

'He asked me to come. He's ready to fight this thing, I think.'

Paula frowned at her. 'What do you mean?'

'He's talking about launching an appeal. Seeing lawyers. You know, everything we wished he would do last year.' Maeve peered at her. 'That's good news. Isn't it? If he wants to appeal?'

'I . . .' Paula gestured helplessly. 'I'm so afraid, Maeve.

They might not even agree to an appeal. All the evidence, it's so damning, and I'm afraid – I'm going to lose him forever.' And why the change of heart? Aidan had been dead set on going down for the crime, even though they couldn't be certain he'd actually killed Conlon. She wasn't sure she could allow herself to hope again. Once you opened up a chink of light, it could sometimes show you just how bad things were.

'Ah, come on. There's a chance, still. He didn't do it, that has to count for something.'

'But . . . he might have.' Her voice was a whisper. 'Anyway, it looks as if he did. Maybe that's the same thing, in the courts.' She got a brief flash of what her life might be if these leads on her mother came to something and she was dead. If Aidan's appeal failed. Once the tiny, struggling bit of hope she had was truly stamped on and dead. If her mother was really gone and Aidan was in prison for years, what then? What was Paula's life?

Maeve brushed back her hair, and Paula saw the scarring on her lovely face, from where she'd been caught in a petrol bomb attack a few years before. Something in Aidan had broken seeing his friend like that. *It's me*, he'd said to Paula. *These things keep happening to me. My fault.* And she'd told him not to be so daft, and they'd tried their best, fought for their two years of happiness. Just ordinary happiness, a couple in a terraced house with jobs and a child, but even that they hadn't been allowed to keep.

'I thought my life was over when this happened,' Maeve said, tapping her scar. 'Wouldn't be able to chase down stories, climb over fences, all that malarkey. But I'm fine. Hey, I'm going to be a mammy! Where's that Paula Maguire stubbornness? There's still a chance. Aidan's always got in his own way, he's as contrary as you are, but if he's willing to fight at last, who knows what'll happen? Just have a little faith, Maguire. Don't give up on him.'

Faith. A town like Ballyterrin was steeped in it, faith in marriage and family and God and tradition. Paula had never had much, which was why she'd run away when she could. Now, she found herself wishing she could borrow some. Just to believe that maybe one day, her life would be OK again. She smiled at Maeve as best she could. 'I'll try. In the meantime, how about you tell me something useful on Paddy Wallace? Ghost or no ghost, he's a real-life man, and that means he has to be hiding somewhere. He must have help, to stay under the radar for so long.'

'OK,' said Maeve reluctantly. Even with close friends she liked a little quid pro quo for her information. 'Paddy Wallace used to run an IRA punishment squad, yes? He's been gone for years, and now he's back in town, putting himself at risk of arrest and a long spell in prison. So, why?'

'You tell me.' She'd been wondering about that herself. The timing of it all, the bodies at the farm, Paddy snatching Carly then giving her back. All to get at his sister?

'Have you come across the name Mark O'Hanlon?'

'Hmm, maybe.' It rang a bell, though she wasn't sure why. 'How come?'

'Oh, it's probably nothing, but . . . ask your mate Gerard about him. He turned up dead a few weeks back. Anyway, he was one of Paddy Wallace's pals way back. Helped interrogate people.'

'And he's dead?'

'Aye. He's dead, Sean Conlon's dead, and Paddy Wallace is back.'

Paula waited for more information. 'That's it?'

Maeve raised a hand. 'Like I say, probably nothing. Just ask Gerard, though. And when Carly's ready to talk, you know where I am.'

Chapter Twenty

'He didn't say anything,' Carly insisted. 'We was drinking tea and then he grabbed me. He's so strong! I couldn't . . . I couldn't do anything.'

'He took you in a car?' Corry asked. 'Or was it a van?'

'I dunno. He put this thing on my head, a bag or something like. All rough.' She fingered her shiny dark hair. 'Then we was driving out of town and he pushed me down in the footwell like. Think it was a van or something, maybe. He had to help me up into it. You know.'

'And he never said anything else, didn't mention any other locations?'

'He never said a word to me after that, except for the video. It was . . .' She shuddered in the hospital bed, pulling her jumper around her. 'It was spooky. He never said a thing.'

'All right, Carly. If you think of anything else, please let us know.'

'Where's my mum? Are you looking for her?'

'We . . . we're going to do everything we can.'

'But you had her!' Carly looked between them, incredulous. 'How could he just get her?'

Corry paused. 'I'm sorry. We'll do everything we can.' Her eyes met Paula's – it was a good question. How could they have let this happen? Police roadblocks all round the area had turned up nothing, and the surveillance helicopter was drawing a blank. It seemed as if Mairead and her brother had simply vanished into the landscape, the bleak, forbidding bogland that had swallowed so many secrets before. The next step was to go public, replace the alerts for Carly with ones for Mairead, and that meant explaining to the press and everyone else that they'd managed to find the girl and in the process lose the mother, right under the noses of the police. And Paula knew, deep in her stomach, it was her fault. She'd put Mairead in danger – it was up to her to fix it.

On the way into the station, Paula took her phone out to check for messages, and saw she had two missed calls. She saw the name *Davey*. The PI only ever contacted her when he had news. Her stomach fell away. Today of all days, she really didn't have time for this. She palmed the phone and slipped off to a quiet spot beside the interview rooms.

Once alone she dialled him back, noticing how her fingers left smudged marks on the screen. Her fingerprints, the unique combination of whorls and arcs that only she had. What they used to identify you, if you turned up dead. 'Davey?'

'Well.' His raspy smoker's voice was unusually sombre as he got straight to it. 'No easy way to say this. I've bad news.'

Oh, shit. She leaned against the wall for support. This was it. Her mother was dead, killed in that farmhouse after all. So where was her body? Would they find it somewhere else on the land? Had she been walking about on top of it?

'Your man Edward. Found an obituary for him in *The Times*.'

'When?' Her voice was croaky, strangled.

'Back in 2006.'

'Wh-what happened?'

'Car bomb, outside his house in Croydon. He survived a while but pneumonia got him in the end. His ones must have put this in – father was a major or something in the Army. There's more.'

'Oh?' She couldn't bear to ask it. *Was my mother with him? Did she die too?*

'In the obit – I'll scan it over to you – it says he leaves a wife and child. No names.'

'Do you think . . . ?'

'Aye, it's possible it was her.' Her mother, and the child she had been carrying when she fled Ballyterrin. Paula's half-sibling. It seemed insane.

'There's no other family left, I take it?' It was too much to hope for.

'His ones are long dead now. But I'll keep digging. Somebody'll have known them during that time, be able to look at a photo. Sorry for the bad news.'

'It's OK. Thank you, Davey.'

He rang off with another coughing fit. So, her mother's lover was dead. A man she'd never met, obviously, but all the same she found she was trembling. She shoved the phone into her trouser pocket and tucked her hands under her armpits to stop them shaking. This was stupid. She'd thought she was ready – all those years with no answers, the day the police had dug up the garden looking for a body, the three dead women she'd had to try and identify over the years, none of them her mother. But it turned out you couldn't ever be ready to hear that someone you loved was dead. Your mind could try, but your body, your heart and stomach and heaving lungs, they would always get the news like a physical blow.

'You OK, Maguire?' Gerard was coming up behind her, filling the hallway with his overpowering cologne and hulking shoulders. She remembered she had to ask him about the case Maeve mentioned, but for now everything was focused on finding Mairead.

'Oh, yeah. Any news?'

'We got the results back on that DNA sample from Mairead Wallace.' He held up a sheet of paper. 'Let's go find Herself.'

Corry was staring at the papers lying on the table in front of her. 'This is for definite?'

'Far as they know.' Gerard scratched at the back of his head. Across the room, Avril was on the phone, calling off the search for Carly, co-ordinating with the search teams looking for Mairead. The wedding was in a few days, and this type of case wasn't what they needed. The kind that was like ever increasing circles, answers turning into questions and spinning away.

Corry shook her head. 'So Mairead's a direct familial match with our Jane Doe. I suppose that explains why she wouldn't give the sample.'

That was what the results said. A close relative, but exactly of what type they couldn't be sure. Paula wasn't surprised; ever since she'd seen the likeness between the dead girl and Carly Jones she'd suspected as much. She said, 'Does this mean Mairead lied? It is Aisling Wallace in the morgue after all?'

Corry shook her head, still staring at the paper as if willing it to give a different answer. 'Not necessarily. This, the reconstruction – none of it's conclusive. And Mairead couldn't ID the body.'

Couldn't, or wouldn't. Paula was frustrated. 'Then who else could it be? It must be her, surely.'

'We should visit the mother again, see if we can get anything more out of her. Monaghan, do you want to take that? See if you can charm the wee girls that work there? You used to be good at that sort of thing.'

He stifled a groan. 'The old folks' home? Seriously?' He saw her face. 'Of course, ma'am.'

Corry turned back to the papers. 'Even if it is Aisling, doesn't mean Mairead lied. I see it all the time, people make the wrong ID. They don't want to accept someone's dead, so they see things that aren't there. I'd like to also compare this result with Carly's DNA. A fresh sample would be better. Wright?'

Avril came over sharpish. Paula saw how tired she looked. The run-up to weddings was stressful. She'd worked herself into the ground before her own, scared to face the truth of what it meant to finally tie herself to Aidan forever. Then, of course, it hadn't even happened. 'Carly's been discharged from hospital, ma'am. We've sent officers to take her to a different safe house.'

Corry looked at her watch. 'Let's send someone to swab her for DNA. We've pussy-footed around that family for too long, and Mairead's been taken because of it. So get cracking, everyone, lots to do. I think we better face the press now – the more we delay the more chance Wallace will get away. Maguire, you staying? Or do you have pressing cartoons to watch at home?'

It was late, already after six. Paula sighed. Of course she was staying – sheer guilt would have seen to that, if nothing else. Every time she thought about Mairead her stomach lurched. She'd promised. And still this had happened. The way the woman's hands shook when she talked about her brother. They had to find her. 'I'll come. Let me just ring Dad and Pat.' Maggie would be fine for another night, but it was this kind of thing which had eventually made her leave Ballyterrin. While she was here, every case was so personal she often couldn't let them go, and it wasn't fair on Maggie. She had to go back to London, whatever happened here. If she stayed in this town she would never get out from under its shadow.

Chapter Twenty-One

The next day Paula was up early, back in the office. It was buzzing, the search for Mairead and Paddy Wallace at full gear, phone calls coming in from the press who were avid to know how on earth they'd cocked this operation up quite so badly. She'd been turning it over in her mind all through the sleepless night. How could two people just disappear like that? Then there was Maeve's question – why had Paddy surfaced now? Surely they would find him, now he had his sister in tow. She made a mental note to ask about Gerard's case, and check up on Paddy Wallace's old associates. No fans of the police, there was a good chance some of them would be helping him hide. She went to Corry's office and knocked, expecting to get her orders for the day. Tozier was there too, sticking his oar in no doubt. Today he wore a jumper over a striped shirt, and sensible trousers.

'Is there anything . . . What's the matter?' In the room an atmosphere, a charge. Something to do with her? She couldn't place it.

Corry was stony-faced. 'Paula, there's no good way to say this . . .'

Her knees were weak. She was sinking down. What was it – Aidan, her dad, Maggie? No, she'd just left Maggie safe with Pat, it couldn't be that.

'We had a tip-off via the Commission this morning,' said

Declan Tozier. He looked uncomfortable with the sudden emotion in the room, standing awkwardly by Corry's desk. 'Maybe you'd like to sit down, Dr Maguire?'

'I'll stand.' She threw the comment at him, eyes on Corry. 'Just tell me, Helen.'

'This informant – obviously we don't know who they were – claimed your mother's buried there too. On the Red Road farm.'

She waited to see how deep the wound was going to go. Nothing. She felt numb. 'Did they say anything else?'

Tozier spoke again. 'They said she was brought there in 1993, abducted from your house as suspected, then kept and interrogated there for several days. They – well, they've given us quite a specific area to search, Dr Maguire. If the information's true we should know in a day or two.'

She tried to picture it. Old bones, coming up dirty with soil. Strips of tattered clothes attached. What had she been wearing that day? Paula had never known; she'd left for school before her mother was dressed, but it was usually some kind of suit for work, or baggy jeans and a sweatshirt in the house. Nineties mum clothes. Nothing special.

But still, she couldn't picture it at all. 'Have you told my dad yet?'

'Not yet. I felt we should bring you both in and—'

She cut Tozier off. 'Let me do it. Did they seem . . . credible? This informant?'

A glance went between the two. Corry spoke gently. 'They knew details we hadn't released about the other two bodies. That it was the barn used for burials and how they were placed, even.'

'Did you get a name for her, the dead girl?'

'No. No name was given, sadly.'

An awkward silence settled. Tozier swallowed, his Adam's apple bobbing. 'Dr Maguire, if there's anything we can do – we have counsellors, teams of people used to supporting families in these kinds of—'

'I'm fine.' She cut him off again. No time for politeness now. 'Could you give me a wee minute with DI Corry, please?'

He went, casting backward looks as if irritated to be put out of the room. 'He's just doing his job,' said Corry neutrally.

'Yeah, yeah, I know. But I'm not some outsider. No need to use the special voice and the tissues, for God's sake.' She saw with some disgust they'd placed a pastel-coloured box on the table, one pulled out suggestively. For what? She wasn't going to cry. Why would she cry when there was an answer, finally? Maybe, anyway. 'The pendant,' she said impatiently. 'The one from the girl's body. I had one just like it in the nineties.'

Corry stared at her, frowning. 'How can that be?'

'I don't know. I lost it, I think. I can't remember when. Everything was topsy-turvy that autumn, when Mum went.'

'Where did you get it from?'

'On holiday in Kerry, I think. I was into all that sappy stuff. Dolphins, kittens, cute animals. My dad bought it for me.' She could remember the feel of it in her hand, chunky and cold. She'd been like a dolphin herself back then, plunging fearless into the cold Atlantic waves. Her father was not a demonstrative man – her mother sorted the presents, always had – so it was a surprise to receive it on her thirteenth birthday a few weeks after their holiday. *Just a wee something extra*, PJ had said, embarrassed. *Know you like those wee things.*

Then of course a month after that her mother was gone, and everything else was forgotten, and her normal teenage world of necklaces and TV and sleepovers with Saoirse was abruptly shattered. She hadn't missed the necklace, couldn't remember when she'd last seen it.

'So . . . how could it have ended up there? Have you been to that farm before?'

She shook her head. 'No. I'm sure I haven't.'

'Ever have a burglary, something like that?'

'No. Dad was a cop, you know. The place was locked up like Fort Knox. Anyway it wasn't worth much, it was just a wee thing.'

'So maybe . . .'

'She could have taken it,' Paula heard herself say, and as she did she knew it made sense. 'My mother. She could have taken this with her when she went. I didn't notice at the time it was gone but . . . she could have.'

Corry digested this. 'When she "went"? I thought you didn't—'

'I know,' Paula interrupted. God, she was tired of this. How could this still be going on, twenty years after her mother had been lost? When she'd been ready to give up, get on with her life, why were these clues surfacing, the note and the pendant and now this tip-off? 'Listen. Last year, I found something.'

And she explained it all: the renovations to her kitchen, the note the builders had found down the back of the worktops, knocked there by her younger self all those years ago, careless and unseeing.

Silence. Corry had stopped pacing and stood staring, her arms folded. 'She left a note.'

'Yes. But I don't know if – I don't know if they still came

and took her anyway. There were men at the house that day. Our neighbour said, but the report . . . well, it doesn't matter. So she might have got away, she might not. If this pendant was found in a place they used for interrogations, and someone's saying they killed her there . . .'

'We'll know soon enough if it's true or not. But this pendant – you should have told me. You never know, it might be the evidence we need to reopen your mother's case.'

'Do we have to do that?' Paula said quickly. 'It's just I haven't told anyone about the note. You know, Dad and Pat. If they found out . . .'

If Paula's mother had got away – if she was alive, maybe living in London – then Pat and PJ's marriage was invalid, their hard-won happiness destroyed. And she couldn't do that to them. Corry understood. 'OK. We'll keep it under wraps for now. It's not really enough to go on anyway – like you said, these necklaces are pretty common. But you can't hide these things from me, Paula.'

'I wasn't sure. And, you know, the case—'

'You wanted to stay on it.' Corry wasn't even cross. 'I see. Well, even put together there's no real proof. But we'll look, of course. They'll start digging tomorrow. You realise what this means, though?'

She nodded. 'No more investigations.' The law was very clear on that point – if remains were uncovered because of a tip-off via the Commission, they were not allowed to use that information to prosecute. Their other two dead bodies, found at the same site, might even fall under that remit too. The chance to prosecute their killer, or killers, was perhaps gone.

'We can try to find out who the girl is, but that might

be all. I know that goes contrary to your nature, Paula. It goes contrary to all our natures – Monaghan's got some choice things to say on the subject. But it's what we have to do – the price we have to pay for all this being over. We'll look for a name to put on that girl's grave, and that's about all we can do.'

'I know that.' She'd known it in practice, of course, since the law came into being, but now it seemed to settle into her how deeply wrong it was. They were the police. How could they find a murdered girl and not put anyone in jail for it? It went against the order of the world.

'And your mother – if she is there, and we find her, we can't do anything either. We can bury her, that's all. We can give you answers. I know you've been looking all this time. I know you think she went to London.'

Paula looked away. Corry saw too much, always had. *But*, she wanted to say. *A psychic told me she was alive, and over the water. But, Edward got out alive, and he was living with a woman and child in London. That could have been her! It could have! She was pregnant when she disappeared.* Another horrible thought came. 'If they do find her – can you tell me first? There's things that my . . . my dad doesn't need to know, maybe.'

'We'll have to see. You know I can't offer special treatment, Paula.'

Did she know it? She stared at the carpet. It needed a good vacuuming. Who was doing the office cleaning these days? 'Are you sure it's even true, this tip-off? I mean, everyone knows about this law, right? So if you wanted to slow down this investigation, and stop us finding out who's in that grave, wouldn't it make sense to phone in a false tip? They probably know I'm working on it. Or at least enough about the case to make it credible – everyone thought the IRA came for her, back then.'

Corry looked at her patiently. 'It could be that. We'll know soon enough, like I said. If you want to hang onto that belief till you know something concrete, that's OK. In the meantime you should go and talk to your father. This is something at least, isn't it? Even if she's . . . you told me once you just wanted to know. Either way.'

'Right.' It was something, but all the same the idea made the bottom of her stomach hollow out, and she realised that when people said that they just wanted answers, they must be kidding themselves. As long as you didn't know for sure, there was hope, and hope was like bindweed holding up the crumbling walls of her life. Without it, she didn't know who she'd be. 'I guess I'm off the case now, then?'

Corry made a face. 'Officially. You can keep doing background stuff, if it'll stop you haring off like a madwoman, but keep your head down. No private investigations. Deal?'

'OK. Deal.'

They broke new ground at the farm at first light, a grey Irish dawn, rain sleeting down on the diggers and workers in their high-vis jackets. June in Ireland. Paula had gone to see it start, her hands shoved deep in her trench coat, red hair damp through as she watched the clods of soil being turned up. Declan Tozier was there too, strands of dark hair plastered to his head with the rain, his glasses steamed up. He wore a high-vis jacket with the logo of the Commission on it, sensible and dull, and Paula was internally mocking him to keep from thinking about what was going on.

'You sure you want to be here? We'll tell you as soon as we know anything.'

'I just needed to see it begin.' How long had she thought of this moment – someone to take her seriously, someone to actually look for her mother? Say that she'd been a person who mattered, who was worth searching for even twenty years on? It meant a lot, she realised now. 'I won't watch all of it.' Because they might turn something up – a bone, a shred of cloth – and then what would she do? She looked away from him, blaming him for all of this, knowing that was unfair.

He took off his glasses and polished them on his jumper. 'I know it's hard about your case, that this might affect the investigation. I'm sorry. The police officers we work with often find it difficult. And with your witness missing as well.'

Paula sighed, relenting. 'It was all my fault. I persuaded Mairead to go and meet her brother and now look. He's got her.'

'She knew the risks. It was worth it to her to get her daughter safe, I'm sure of it.'

She looked at him from the corner of her eye, surprised at his perspicacity. 'How many of these have you done?' She nodded to the diggers, the Commission's own.

'Five. We're still looking for one – not sure if the information was bad or they just couldn't remember exactly where the burial was or what. That happens, you know. People can't always remember. It was a long time ago.'

'I know. You used the GPR here, though, right?'

He hesitated. 'Yes. It did show disturbed ground. But it doesn't always mean there's a burial site. Like I say, people forget, or they call to assuage their conscience but they don't give the right info, or they ring to make mischief. We get a lot of crank calls, if you can believe it.'

She nodded again. She was trying to keep her emotions in

check as best she could, view it as another case to crack. She'd told her father the night before, while Pat put Maggie to bed, in measured tones with the TV muted behind them, men hitting each other with hurling bats. PJ had taken it in, in that quiet way of his, like rain soaking into the ground. 'They'll be digging, then?'

'Yeah. They have to at least look. But Daddy . . .' She'd tailed off, not sure what she wanted to say. 'I don't feel she's there. You know? I just don't.' Her father, she knew, had long ago decided her mother was dead. Had made the choice to move on and marry Pat, aim for some happiness in his life. It was a big leap for them. Paula had heard Pat crying in the bathroom later in the night.

'You don't feel she's gone.' He stared at the silent TV.

'I – I don't know. I never did.' Would she know, if her mother was dead? Would she feel it? She'd no idea.

'Pet, I don't know either. All that stuff people say about having a feeling, I used to hear it a lot on the force. *I just feel he's alive, officer.* When I knew rightly the son was lying dead in our morgue. It's not something we can know until we know. Maybe this'll be it. The way we find out.'

'Or maybe we never will.'

'Aye. I had to face that too.' He'd squinted at her. 'I'm not sure you have, pet.'

She fell silent. It was true, she hadn't. She'd been turning over stones for years now, even hiring Davey Corcoran to ferret out the truth, urging him down dead end after dead end. Was she ready for it, if it came?

Another skiff of rain started her back to the present, the cold day, the noise of the diggers, the wet slap of soil. She hunched her shoulders. 'It's awful weather, I better go in.'

'I'll stay. I like to supervise.' Tozier squared his shoulders into the wind.

'Listen,' said Paula grudgingly. 'Thank you. For looking for her. It means – well, I don't think I realised what it would mean. So, thank you.'

He shrugged. 'We have to pay a high price for it, sometimes. To get them back. I ask myself every day is it worth it, and so far, I always come up with yes. But if you come up with a different answer, I get that.'

Paula still didn't know what she thought. She trudged off, her boots squelching in the mud. The house was shuttered up, the brand-new windows still with their stickers on. She felt sorry for the poor couple who'd bought the place. When she'd sold her own house a few months back, she wasn't sure how much the estate agent had told the buyers. Her mother hadn't died in there, of course. Just disappeared from the kitchen. But maybe now it wouldn't be the last place she'd been seen. Maybe this was, this raw stretch of land, flat and green. She found she'd come to the first pit under what had been the barn, its sides neatly squared off like a grave waiting for a corpse. It was empty, of course, marked with police tape, the bottom filled up with brown water, but she stood and peered into it. Trying to imagine how that girl had been placed in there, with her grave goods about her, the cheap little pendant, her arms folded over her chest. A relative of the Wallaces, but no one prepared to say who. It must have been Aisling, surely. Who else? Her mind went round in circles. If it was her, why had Mairead not admitted as much, let them bury her? *Who are you?* The earth gave nothing back, only the increasing patter as the rain fell into it, swallowed back up by the pit.

Margaret

'What's this?' The girl's nails were uncut, sharp as claws. She snatched at Margaret's neck, scraping the skin there. She'd taken to coming in most days now, and Margaret had learned to dread the fumbling with the lock on the door, knowing what it meant.

She tried to keep her voice reasonable, but fear had dirtied it beyond pretence. 'It's a necklace. My daughter's. She's about your age. I . . . I took it with me when they came for me.'

The girl turned her nose up at that. She appeared untouched by emotion, only curiosity and a certain interested cruelty. Margaret wondered was something wrong with her. She never seemed to be at school, for a start. She wondered if Paula was back – had she taken time off when her mother went missing? Would they be searching for her, out beating hedgerows and dredging ponds? Why hadn't they found her yet? It wouldn't be hard to make the link – they were clearly some kind of IRA squad, these lads. Someone must know their names. They weren't even trying to hide her that well. So why had no one come? Had Bob kept his bargain too well, and sent them on a wild goose chase? She'd thought she might be able to run, just for a while, till everything died down, and she didn't want the police looking at her too closely. She'd been so stupid. And now here she was.

It was surreal, thinking of them all going on with their lives, Paula going to school and PJ to work – with the police! – and Edward with all the resources he had access to, soldiers and spies and manpower. Yet he had not come for her. Sometimes when she drifted off she dreamed about Paula sitting in the kitchen, her red head bent over her homework.

She dreamed she made it back to her door, that same house door she'd opened thousands of times, the paint peeling, the roses in the garden. *I'm back. I got away!* And Paula turned slowly to look at her, her face pale and distant. *Who are you?*

She knew what this dream was telling her. There was no going back, even if someone did come for her. She'd made the choice between her family and the new child she was carrying. Could she bear to see PJ again, and have him look at her differently – not just a tout but a whore, a cheat? Like someone off the soap operas she used to watch during the day when Paula started school, alone in the living room, wondering if her husband would make it back alive that day or not.

Her head jerked up. She had passed out for a few moments. It was happening more and more. The girl was leaning over her, her thick dark hair falling into Margaret's face. She smelled like baby shampoo and cows, an incongruous combination that somehow made Margaret very frightened. For the last two years Paula had smelled of body spray and complicated potions from the Body Shop, all synthetic fruit and flowers. Who was this strange teenager? She had her hand clasped on the pendant round Margaret's neck, the cheap silver dolphin leaping in mid-air. 'I'm taking this. I want it.'

Margaret remembered buying it, in the small gift shop on that island. Only months ago, only in the summer, but how very far they'd come since then. Paula still twelve, right on the edge of being a teenager, young enough to plunge into the sea with no self-consciousness about her swelling chest or long, pale limbs. PJ marginally relaxed for once, the lines from his face gone, not checking under the car every day for bombs before getting in. She'd known even then she would have to face things soon – she wasn't stupid; she knew the signs that she was pregnant – but not yet. A few minutes more before it had to be shattered. It was PJ who had chosen the pendant. He wasn't a man who noticed such fripperies, but on that holiday, far enough away from daily bombs and shooting, he'd pointed to the kiosk near the ferry stop. 'She likes that kind of thing, doesn't she?'

Paula was out of earshot, mooning over a display of mood rings. 'Developing a taste for jewellery?' She hadn't teased PJ for a long time. The lightness that had once been between them had dwindled a bit more every year, dampened down by fear, and the way the long nights waiting for a phone call had soured into anger. Why did he put her through this? Could he not find another job, or move away, leave this bloody town? It was this, in the end, that had pushed her to Edward. She couldn't stand to love PJ and have him killed, like his friend John O'Hara. Easier to run, burn the marriage down herself. But the baby. She'd never meant for that to happen. Did she even know Edward? *Why hadn't he come for her?*

'For her birthday.' PJ had been embarrassed, the silver necklace held in his big RUC man's hand.

'She'll love it. I'll distract her and you pay.'

The necklace had been sitting on the kitchen counter when Margaret heard the car outside, and she'd snatched it up, wanting something of her daughter's. She wondered if Paula would miss it. Probably she wouldn't notice right away. She was careless with her things, like all teenagers, leaving her PE bag on the bus, her purse in the corner shop.

Now the girl was pulling on it, so the chain dug into the back of Margaret's neck. She winced. She told herself it did not matter if she lost it. It was only a bauble, not even worth a fiver, and Paula had just left it lying around. She wasn't allowed jewellery at school and it was chokers that were all the rage now. But all the same it hurt, seeing it grasped carelessly in this girl's dirty hand. Thinking of PJ, ashamed to buy something like that, but wanting to please his daughter. He was a good man. If it wasn't for this war, the endless bloody violence, they could have been happy. She closed her eyes.

'Emer! Fuck's sake, get out of here.' A man's voice. A boy, really. It was the brother, she thought – he must be, he was so like the handsome man. In her head she was trying to keep track of them all. Paddy, the leader. Sean, older, harder somehow, who gave her strange looks like he might want to help, but then never did. Fintan, the dogsbody, who just fetched and carried, hardly meeting Margaret's eyes. This boy, Paddy's brother, she thought, was younger. Nineteen or twenty maybe, his cheeks still boyish with bumfluff and acne. He'd be handsome too in a few years. He'd only been in the barn once, dragged in by his brother. He didn't like what they were up to, clearly. But he didn't stop it.

The girl had dropped the pendant, and it fell back lightly against Margaret's chest, the sweat of the girl's fingers still on it. The brother pushed her out the door, protesting, and Margaret realised she didn't have the strength to appeal to him for help. As the days went on, she was giving up. He turned into the light, his face in shadow. 'Sorry,' he muttered. Then he closed the door again and she heard the padlock click into place.

Chapter Twenty-Two

The phone was ringing. Paula blundered about the bed, groping for a table that wasn't there. Of course, she wasn't in the rented London flat, with the Ikea furniture and orange glow all night long from streetlights. She was in Pat's guest room – which had once been Aidan's room. She found her phone in the covers and silenced it. Maggie stirred restlessly on the other side of the bed. 'Maguire.'

'Dr Maguire?' The voice was shouting over some background noise – the clank of machinery, the roar of the wind. 'It's Declan Tozier.'

Her stomach turned over. The house was so quiet compared to the noise coming down the phone. She spoke softly. 'Have you found something?'

'We've uncovered some bones. I thought you might like to know – normally I wouldn't tell the family until we were sure, but—'

'Can I come there?' She was already out of bed, whispering, trying to find her jeans and hoody in the dark without disturbing the sleeping child. 'I'm coming.'

'DI Corry said there was no point trying to stop you. It might not be her, you know.' But he didn't sound convinced.

'I'll be there soon.' She cut the call, stooping to fumble some clean socks out of her case. She paused for a moment to smooth the hair off Maggie's hot face. Was this it? Was this the moment they'd waited twenty years for, when they'd finally know what had happened? Her mind was trying to mould around it. If it was her mother, and they found evidence she'd been pregnant – could she keep that from her father? It wasn't his child – she couldn't let him find that out. It wasn't fair on her mother, who had no one to speak for her. Maybe she'd had her reasons. Paula knew that the cold facts of a case never explained what had gone on in a person's heart, the steps that had led them there, to the point of no return. Like her, with her fatherless child and the man in London who saw her every day and had no idea Maggie was his. Not so very different from her mother, after all.

She wondered for a second about waking her father, telling him they'd found something. But she wasn't sure she could bear to. And maybe it was nothing. Sean Conlon had told Bob he'd helped her mother escape. But then he'd also told Paula he'd never taken her mother in the first place, said it to her face when she'd gone to see him, heavily pregnant and desperate. He was a liar, he could not be trusted in life or in death. And the pendant, the stupid dolphin pendant. Her mother had maybe been at this farm. Died there, perhaps. But the face of the psychic. *Your mother's alive.* A stupid piece of hope to cling to. Seeing shapes in the shadows – the man Edward living with a woman in London, after her mother had vanished. So what? It was probably his wife. He'd probably run as fast as he could from the mistake he'd made, the local woman he'd used as a source and then got pregnant. He was dead now anyway. It was all so tenuous, whispers in the wind. She was so tired of not knowing. Maybe tonight would be the end of that.

She left the door open, knowing Maggie would run to Granny and Granddad if she woke up. She settled the child gate across the stairs and went down, scrawling a quick note on the back of the *Ballyterrin Gazette* that sat on the table. Aidan's paper, once. Then she pulled on her coat, found her car keys, and slipped out of the dark, sleeping house into the night.

The farmyard was bright as day from the lights they'd rigged up, the blue flash of emergency vehicles washing gently across the scene, making everything look like it was at the bottom of the sea. Paula pulled her coat tight round her as she struggled over the boggy ground, marked with tyre tracks now. Huddles of people in high-vis clothing. She spotted Declan Tozier in his bright jacket and a hard hat, and noticed how he approached her, shielding her with his body from the new pit they'd opened up, over near the fence of the property.

'What's going on? Why have you stopped digging?'

'Dr Maguire . . . maybe we can talk in the car. It's cold.'

She pushed past him, stumbling over to it. A pit of light, swallowed in the dark. In the bottom, clagged in soil, some white things like branches. Bones. These were the bones. She looked for the tell-tale human signs, the long femurs and the shape of the skull. She blinked. The bones were too small for an adult, surely. 'What is this?'

Tozier caught up to her, panting a little. 'I was trying to tell you. There's been a burial here all right, but it's not human.'

Something in her gave way, and she registered it was relief. 'What do you mean?'

'Well, it looks like the intel was solid as to the burial place – remarkably so, in fact – but the grave has – well, we think it's a sheep in it.' He sounded almost embarrassed.

'I'm so sorry to drag you out here. I've never seen anything like this before.'

Paula realised how cold she was now the adrenaline had worn off, the wind cutting right through to her sleep-warm skin. 'No, it's OK. Don't be sorry. I needed to see. So . . . it's not her?'

'We can keep looking, but there's no evidence of anything else buried nearby. It looks as if they dug a grave then buried an animal instead. Why someone would do that, I have no idea.'

'So you're going to stop?'

'We can look a bit more widely, but then . . . I'm sorry. Yes.'

She looked away, feeling the sting of it harder than the wind.

He took off his glasses and rubbed his eyes. 'I'll send everyone home for the night. You should get some rest too.'

He trudged off, and Paula stood again and stared into the pit, the heap of animal bones in it. No sign of her mother, a ghost again after all these years, like someone you can only ever glimpse out of the corner of your eye. She murmured, 'You were here, weren't you? I can feel it. Where are you now? Where are you?'

For answer, there was nothing but the moaning of the wind over the mountains, lost and lonely and cold as ice.

Chapter Twenty-Three

Walking into the office the next day was hard. The little looks of sympathy pricking on her skin. She didn't want that. The hurdle had been got over – it wasn't her mother buried there – and all she knew was she was relieved. All those years of telling herself she just wanted answers, even if her mother was dead. Turned out she was pretty good at lying to herself.

She sat down at her borrowed desk, looking with distaste at the dull reports she was typing. If only she had some insight that might help. Find Mairead. Find her mother. Anything. On impulse she fired off an email to Guy in London. *How's it going there?*

He came straight back, and she hated the little lurch her stomach still made. *Quiet without you. How's the case?*

Messy. Actually maybe you could help with something. Can you find out anything about a murder ten years ago in London – Ciaran Wallace was convicted of it? Thanks.

She clicked out and stood up, knowing that sitting email-ing Guy all day was a sure-fire disaster waiting to happen.

Gerard was hunched over his desk, eating a pasty from a paper bag, filling the air with the smell of beef and onion.

'Any news?' she asked him.

He shook his head, spraying crumbs. 'Search teams are out, alerts are out, all that jazz. No sign of Mairead or her brother yet. And I got nothing from the mother, except a feed of cake from the carers in the home.'

She sighed. That meant nothing for her to do. And if she couldn't justify her presence there, she'd have to go home.

'What are you working on?' She perched against his cubicle, remembering Maeve's tip-off. 'Heard you had a murder recently?'

Gerard rubbed his eyes. She noticed another new suit, the influence of Willis Campbell, no doubt, who was a great man for a cufflink. 'Two murders. One a few weeks back, one got rubbed out the other day.'

'Rubbed out?' Paula raised her eyebrows. 'You been at *Scarface* again, Monaghan?'

'Ah, leave me be. You try planning a wedding that's up there with the peace process and also dealing with dead bodies and missing women, then take the piss.'

She had planned a wedding while working a case, of course, right up to the wire, but she let him have that one. 'Who is it this time?'

'Some thug by the name of Prontias Ryan. Low-level drug-dealer, general crim.'

Paula was suddenly paying attention. The bell was ringing again. Where had she heard the name? She frowned, trying to remember.

'You OK?' Gerard looked up from stabbing at his computer keyboard. 'Yesterday, that must have been . . . shite, like.'

She smiled faintly at his attempts to empathise. 'It was only a sheep.'

'No, but still, you thought it could've been . . .'

'It wasn't. I'm OK. It's just so frustrating, not being able to investigate the Red Road case properly. I feel like my hands are tied behind my back.'

'Tell me about it. Bastards are gonna go free, again. Makes me wonder why we bother, sometimes. I'm knocking my pan in trying to catch these fellas and half the time they won't even go down for it.'

'How was he killed, this Ryan?' She was looking for distraction, another case less close to home, something that didn't begin and end in red, clinging soil.

'Usual – knocked about a bit, then a bullet behind the ear. That's interesting though, maybe.' He chucked her a piece of paper.

She scanned it. 'He'd money thrown on top of him?'

'Yeah, thirty quid. Why'd they do something like that? Seems a waste.'

'Fintan McCabe . . . didn't he have the same amount in his pocket?'

Gerard squinted. 'It's just money though. Why, you think it means something?'

'It was something the IRA used to do to . . . informers.' *Touts*. 'Thirty pieces of silver, that kind of thing. Telling everyone what they'd done, that they were traitors.' Sometimes they would make tapes of people too, tortured into confessing, and send them to the victims' families. Then the family would not only have a dead loved one, they'd also be shamed and shunned, knowing one of their own had betrayed their side. She'd been spared all that at least. Nothing from her mother – no body, no tape, no phone call admitting responsibility. A note she hadn't found for twenty years. And now this tip-off, and a grave she wasn't in. 'Was he ex-IRA, do we know?'

'I reckon so. Sure most of the lowlifes in town were wrapped up in it, back then.'

'Well then. Is that worth looking into?'

'Suppose.' Gerard took the paper back with a sigh and plopped it onto a large pile on his inbox. 'Christ, you'd think we'd be done with these by now.' Under it, Paula spotted something that looked like a scrawled wedding to-do list. *Cousin Sarah vegetarian?? Will eat FISH?? Auntie S not to sing in church.* She was glad that wasn't her again, however much she missed Aidan.

She said, 'It'll never be done so long as there's lunatics about. Like Paddy Wallace for one. On the run for twenty years, long after everyone else stopped giving a damn. Kind of sad in a way.'

'Just kinda wish we'd get some normal murders now and again. You know, crimes of passion. Housewife rearing up and stabbing her ould fella. A bit of mystery, you know? These ones are so predictable.'

'Er, you're forgetting that the interesting ones always seem to end up with someone putting a gun to my head, or your guts leaking out over my good jumper. Or Avril drugged and kidnapped.'

He glowered protectively across the room at his intended, who was patiently taking down notes from a caller who seemed convinced the Pope was hiding in their shed. 'Aye, well, maybe you're right. Suppose we've not got the time right now for an interesting one, not with these bodies and Mairead missing.'

There was something interesting in this case for Paula, though, who had suddenly remembered where she'd seen the name Prontias Ryan before. She eyed the sheets Gerard had spread haphazardly over his desk. His idol Willis Campbell would have something to say about that, and the greasy pastry bag littering crumbs among the pages. 'The first murder, his name was Mark O'Hanlon?'

'Aye. How'd you know that?'

'And was it similar to this one? He was ex-IRA too, right?'

Gerard narrowed his eyes, trying to remember. 'Aye. And he was shot in the head in his flat, right enough.'

'At the door?' That was often the IRA MO. Knock on the door, shoot, be gone in seconds, leave your victim dying in the hallway.

'In the lounge, I think. Why?'

'Sorry, Gerard, bear with me. Was there cash on him too?'

A long pause from Gerard, puzzling it out. 'There's a connection? What've you got, Maguire?'

'I don't know. Maybe nothing. Mind if I borrow this file for a minute?' she said casually.

He waved permission. 'Just put it back when you're done. Need to clear all this before we're off on honeymoon.'

'I'd start with the pastry,' Paula advised. 'Otherwise they'll have to call in pest control while you're off sunning yourself on the beach.'

Back at her desk, she leafed through the pages, noting greasy thumbprints here and there. Ryan had been in his fifties, overweight and unwell, living alone in a squalid council house. 'Rambo' had been his nickname in his IRA days, and it seemed a sad joke now, looking at the pictures of his bloated pale body, tattoos on sagging flesh.

O'Hanlon was similar, separated from his wife and living on benefits, out of condition and dicing with Type 2 diabetes. He'd also been active in the IRA back then. A few weeks back he'd been found dead after neighbours complained about the smell. Paula scanned the report on the system. Defensive injuries. Evidence of restraints, wounds to his hands and face, money tossed onto the body. These really were the cases no one cared about, shoved to the bottom of the pile. The last casualties in a war that had ended in 1998. Bad men, men who'd done terrible things and walked free, or had their sentences cut as part of the Agreement. No one would mourn them too much. But she'd seen the names Mark O'Hanlon and Prontias Ryan before – on the list Sean Conlon had given to Bob before he died. Just coincidence, maybe. These men had lived and died by violence, and it was hardly unusual to find a murdered ex-IRA member even these days. But they'd been on Conlon's list . . . and they were dead, and so was Conlon. Aidan was in prison for killing him. So Aidan had been in prison when these two men were rubbed out, as Gerard put it. Too much coincidence, Conlon, O'Hanlon and Ryan killed by different people within a year of each other?

She called over to Gerard. 'When was this guy Ryan killed, do we know?'

He scratched his head, consulting the smeary whiteboard on which they wrote unsolved cases. 'Pathologist reckoned a week or so ago. Why?'

'Oh, nothing. Just an idea.' But her heart was beating faster. Three names on Bob's list. Two recently killed, one on the run having kidnapped his sister. And the writer of the list dead as well. Maybe that would qualify as interesting enough for even Gerard's tastes. 'Monaghan.' She put on her most winning smile.

'What do you want now?' he said suspiciously.

'Oh, just a wee favour. What are the chances I could visit this crime scene?'

Chapter Twenty-Four

'This is it.' Gerard lifted the police tape to let her through and into the council house. The estate it was in was notorious for Republican crime, and they'd parked the car a good distance away to avoid coming back to four slashed tyres or worse. All the same Paula could feel eyes on her as they walked to the house, peering from behind darkened windows and out of every shadow. Prontias Ryan had lived alone in a drab little one-bed, weeds poking up from the gravel in his front yard. There was no chance of getting into O'Hanlon's place; it was long since cleared out and tidied away. 'Forensics are done now, so we don't have to suit up.'

Going in she noticed the smell at once – damp and fried food, overlaid by a sharper, more insistent reek of death, and the metallic note of blood. She wrinkled her nose. 'You said he was here a while before they found him?'

'A day or two. No family, not many friends, that's what happens.' Gerard tucked his tie into his shirt to stop it swinging. 'We found him here.' He pointed to the floor by the TV, where a large dark patch on the orange carpet indicated the body had lain there. A mixture of body fluids and blood. Paula breathed through her mouth, looking about her. It was a sad and squalid place, no pictures on the bare magnolia walls, the carpet frayed and now destroyed entirely, the furniture sagging and stained from various takeaways. A stack of dirty cartons could be seen in the kitchen. 'Did you find anything interesting?'

'Nah. We get these every so often, that shower bumping each other off. Old scores, you know. This one was a wee bit weird, though.'

'Weird how?' She examined the small collection of knock-off DVDs on top of his TV – horror, porn, martial arts.

'Well, in a feud like that, what they'd do is ring your bell then shoot you and run off, like you said. Have a driver waiting. But that's not what happened here.' Gerard pointed to the stain. 'He'd those cable tie things on his ankles and wrists. Cuts all over his arms and chests. Finger missing, even.'

'What?'

'Chopped off with a bolt cutter or something.' Gerard said this with a certain relish. 'Nasty.'

'Why would someone do that? Torture?'

'Wanted to know something, s'pose. Or revenge. Or both. Then there was the money lying on his chest too – thirty quid in notes. You said that was an informer thing?'

'Yeah. Thirty pieces of silver. And the other case, O'Hanlon, it was the same?'

'Aye. I'd have made the link,' he said defensively. 'I hadn't had a chance to look at it properly.'

'I know. You didn't lift any prints from either scene?'

'Nope. Not a thing we can use. Whoever did this knew their stuff.'

And perhaps they were good enough at evading the police to have earned the nickname 'The Ghost'. If he'd been tortured for information, what had Prontias Ryan told his killer before he died, in agony, his last sight this nasty, smelly room that reeked of loneliness? She was glad to have Gerard there, his hands shoved in his pockets and his big red country face. It was a horrible place, full of death and suffering and the waste of a pointless life. 'Let's go,' she said. 'Thanks for letting me see.'

'Amazing.' Paula cocked her head at the ceiling. 'She goes down like a lamb for Pat. Back home it's an hour of baths and stories and drinks of water and Mummy can I act out bits of *Frozen* for you.'

'Aye, Pat has the touch all right.' Her father was in his usual spot in front of the TV, while Pat was upstairs putting Maggie to bed. Paula had murmured protests, then gratefully accepted the break, telling herself Pat probably liked it. She didn't see Maggie enough. And they'd be gone again soon, back to the place she'd just described as *home*. Her father hadn't commented on that, but she knew he would have noticed. Instead he said, 'So they're still digging. At the farm.'

She stiffened, caught off guard. 'I think not for much longer. Unless someone else comes forward.' But why would they? Why would anyone care about a woman who'd gone missing twenty years before? 'Dad – you know we've another missing person now. Paddy Wallace's sister – he took her.'

'Saw it on the news. God love her.'

'He must have help, to hide like this. Anything you can tell me about him, his old mates, his associates?'

'Well, there was a gang of them in town in the late eighties and nineties. Lots of young fellas dabbled in the Provos, but we always knew who the main command were. Or whatever they called themselves. Playing soldiers. There was . . . Conlon.'

She nodded. That name was painful in this house ever

since Aidan had gone down for his murder. 'He was older, in his thirties. But Wallace was in charge, all the same. There was thon one you've just found, Fintan McCabe. I know his Mammy's been on the TV weeping and wailing, her innocent wee boy, wouldn't have known a thing about the Provos, but he was up to his neck in it. You know, I always thought it was the two of them did for poor John. Him and Conlon.' He glanced up at the picture on top of the piano, John O'Hara with his hand on Aidan's shoulder, Aidan dressed in a white suit for his Communion. Under happier circumstances she might have nudged and slagged him for that, the pious expression on his face, hands raised in prayer. But John O'Hara had been murdered only months after the picture was taken, and Aidan, that innocent boy, was sitting in prison.

'You couldn't get them on it?'

'We tried. Well, I wasn't allowed to work the case. Hamilton was the lead.' His voice flattened out. Still no love lost there, and Paula hadn't been able to tell him Bob had been working behind the scenes all this time to protect them from the truth.

Whatever that was.

'And Wallace?'

'We knew they were the punishment squad. Brought people in and tortured them for info, knee-capped them, went after so-called informers. Interrogation, they called it. When your mammy . . .' His voice failed. It was still hard to talk about. 'When she went, I wanted to bring Wallace in for it. If they had her, they'd have been interrogating her. Taken her somewhere for questioning. Then they'd shoot her, like as not. Dump the body. It was so close to the other ceasefire, though – I always wondered did they maybe just hide her. So as not to rock the boat, you know? But nobody heeded me and I could hardly go after him myself.'

'You thought they took her, then. Wallace and that lot.'

He shrugged. From upstairs, Paula could hear Pat's soothing voice, reading a bedtime story. Safe, cosy, everything she wanted for Maggie. 'I don't know. Why wouldn't she have told me, if she was in trouble? I could have helped. For God's sake, I was in the RUC. If anyone could have helped, I could.'

Paula thought she might know why – the answer hidden in her mother's medical records, which Davey Corcoran had unearthed for her. Her mother had been pregnant when she disappeared. The baby not PJ's. So. There were those facts, facts which were as heavy and leaden as bullets, and so far she hadn't quite been able to fit them into the empty slots in her mind. But she was getting there. 'And did they even interview him, Wallace?'

'Hamilton said they did, but I was never sure. He blocked me at every turn. Even came to our place and dug the garden up. Suspended me and all.'

She remembered that. Her father, who'd never been home throughout most of her childhood, suddenly at home all day in his dressing gown. Another frightening shift in the bedrock of her world, always so solid before. 'Maybe there was a reason,' she ventured.

Her father's face hardened. 'Hamilton and myself, we never saw eye to eye, not really. But there was a time we worked well together. Partners. I respected the man, in his way. But then it's my own wife gone and he's cutting me out, barring me from the incident room, sending me home, refusing to tell me if they'd even any leads. I could have helped! Nobody knew the local Provos like me back then.

They were out for my blood, so of course I knew them well. But he wouldn't even talk to me. God only knows what that was about.'

Paula knew now, but she could hardly explain that Bob had been deflecting attention as best he could, hoping her mother had managed to escape, praying that an investigation that didn't look too hard might give her the chance to get away. 'Daddy, you know Bob . . . I think he's a good man.'

'Aye, I thought so too one time.'

'I know it was hard. I know he did some things that were . . . strange. But I think we can't understand why. I think he did the best he could at the time.' She held her breath – she couldn't say more in case her father suspected what she knew. But equally she couldn't bear for Bob to take the blame when none of it had been his fault. When he'd only ever tried to spare them, her and her father, from whatever it was her mother had done that meant she had to flee.

PJ looked at her sharply. 'Thought you were no big fan of his. It was you nudged him over to retirement.'

She felt ashamed of that now, the fuss she'd kicked up when she found out he'd suppressed the report from the neighbour. Not knowing it was all done for a reason. 'I know, but . . . he cared for you. He speaks very highly of you still. He's just . . . he has his own code.' A code that she now knew had involved protecting her mother at all costs, including her darkest secrets. She changed the subject back. 'So. Wallace. He might have been the one who . . . came for her.'

'He'd have known something about it at least. And he'd recognise your name, pet, I'm sure of it. So tread carefully, aye?' He wasn't asking her to come off the case – he knew she could never do that – but he was reminding her that here in Ballyterrin, everything was personal. Everyone knew you. And that was maybe the best thing and worst thing about the place, both at the same time.

'OK,' Paula lied. Her father had never thought of his own safety all those years in the RUC, but she'd pretend to listen, all the same.

After a long moment he said, 'You know, it was maybe Wallace rang in that tip. About your mother. The farm.'

'I know.' A tip that wasn't correct. 'What happens, Dad?' she said, looking at the TV and not him. 'If they ever do find something. Did you ever think about it?' He must have. There'd been the other three bodies, dead women surfacing in bogs and drains and building sites, bodies he'd had to go and look at. None of them her mother.

'I don't know, is the honest truth. Even now, with the tip-off . . . I could never picture her gone. Had to try – I owed it to Pat – but no, I've never been able to see it.'

Paula knew what he meant. Although she'd told herself time and time again to be prepared, that anyone who disappeared for twenty years was surely dead, some part of her couldn't take it in. Perhaps that was why they made you look at the body in the morgue, see with your own eyes that they were dead and gone, try to accept it. Maybe everyone with a long-missing loved one felt this way. It was something she'd heard the families of the Disappeared say a lot, that they just wanted a body, just wanted closure. Were they really after a way to kill that terrible treacherous hope? 'I don't know either, Daddy.'

Her father was quiet for a long time, focused on the flickering TV. Eventually he said, 'It's in the past now. All we can do is try to get on with our lives. You too.'

'I am!'

'You might have moved away, but any fool can see your mind's never left this town. And your man down the road.' Meaning Aidan.

'I can't just forget about him. Would you?'

'I'm not saying forget. But you know as well as I do he'll be in there a long time, unless something new comes up.'

'You think he did it,' she stated, quietly.

Her father shrugged. 'Never said that. But see if I was still working up on the hill, and I'd arrested him? I'd have made damn sure he went down for it, and stayed down. Whoever it was he killed, terrorist or not.'

But he's innocent, she wanted to say. *But it isn't fair.* 'He deserves a chance,' she said weakly. 'Maybe an appeal . . .'

'Aye, I know, and Pat'll stand by him no matter what, and I'll stand by her, but you've got your whole life ahead of you, and that wee girl to raise.'

'I went, didn't I? I took the London job.' Paula knew she sounded petulant, something her father could always bring out in her. She also knew it wasn't much of a fresh start, working alongside Guy Brooking every day, and failing to tell him the truth about Maggie.

'Aye, and you're straight back here like a boomerang. I don't like to see you so far away, pet, you know that, but I want to see you happy. I don't know if there's any happiness for you here, waiting for Aidan.'

'I'm not waiting for him,' she muttered. Her father just raised his eyebrows. 'We're going back after Avril and Gerard's wedding. I'll try to settle in more. I hear what you're saying.'

'You went through a lot,' he said, eyes back on the TV. 'With your mother. No wean should have to go through that, and it may be we'll never find out why. I just want to know you won't spend your whole life chasing a ghost.'

She'd have liked to say she wasn't, she wouldn't, but for years now it had been so close, just beyond the reach of her fingers. The note, a real and concrete thing. Davey's invest-igation. Now this phone call, the claim her body was there. Only to find an empty grave, another dead end. 'But Daddy—'

'What would you even do if you found her?' The question floored Paula.

'Well, we'd bury her, and I'd—'

'Not her body, pet. *Her.*'

Her hand was shaking. Slowly, she put the cup down on the side table. 'I don't know.'

'I told myself a long time ago I'd let her go,' PJ said. 'Whatever happened to her. I'd let her go in peace and live my own life. Can you do the same, pet?'

She stared at the floor, Pat's swirly carpet blurring under her eyes. The truth was she didn't know what she'd do if she found her mother. Because if she wasn't dead, she'd been alive all this time and never once contacted her daughter, and how could you ever forgive a thing like that?

In the silence between them, the TV burbled. PJ's eyes fixed on it. 'You'll be OK, pet,' he said. 'You'll be OK, no matter what.' She wished she believed that.

Margaret

Another day. The sound of the door rattling up again, and blinking against the light. But this time there was hurry, urgency. The girl, Aisling, was kneeling behind her, fumbling with the knots. 'You have to get out of here,' she whispered urgently. 'I heard him say he's going to do it today. That you won't talk so he may as well finish it.'

Her stomach in knots of terror. 'What?'

'They were talking about it. Deciding, like. So close to the ceasefire, should they give you back – but Paddy said it's too far gone for that. You've seen us all. You know where we are.'

'I don't! Where are we?' Her arms were free now, aching and numb, and Aisling was starting on her feet.

'Near the border. Red Road. Go over the back fields till you come to the road.'

'But – what will happen to you?'

Her dark hair hung over her face, hiding it. 'Doesn't matter. I can't let them do this to you. I'll get away – my sister's after running off a few months back, over to England. I can leave too. And you get out of the country, as fast as you can, OK?'

Margaret stumbled to her feet, stiff and aching. 'Aisling, I can't just leave you here. What if he hurts you?'

'I'm his sister.' She smiled, showing crooked teeth. 'Has to count for something. Anyway, he'll think it was one of the lads. Go now. He's out but he'll be back soon.'

Outside was so dazzling she had to close her eyes, leaning on Aisling for support. She hadn't been sure she'd ever see the outside again, the sky so grey and wide. All around were fields and hedges, nothing to tell you what way was north or south. 'That way.' Aisling nudged her. 'You'll get to the road. Flag someone down and get them to ring the police.'

'I can't. I . . . I can't ring the police.' How could she, after all this? Tell PJ she was carrying another man's child?

'Ring whoever you have, then. Just get out of here.' The girl turned to go.

'Wait! Thank you! How can I . . . God, I don't know . . .'

'Never mind that.'

Margaret tried to hug her, feeling how thin the girl was under her T-shirt, her shiny dark hair whipped in the wind. A sudden instinct made her take the necklace off, fumbling agonisingly with the clasp. 'Here. Just . . . here.' A cheap trinket, but it was all she had to offer. Small thanks to give for her life.

The girl stared at it, then slipped it into the pocket of her jeans. 'Go.'

Then Margaret set off, hobbling over the farmyard to the field behind, her legs cramped and sore. Her shoes were long lost, and the ground strangely soft and soothing under her bare feet. She could hardly run, and the light was so bright, the land so open. They'd see her, surely. She didn't look back. There was a tree. She just had to make it to the tree. She could hear her own breath ragged in her ears. Oh God, the fear. She'd never known anything like it. Had it been worth it? Her rage at this country she lived in, burning up and consuming everything, her own quiet life, her husband, silent and broken, her daughter. Even days ago – only days she'd been here! – a chip shop had been blown up on the Shankill Road, two children dead. One seven years old, one Paula's age. A sickening spiral of violence going on and on. In trying to stop all this she'd blown up her own life. She'd never see Paula again.

Margaret reached the tree and leaned against it for a second to catch her breath. The farmhouse was indistinct, a typical two-storey house in cream paint, surrounded by outbuildings. Her prison, where she'd been convinced she'd die. She wasn't sure she'd even be able to find it again if asked. A phone. She had to find a phone, a road, a person, anyone she could tell she was alive and not vanished into the air.

She was about to set out again when a hand clamped over her mouth, cracked and calloused, and she was lifted off her feet by two burly arms. A voice in her ear said, 'What the fuck do you think you're doing?'

Chapter Twenty-Five

Willis Campbell stared at her across the desk. Paula fought down the dislike she'd always had for the man, drafted in to replace Corry when she'd been demoted a few years back. His smooth tanned skin – sunbeds? – his hand-made suits, the cloying smell of his aftershave. 'Tell me this, Dr Maguire. How could Monaghan's murder case be an IRA punishment killing, if the IRA disbanded nearly twenty years ago?' He was splitting hairs, and it irritated her. Everyone knew there'd been recent murders linked to the Republican movement – just the year before, a former informer had been gunned down in his Donegal home. Bad blood from the past. Scores to be reckoned. People who knew more than was good for them – literally where the bodies were buried. People who'd done the unthinkable and touted during the Troubles, thinking themselves safe almost twenty years after it was all over, only to answer the door to a man with a gun. There were always rumblings when such deaths happened, since the terrorist groups were supposed to be disbanded in order for the peace process to hold, but as long as it could be written off as isolated violence, a personal grudge of some kind, it was usually overlooked. Because those groups had officially given up, cleaned up their acts, handed over the guns, so they couldn't be behind it. A delicate balancing act, aimed at keeping the peace.

'I don't know,' she said, a touch grouchily. 'I don't know who did it. I'm just saying it fits the pattern. The money left on the body, the bullet over the ear . . . This has all the hallmarks of a punishment killing. It's like a throwback to the seventies.'

He sighed. 'Dr Maguire. I know you've been away . . .' She bristled at that. This was her home, and a few years away didn't mean she'd forgotten how things worked. Did it? '. . . but we're on very shaky ground with this. If we say these murders are linked to the IRA, the DUP won't continue to govern with Sinn Fein. Those are our two largest parties.' Paula rolled her eyes; as if she didn't know that. The DUP were the ultra-conservative Protestant party, and getting them into government with former terrorists in the first place had been a remarkable achievement, only possible because the bad old days were supposed to be entirely over and forgotten, Sinn Fein's links to the IRA thoroughly dissolved and denied. He went on. 'If our two largest parties won't work together, our entire system of government will fall apart. The peace process will crumble. There's a good chance we'd be right back to pre-Agreement violence and direct rule from London.'

'I know, but don't you think there's a link? We've uncovered two dead bodies on that farm, the place the punishment squad used to use for interrogations, and meanwhile someone's going around shooting former IRA members.' Not to mention that Sean Conlon had been murdered the year before. Paula was trying to keep a lid on the beat of excitement in her stomach. Hope, shooting out leaves to the sun. If someone else had killed him, if Aidan could be cleared . . . but she knew Willis would have her off the case as soon as she breathed a word about a possible link to that.

She had to be careful. 'And Paddy Wallace, the Ghost, is back in town, and he's taken his sister. Him, and Fintan McCabe, and these other two murders . . . They all knew each other. They were friends – colleagues. They saw themselves as soldiers together. What if someone's trying to settle old scores, or cover something up?' Was that why Mairead had been taken – did she know something about what had happened back then?

Willis was scowling. She hoped he wouldn't bring up Sean Conlon. She needed to stay on this case, for her own sanity. Finally, he sighed. 'This is going to cause an almighty mess, Dr Maguire. I hope you're ready for it. Easy for you to drop this then skip off back to London next week, but we'll be cleaning it up for months. Years, maybe.'

She tried to look contrite. 'But sir, we're finally getting somewhere. If Wallace didn't get to everyone yet, someone might know where he is, where he's holding Mairead.' She sat back in her chair. 'I'd like to go and speak to Ciaran Wallace again, if you'll let me. He must know more than he's told us.'

Willis sat back too, sighed again. 'Your job in London – it's a good one, yes?'

'Well, yes. It's . . . prestigious. Interesting.' She tried to sound convincing, hide the fact it bored her. 'Working with DI Brooking, of course, is a real privilege.'

He narrowed his eyes at her. 'Well, then. Perhaps after this case you'll stick to that? Your actual job?'

'Perhaps.' Paula gave nothing away.

He muttered, 'Things were a lot quieter around here once you went. Fine, fine. Go and see what Ciaran Wallace has to say and we'll review it then. Though God alone knows who I'm going to put on it with Monaghan off getting his hair and nails done for this wedding of his.'

He was one to talk – Gerard had learned his fussy grooming habits off Willis. But Paula just said, 'Thank you, sir. I'm only trying to find Mairead. I feel responsible, as you can imagine. It was me talked her into going to meet her brother.'

'Hmph. Fine. I just hope you can handle the subsequent media attention. If I say we've spotted an IRA link to these murders, all holy hell is going to break loose.'

Chapter Twenty-Six

Paula tried to stay calm as she approached the prison visiting area. Not her first time, or even her first as a non-professional visitor, but still she felt queasy and hot. The other women in the queue seemed calm and resigned, holding their belongings in little plastic bags, having surrendered phones, cash, food, headphones, mirrors, sprays, and any other items that weren't allowed.

She'd dressed up a bit, foolishly, in a red print dress and boots, just on the off-chance Aidan might be there, and as she was patted down by security, she saw the other women had done likewise, though some had interpreted 'dressing up' as leggings and hoop earrings or skin-tight jeans and spiky, tottering boots. They were just the same as her, for all her doctorate and fancy job.

She moved into the visitors' hall, its high ceilings echoing like the canteen at school. A quick scan revealed no Aidan, and it was stupid how much her heart sank. How had it come to this? They'd lived together for two years, and now she had to hang around the prison in the hope of spotting him. Pathetic.

Ciaran Wallace was waiting for her at a table, rolling a cigarette in his hands. 'Thanks for seeing me again.' She sat down.

He shrugged. 'Dunno what I can tell you.'

'Prontias Ryan.' She launched right into it. 'That name mean anything to you?'

Ciaran nodded cautiously. 'Mate of our Paddy's, way back. One of that lot.'

'Mark O'Hanlon?'

'Same. Never knew them that well. Why?'

That lot, he said. As if he'd himself had nothing to do with the IRA. And yet here he was, serving a sentence for killing an Army officer. Guy had said he'd look into it for her, though she couldn't say what she was hoping to find. 'They've been murdered, Ciaran. Shot and likely tortured in their homes. Same method as the dead man at your farm – you've been told that's Fintan McCabe?'

He tapped the roll-up off the table. 'So they say.'

'Another of Paddy's mates?'

'Yeah. Short life expectancy, those fellas. Another reason I got out of this country while I could.'

'Ciaran . . . I know you want out of here. You're innocent, you say?'

'I've been saying that for ten years, missus, for all the good it did me. Just have to keep my head down now and do the time.'

'What if we could help you get out sooner?' she risked.

He narrowed his eyes. 'How?'

'Well, opening an appeal. Early probation, even. We just need information. On these fellas, Prontias and Mark, why somebody would kill them now, after all this time. Who might want them dead, that sort of thing.'

'Any God's amount of people,' he said, coolly.

'Including your Paddy?'

'Aye. Could be.'

'You know he's taken your sister.'

'They told me that too. That's between the two of them.'
Not a flicker on his face.

Once again, Paula was astounded at the alienation between these siblings. 'It's not, though, is it? Mairead didn't want to go. She wants to be with her daughter, your niece.'

The words seemed to mean nothing to him. He folded his arms. 'You want something from me, missus, you better just say. Don't like to be seen talking to the peelers too often in here. People start to talk.'

'We need to know places Paddy might go. Where he could hide, keep someone against their will.'

He shrugged. 'Can't help you there. He had loads of places. That's why they called him the Ghost.'

'You never went to any of them with him?'

'Told you, I wasn't involved in all that. He wanted me to be, but I kept out of it. Moved away when I could.'

'About that.' She flicked a fragment of tobacco off the table. 'As you know, it's Fintan McCabe in that grave we found. The girl, we still don't have an ID. You don't know anything about that?'

'No.' The closed-off look, the same one on Mairead's face when asked about the dead girl.

'We had a tip-off that a woman was brought to the farm for interrogation in 1993, around the time Fintan McCabe disappeared. Older than this girl. Her name was Margaret.' Paula took a breath. She was on shaky ground here. 'She was my mother, Ciaran.'

A flicker of surprise at that. She saw him glance at her hair and her heart leaped. Did he recognise it? Everyone said how much she looked like her mother. If he'd still been at that farm then, had he been involved in hurting her mother?

'We never found her body. The tip-off said she was buried at the farm too, but – no. She wasn't there.'

'Sorry for you,' he said, gruffly. 'Must have been hard.'

'It's still hard. The not-knowing, that's what hurts. If I could get some answers, find out what happened to her, that would really help.'

Ciaran seemed to think about it for a long time. Then he sighed. 'Listen, I'm sorry about your ma. But I don't know what happened to her. I told you, I went to London before all this.'

'Before what?' she said quickly.

'Fintan and . . . whoever. He was grand when I left. Best pals with our Paddy, round the house all the time. I went off, lived my life, then next thing I know I'm being arrested for killing some fella I never even heard of. They'd evidence. I dunno how, but some things of mine were at the scene. My hoody and that. Then I was brought back here and banged up for years.' As he spoke she saw the bitterness on his face, and imagined it for a second, serving all that time for something you hadn't done. Would it be the same for Aidan? She shut it down. They always said they hadn't done it. Didn't mean it was true. He was getting up now, scratching at his thin, tattooed arms. 'Sorry,' he said shortly. 'I can't help you. Dunno where our Paddy would take someone.'

'Aren't you worried?' she tried, desperate now. 'She's your sister.'

'My sister who I've not seen in twenty years. And our Mairead and Paddy . . . well, it's maybe not what you think.'

'What do you mean?' She frowned, puzzled.

He turned to go. 'Dunno. Can't help you. Sorry.'

Paula stood up too, her heart sinking – she'd thought this

was a good move, that he'd tell her more – and as she lifted her little plastic bag of possessions, she saw Aidan.

He was sitting at a table, composed, and her heart gave out. Just the sight of his face, the familiar lines of it now more scored with age, his stubble grey round the edges. *Oh, Aidan.* She swallowed down her tears and before she knew it she was walking towards him. He sat very still, not running away this time. 'Hi.'

'Hiya.' For a moment they just looked each other over, taking in the way they'd changed, the way they were the same. 'You look well,' he said cautiously.

'Thanks.' She glanced over at the guards, but they were occupied with seeing people out. Maybe she could grab a few minutes with him.

'Being away from here suits you. I knew it would.'

She looked at her hands. She hadn't wanted to leave Ballyterrin, had hated him for suggesting it, but perhaps he was right. 'It's . . . well, it's not home. But the job is good. Bit dull after here, but good.'

'Dull is under-rated, Maguire.' He paused. 'Does Mags . . . does Maggie like it?' He stumbled over the child's name, and Paula felt it like a knife.

'Well enough, I suppose. I feel bad taking her away from Dad and Pat, and Saoirse. Did you know she was having a baby?'

'Aye, great news. They come in to see me the odd time.' Aidan almost looked like his old self when he smiled. 'God knows they deserve it.'

'I could bring Maggie to see you,' she said carefully, and he darkened again.

'Come on now. She's only three, she doesn't need to be

seeing me in here. With a bit of luck she won't even remember me.'

Paula said nothing, didn't tell him Maggie still thought she saw him on the street, still asked for him. Maybe it comforted Aidan to think otherwise. She didn't pretend to understand what it was like for him, locked up in here, the life he'd almost had gone in an instant of madness. 'I hear Bob's been in to see you.' She wanted to ask who was visiting him today. Not Saoirse or Pat, they'd have told her surely; anyway, Pat was minding Maggie. Who?

'Aye, he's not such a bad old stick when you get to know him. He has some cocked idea that Conlon was a marked man and someone else was there that night to finish him off.'

Paula too had always pinned her hopes on this. The problem was, how could they ever prove it? 'Yeah.' She waited to hear what had changed. Aidan had never believed this before.

He shifted in his seat, not meeting her eyes. 'Here's the thing. You told me that last year and I never believed it, not really. I knew what I did to the man – punched him, kicked him, stamped on him even. He could have been dead when I left him. I don't know that he wasn't. But . . .'

Paula's heart, stupid as it was, leapt up.

'. . . Maybe someone else did come and do it. And Bob, he had some ideas about who that could be.'

'I know. He had a list. Sean Conlon gave it to him.' Did Aidan know that, that Bob had been working with the man who'd likely murdered his father?

It seemed he did, because he didn't react like she expected. As if it had drained out of him, all the rage and loss that had led him to beat Sean Conlon to a pulp while he lay on the dirty ground of a pub car park. 'There's a lot of bad blood,

Maguire. Conlon and my dad. Me and Conlon. Ould Bob and Conlon, and I don't know what they had between them . . .'

'My mother,' she said. It was surreal, how they were speaking to each other, laying the truth out between them on the scuffed table. 'Bob knew something about where she went. Why she was taken, or had to run, or . . . whatever happened.' She couldn't tell Aidan everything yet, about her mother being pregnant, that her mother's handler and lover had been living in London in the nineties, with a woman and baby. Because Pat was Aidan's mother, and it would destroy her if she thought PJ's wife might be alive after all. 'He loved her, I think. My mother. He did something for her. I don't know what exactly.'

'That's why he hushed up all the reports, bungled the investigation?'

'I think so.' Poor Bob. Being thought a failure all this time, when he'd only done it to bury Margaret Maguire's lies. 'So. What now?' She faced him across the table. His eyes were so green. She wanted to touch his face, smooth away those new lines, run her hands through his newly short, newly greying hair.

'If I could find some proof another fella went after Conlon that night . . .' Aidan murmured.

'A witness?' They were almost whispering now.

'Maybe. But if I could, would they reopen the case? The PSNI?'

Her heart was hammering. It was happening, actually happening. Aidan was going to fight, at last. 'They'd have to. There's no proof you were the one killed him. If someone could say he was alive when you left . . .' But who would do it? She looked quickly round the room. 'Is it someone in here? Someone talked to you?' That would explain his sudden change of heart.

'Shh. Not a word, Maguire. It's delicate.'

'But you'll try?'

'Let's see. Will you back me?' His words were rough, awkward.

'Will I . . . God almighty, of course I will. I've been saying that all along. What's changed?' The guard was looking her way; she hooked her bag over her fingers. 'Why now?' she said quickly.

'Well, I suppose . . . With you being gone. I thought you'd have your own life now, without me holding you back, good job, better life for Mags . . . And then I started thinking, maybe actually I didn't want to sit in here for years, if it wasn't me who did it after all.'

'Oh.' So all this, the desperate atonement, the refusal to provide mitigation, had been to make up for what he did to her. The lie about being Maggie's father.

'Did you tell him yet? Brooking?' As if reading her mind.

She sighed. 'He's having another baby. With his wife. It didn't seem right, not yet. But I will. I've promised myself I will, when the time is right.'

He nodded. 'You and him—'

'Colleagues. We always worked well together. Should have left it at that.' Both of them were speaking lightly, but her chest was fluttering like a bird. Was this really happening?

'I'm sorry, Maguire. I'm so bloody sorry I didn't tell you about the DNA test. It was unforgivable. I just . . . I wanted you. And Mags. I wanted us all together.'

The guard was unlocking the door. Almost time to go, the seconds trickling away. Paula gathered her bag close. 'What you didn't realise,' she said quickly, 'was that it would have made no difference. Even if I'd known you weren't her dad. It was always you. Always. There's nobody else, Aidan. There never will be.'

'Time to go now, folks!' The guard was calling over.

Aidan stood, his face blank. 'I . . .'

'Just try, please? For me? For us?'

He nodded. She turned to go, and then she was back, hurling herself at him, and his arms were around her, stronger than before, wired with muscle, and her lips were on his, just for a moment. 'I will,' he said fiercely, into her mouth. 'I will. I promise, Maguire.'

Chapter Twenty-Seven

Paula almost floated out the gate. She'd spoken to Aidan, for the first time in months, and he'd kissed her. It was unbelievable. Something had changed. She wished she knew what. It couldn't just be Bob's visits, surely. Someone in the prison, perhaps, helping him. Someone with information.

On her way out she saw a familiar figure hobbling towards the visitors' centre, stick in hand. 'Ah, did I miss it?' Maeve said. So that's who was visiting Aidan. 'Got held up at a bloody press conference. Hope he won't be raging.'

'I don't think he'll mind too much.'

Maeve saw her face, which Paula knew was impossibly flushed. 'You spoke to him?'

'Maeve, he talked to me! He's really going to try and fight!'

'Well, I know that, sure aren't I helping him?'

Paula squinted at her. 'You what?'

Maeve sighed. 'Come on. I'll tell you mine if you tell me yours.'

They sat in Maeve's car, which as always was a skip on wheels. Paula had to move three crisp packets and a cat collar before she could get in. Rain skiffed against the windows as she told Maeve about the possible link between

Paddy Wallace, Mark O'Hanlon and Prontias Ryan. Maeve listened, nodding along.

'So. Why'd they get shot now, with Wallace back? Seems too much of a coincidence.'

'It's a huge story,' said Maeve, propping her crutch against the window. 'Been rumbling on since that informer got shot last year, down in Donegal. If it's proven that the IRA are still active, ordering executions, the DUP have said they'll leave the executive. Then the whole thing collapses. So the police have to turn a blind eye, kind of. Write it off as just random murders.'

Paula was silent. The peace process had been in place since she was seventeen. A part of her life she'd taken for granted. It was sobering to realise how fragile it was. 'So it's simpler to pin Conlon's death on Aidan, is that what you're saying?'

'I'm sure Willis Campbell is straight. But if he can make it a nice clean normal murder, a drunken fight, why would he go digging to find out if the IRA are involved? The IRA who officially disbanded years ago? You see what I mean. Why upset the whole house of cards?'

Paula nodded. 'And if I find evidence someone else did the murder, and Aidan gets out – it could spark off an almighty row?'

Maeve nodded. The grey light picked out the scars on her face – marks from a petrol bomb, thrown by members of the Republican movement that officially didn't exist. She'd been caught in the crossfire when someone tried to kill the former Sinn Fein mayor of Ballyterrin, himself ex-IRA. He was dead now too. A lot of people were dying, even decades after the Troubles. 'It's no exaggeration to say it could take us back to civil war.'

'I see.' It would be so easy to give up. Even Aidan accepted he'd probably killed Conlon, or at least that he could have. No one else cared if he spent the next few years in prison. But Paula had never been good at giving up on lost causes. 'What would you do? If you were me?'

Maeve made a face. 'Aidan's my friend, as you know. I love the bones of him, useless bastard that he is. I'd find someone to confess to killing Conlon. But why would they? And how could you ever get close to these guys? They don't just talk to anyone, and you're police, and they know who your mammy was.'

Paula nodded. She knew that was a non-starter. Besides, it was too risky, and for Maggie's sake she had to be careful who she sniffed around. 'I need some kind of leverage. Someone with something to lose, or gain.'

Maeve fixed her with a stare. 'You got someone in mind?'

'Maybe.' She was thinking of Ciaran Wallace. He was still a young-ish man. He wanted out of prison, sooner rather than later. Did he even know anything? And could she trust him – was he lying about not being there when her mother was taken?

'Be careful,' said Maeve. 'I know I'm one to talk but – take it from someone who knows. When we have this baby, I'm going to ask for a transfer.'

'What?' Paula stared at her. 'What to?'

Maeve sighed. 'Features.'

'My God.' Investigative reporting was in Maeve's blood. Hunting down criminals, exposing conspiracies, slamming the corrupt – this was what she did. To hear she was thinking of giving it up was shocking. 'Seriously?'

Maeve indicated her injured leg and wounded face. 'I've sacrificed a lot for the job already. Sinead isn't happy. She can't do it all on her own, and I don't think it'll be fair to the wee one to keep on the way I've always been.' She saw Paula's face. 'It's different for you – it's your mother. It's all personal. But I just think it's time for me to live the easy life. One where you're not checking under your car every morning for a bomb, and you can walk through an underpass without running in case someone comes up behind you, not that I can run very fast these days. Where you don't have your own police liaison for all the death threats you get. You know?'

'I know. I understand, I really do. I'm just . . . surprised.'

'We're all growing up, I suppose.' Except for Aidan, who hadn't been able to restrain himself, and was now in jail. Except for Paula, who'd tried to make a new life in London and boomeranged right back here, as her dad said, up to her elbows in the muck of the past.

'I'm just so close,' she said. 'To finding out what happened back then. To her.'

'You could be inches away all your life and never get there. Fact is, people don't want you to find out. You know that, right?'

'I . . .' She hadn't wanted to admit it. 'I don't know.'

'Listen. If the Provos killed your mother back then, they'd have dumped her body for you to find. That's what they did. Unless she was involved in something else – or she was sacrificed to cover up someone else's crimes. Ever wonder why no one even investigated it properly?'

'Yeah. It drove my dad nuts. He thought they were incompetent.'

'No one's that incompetent.'

She knew why Bob had botched it, but what about the people her mother had worked for? Why hadn't the Army come to rescue her, their valued source? 'Yeah. You're right. Protecting another informer, maybe?'

'That's what I'd say. There was something else at stake – someone they didn't want people to know about, and your mother was given up to protect them.'

It all made sense, as if she'd always known it. 'Another informer. Inside the IRA.'

'That's where I'd put my money. You can always sue, you know, if you have proof the Army ran her as an informer. Failure to protect her – a few families are doing that since the Stakeknife stuff came out. Might give you some answers, at least.'

She shook her head. It couldn't come out officially, not without giving up all her mother's secrets. 'I'm going to get there. I know it. I'm going to find the truth.'

'Maybe, Paula. But will you be able to handle it when it comes?'

Everyone seemed to be asking her that. Stubbornly, she looked away. 'Cross that bridge when I get to it.'

Maeve smiled. 'You're just like him, you know. Like a pair of mules in harness. Here, hold this, will you?' Paula grasped the crutch, and Maeve clasped her awkwardly with her free arm. 'Maguire. You know I'm just looking out for you, right?'

'Yeah. Doesn't mean I can take your advice, though.'

'I know. I know. Sure I never took anyone's myself. But when you have a wean . . . isn't it different?'

Paula thought of Maggie. Who did the little girl have? Only herself and two increasingly infirm grandparents, one who wasn't even a relation by blood. A missing grandmother, a father who didn't know he was that. And Maggie was three now. For herself, she could go on living this half-life forever, waiting for Aidan, waiting to find her mother. But Maeve was right. It was different now. She had to sort herself out. 'Come on,' she said. 'Maggie'll be fine with Pat for another while. Let's go and drown our sorrows.'

Margaret

Sean, that was his name. The one who came and went, who was higher up the food chain than Fintan, lower than Paddy. Everyone was lower than Paddy. The man was pacing up and down near the hedgerow, muttering to himself. 'Feck this. Feck it.'

Margaret had sunk down into the dirt, her knees and elbows red with it. She was so tired. Shouldn't this be over by now? 'If you're going to shoot me you should just do it,' she said. Her voice was like gravel. 'It's torture, this, keeping me here for days on end. I don't know anything. I'm no use to you.'

'Shut your mouth,' he said viciously, turning on her. 'Should have thought of that, shouldn't you, when you betrayed your country? Climbed into bed with that Brit bastard? Men are in prison because of you.'

'It's because they broke the law!' she shot back. 'You killed people, what did you expect? It's not worth it. This, this, stupid idea of a united Ireland. Do you not see? Nothing is worth killing people for. It's nearly over, for God's sake. Just let it be over. Let me go.'

'We can't. Paddy's not like that. Once he has someone, he never forgives them. Never.'

'Paddy doesn't have to know.'

He passed a hand over his unshaven face. 'He'll know we let you go.'

'Say I got away. Make it look like you didn't tie the ropes right or something.'

He was considering it. Margaret began to wonder if she had the strength to keep running, to get up and make it to that road in the distance where the cars moved along like toys. Aidan O'Hara had loved wee cars. Until his daddy got shot in front of him, and now he didn't love anything much. Maybe this man had done that. 'You've killed people,' she said. 'I'm sure you have. But I'm just a wife. I have a wee girl. What difference does it make if I live? The war's over. None of this will matter soon.'

'He'll find out.'

'I'm telling you he doesn't have to.'

Sean seemed to think about it for a long time. The light was low, shading his eyes. Afternoon. She had to get help before it was dark or she'd be running about these fields all night, scared and lost. It didn't bear thinking about. 'Please,' she said. 'I know you're not a bad man. You can't be. It's just . . . these things are hard to get out of, once you're in. I know that.'

Maybe it was this that swung it. Or maybe he'd always have done it. She'd never know. He pushed her roughly on the shoulder, and she almost fell on her face in the dirt. 'For feck's sake. Go then. Run to your fancy man. But listen – don't show your face here again, you hear? Not in this town. Not in this country. You need to be gone and gone for good. I'll tell Paddy we shot you and buried you. That's the only way. Otherwise he'll come after you forever. Do you understand?'

'But . . . I have a family . . .'

'You should have thought of that before you did what you did. I hear even a word you're alive, I'll be paying them a wee visit. Your husband, your wee girl. You understand me?'

She was trembling. He was giving her life, but saying she could never see Paula again. 'She'll think I'm dead.' She'd never know what had happened. She'd only know her mother had not been there when she arrived home from school one day. The note, maybe, would explain something, but she'd have so many questions. She was her father's daughter in that respect.

Sean was looking back and forth towards the farm, frantic now. 'For feck's sake, go. Go.' He pushed her again and she winced.

She would die here if she stayed. She would die, and maybe they'd hide her body, like that poor woman in Belfast back in the seventies, and no one would ever know what had become of her. Or she could get to her feet now and run, and never see Paula again, and know that her family would be searching for her while she ran to ground like a rat. That was the choice. Live, or die. Leave her family, or condemn them all to death. Margaret thought of the child in her belly, and she stumbled to her feet. She ran. Across the field, slipping and sliding in the mud, waiting every second to feel the bullet she was sure was coming, be knocked off her feet by it, see her own blood run into the red soil.

Voices behind her. Men, shouting. Margaret did not look back. She just kept running.

Chapter Twenty-Eight

'Package for you.' Gerard chucked the manila envelope down on Paula's desk. She'd crawled into the office with a stabbing headache attacking her temples: bloody Maeve. The woman didn't know the meaning of 'just one drink'.

She reached out to stop it skidding to the floor. 'For me? I don't even work here.'

'Well, it's got your name on it.' And it had, etched in a bold hand with sharpie marker.

Paula took it dubiously. 'These all get screened, yeah?'

'Course, they go through a metal detector.' Another precaution that wouldn't be needed on the mainland but which here was routine, same with the reinforced walls that surrounded the station and the checkpoints you had to go through to get in the door. In London, even in the areas of highest knife crime, you could still walk into the station off the street. She shook the package gently, hearing something shift about. Cautiously, she tore it open and out slid a cassette tape. Nothing else inside.

Gerard was still watching. 'Someone made you a retro mix tape, Maguire?'

'As if you even know what a tape is, all the age of you. Do we have a machine in here?'

'Oh aye, we're still using the old-fashioned ones. Budget cuts. Go in the wee listening room. Wonder what it is?'

Paula looked at the small rectangle. She remembered the brand of cassette from the nineties, when she'd recorded songs she liked off the radio, missing the starts and ends and misjudging the length of the tape so she'd end up with only three seconds of Take That before it cut out. Long before Spotify or iPads. Who would still be using tapes now? It seemed innocuous, with its brown tape spooling inside the clear cover – no writing on the insert card – but all the same she had a bad feeling about it.

She took it into the AV room, which was empty, and spent a few moments figuring out how to work the equipment. She put the large foam earphones over her head and pressed play, ready to hear whatever it was.

Nothing at first. Then the harsh buzz of static. Then a man's voice, Ballyterrin accent. 'State your name and charges for the tape.'

A sound like someone trying not to cry, maybe. Breathing hard.

Same man. 'State your name and charges, I said!'

A woman's voice, faltering. 'My name is . . . Margaret Maguire.'

Paula froze. The blood stopped in her veins. That voice. She hadn't heard that voice in twenty years. *Paula, get up for school now.*

'I'm charged with passing information to the British Army. I am an informer.'

Paula dropped the headphones to the ground and rushed out.

Corry was all business. 'It came in the post?'

'Looked like it. Normal stamps.' They'd already retrieved the envelope from the recycling bin, but it had been touched by so many people that prints were unlikely to be useful. The seal was a sticky one, so saliva was also not likely. It had been posted in the main Ballyterrin office, by the looks of it. Corry had sent someone chasing CCTV already but there were so many people in and out of there each day, it was a long shot. 'Who would send something like this?' *Why*, was what she really meant. Why, after all this time?

Corry said, 'We know IRA punishment squads often taped the confessions of their victims. A few of the families have been sent tapes like this. It's not so unusual. Though that was a long time ago, of course. How much did you hear?'

'Just her name and her . . . what they charged her with.'

'It's definitely her?'

Paula nodded. There was no way to explain how it had felt to suddenly hear her mother's voice, after twenty years of silence. Like she'd been in the room with her, alive and breathing. 'She sounded afraid. Like she'd been crying. I couldn't listen to the rest.'

'I don't blame you. I think someone will have to go through it, though. And you'll have to inform your father, of course.'

She nodded. That would be the worst part. 'Someone wants me to think she's dead. That's it, isn't it? This, the tip-off about her body . . .'

'It certainly seems that way. But they weren't her bones in the grave. We have to remember that. She wasn't buried there. And if someone wants us to stop looking, that means we absolutely keep on looking, because there's something to find.'

Paula had a sudden terrible thought. 'What if she is out there somewhere, alive, and this just stirs it all up? What if I send them after her again?'

Corry sighed. She was twiddling her pen behind her desk, and she looked tired. 'Paula. I said to you years ago that you might not like what you find, if you keep going with this. You seemed determined not to stop.'

'I can't stop.'

'I know that. I've not even tried to convince you, have I? But yes, if you poke around in things buried long ago, the earth starts to shift. You know that.'

She nodded unhappily. 'I can't believe someone had this all that time.' The thought of her mother's screams, her agony and fear, imprinted on that simple brown tape, from so long ago. She shuddered. 'It's so cruel. Such a cruel thing to do.'

'I'm afraid that's the hallmark of men like Paddy Wallace. You're on his radar now, and that makes you a target.'

An even worse thought struck her. 'Maggie?'

'I'm sure it won't come to that. Unfortunately, we get a lot of death threats here, and this isn't even a threat.'

So what was the point in sending it? Information, kindly meant after all this time? A warning? Or proof – *look, we had her. We killed her. You better stop looking, because there's nothing left to find.* She wished she knew.

'What should I do?' she said to Corry. 'I mean now? Today?' It was Avril and Gerard's wedding tomorrow, meaning the station would be stretched even more, every available officer looking for Mairead.

'Honestly, I don't know. We're pursuing all the leads we can. We don't know for sure this is from Wallace, or even a threat. Could be someone trying to help.'

Paula sighed. 'It doesn't seem right, going to the wedding, when Mairead's still out there.'

'Life goes on, Maguire. In this job, it has to, or we'd never enjoy ourselves at all. You go on home. I'll ask a patrol to swing round your way a few times tonight, but otherwise, there's not much we can do.'

Paula turned off the borrowed computer, put on her jacket, and started making her way to the door. Already she was recovering from the shock. Making plans – what to feed Maggie for dinner, what time she'd need to be up to do her hair for the wedding . . .

'Avril?' She stopped by her friend's desk, surprised to see her in a pool of light, bent over her computer. 'Er, aren't you meant to be off today?' Avril was in jeans and a jumper, as if she'd just popped by, and Paula didn't remember seeing her in all day before this.

Avril squinted at her screen. 'I was. I don't know – I was at the house, and everyone was just talking and talking, all this jawing about the ceremony and the hairdresser and who's doing what tomorrow, and I said I left my wallet at work then I just . . . got in the car and came here.'

Paula leaned against the partition. 'Ah, the old night-before-the-wedding freak-out.'

Avril put her head in her hands, groaning. 'Oh God, I'm so nervous. How do you know? That you're making the right decision?'

Paula wasn't sure she had it in her to talk Avril down from a fit of pre-wedding jitters. Clearly, she didn't know about the tape delivery. 'Everyone feels nervous before their wedding.'

'But it's not just that. This wedding, it's been a disaster from start to finish. My mammy's hardly speaking to me; she keeps crying every time anyone mentions the ceremony. Auntie Linda asked me did I mind that it wouldn't be valid in God's eyes. Gerard's mammy keeps slipping me pictures of the saints and asking me who they are. It's like Top Trumps only with miracles. I can't take it.'

Paula tried not to smile. 'Serves you right – you had to be progressive and have a mixed marriage.'

'We should have just eloped. Even to Rome. I'd do it, just to spite Mammy. And Daddy's curate is assisting with the ceremony and he's fighting over every word of it with Gerard's cousin. And I never liked him anyway, his breath smells like egg sandwiches.'

'Las Vegas?' Paula suggested. 'I'll drive you to the airport. Only I don't think Maggie will ever forgive me if she doesn't get to wear her special wedding hairband and shoes.'

Avril gave a watery smile. 'She's a wee dote. It will be nice, having everyone there. Even the boss is coming from London.'

Paula kept her face carefully neutral. 'Oh, Guy's coming in the end, is he? I thought with Tess expecting so soon . . .'

'He said he wouldn't miss it. He'll go back the next day.'

'Lovely.' She pasted on a smile.

'Fiacra's coming too. I was worried he might not.' Avril coloured. Their former colleague Fiacra had been in love with her around the time she and Gerard got together, which had caused some ructions in the team. He was now back with the Gardai, working down south somewhere. 'He's bringing some girl with him, Gisela is her name. Brazilian.'

'He's a new one on his arm every week, the same boy. And your dress came in OK?'

Avril softened romantically at the mention of her dress. 'Oh, it's just beautiful, so it is. Lace. Silk. I love it.'

'See? I bet you want to wear that, no matter what else might be going on.'

'But, Paula – is it stupid? My ones and Gerard's – I don't think they'll ever get on. Is it going to be this way always, fighting at Christmas, and I don't know, christenings . . .' She groaned again. 'That's another thing. What religion would the kids even be?'

'Come on now, Wright, no need to be worrying about non-existent weans, is there? Monaghan's a big eejit but you love him, a blind person could see that. I could see that way back then.'

'Could you?'

'Course I could. It was inevitable, the two of you. And times have changed. If Martin McGuinness can shake hands with the Queen, your and Gerard's families can be civil to each other.'

Avril took a big, shaky breath. 'I'm sorry. I just . . . I *am* having a pre-wedding freak-out, I think.'

Paula nodded knowledgably. 'You'll be gorgeous. It'll be a great day, and soon you'll look back and laugh at all these wee problems. Every wedding is the same. Everyone just has to stick their oar in.' Once again she cursed Saoirse and Pat for talking her into her own failed wedding. All that money wasted. That stupid dress. She had loved it too, secretly, though she would never have admitted it. But she'd known deep in her bones marriage was not something she could trust to. How could she, when her own parents' marriage had been a lie, when her mother had been carrying so many secrets?

As she thought about it, she made a decision: she wasn't going to tell her father about the tape. What was the point, when it still didn't prove anything? It would only cause more heartache, rake up more secrets. She'd carry this burden by herself.

She reached over and switched off Avril's computer. 'Come on. Let's get you home before your mammy sends out a search party.'

Chapter Twenty-Nine

Paula had chosen navy for the wedding. She thought it suggested a middle ground between 'tragic Sicilian widow' and 'flirtatious unmarried mother', one eye on other people's husbands, falling out of a strapless frock. Going alone to weddings was not something she relished. She looked at herself in the mirror, her red hair neatly arranged for once, tucked up under a little navy hat Saoirse had presented her with the other day, bits of lace and flowery strands hanging off it. 'A fascinator,' her friend had explained.

Heels, in deference to the day. Flats to put on as soon as the pictures were over. Maggie would be there for the ceremony and dinner, then Pat and PJ would come to take her home. It was the first wedding Paula had been to since her own cancelled one, and she still couldn't bear to think about that. How stupid she'd felt, standing there in her pouffey wedding dress, seeing everyone she knew through the stained glass doors of the church. Then the moment when she spotted the police car in the street, and Guy was there. The brief second when she'd wondered if he'd come for her, to finally declare himself. Then Aidan hauled away, arrested. Stupid. So stupid. And today she was going to have to sit through a wedding without him, and Guy there too. She took a deep breath and resolved to drink heavily to get through the day.

* * *

A cross-community wedding was hardly rare in these modern, enlightened times, even in Northern Ireland. All the same the atmosphere in the church was strained and hysterical. 'No Mass then,' Pat had said out of the side of her mouth when they'd discussed the ecumenical service, as if this meant they somehow wouldn't be legally wed. Paula slipped into a pew about halfway up, not sure whether to sit on the bride or groom's side. She'd known them both for exactly the same amount of time, since that day she'd stumbled into the small office of the cross-border missing persons team and met Guy Brooking and her life had changed, though she didn't know it then. She saw familiar faces – Bob and his wife Linda Hamilton up near the front, with the family. Today would be hard for them, no doubt, thinking of Ian, their son. Gerard's mammy and daddy were both as red-faced as him, his mother upholstered in some kind of shiny fabric like an angry sofa. She too had bits of leaf and feather hanging from her head; it seemed to be *de rigueur*. Saoirse and Dave were sandwiched into a pew already, no chance of sitting with them. Saoirse was wearing an empire-line dress, though she was hardly pregnant at all yet. Paula gave her a wave. Looking round the church, full of flowers and smiling faces, the thought of Mairead Wallace pulled her down like a current. Ciaran's comment needled in her mind: *it's maybe not what you think*. She'd no idea what he could mean; Mairead had been terrified of her brother. She wouldn't have gone with him willingly.

'There's Mr Bob and Auntie Seer-sha,' said Maggie loudly. She was already rooting about under the church pews, her wedding headband bent out of all recognition.

'Sshh now,' whispered Paula.

'Mummy,' she said, with no reduction in volume. 'Will Daddy be here today?'

Oh no. Not now. 'Why do you say that, pet?'

'We were here when you had your big nice dress and then Daddy went away and I cried and I couldn't wear my new shoes.'

Paula sighed. She'd hoped Maggie, then only two, would remember nothing about that terrible day. 'It's not here, pet. That was a different place. Look, how many people can you count in each row?'

Maggie would not be fobbed off so easily. She too was looking round the church. 'Who's that man, Mummy?'

Paula spotted Fiacra, togged up in a grey suit, fair curls pressed into submission. An unfeasibly tall and glamorous woman picked her way behind him, in heels that pushed her feet up almost vertical. Paula smiled at him, motioning him into the seat beside her. 'You came!'

'Aye, of course. Wouldn't miss it. This is Gisela.' Paula smiled at her politely while Fiacra craned under the seat to see Maggie. 'Hello, pet.'

Maggie stared at him from the gloom. 'Who's that, Mummy?'

'Mummy's friend Fiacra, say hello.'

Suddenly she got shy, returning to her below-seat excavations. Paula wondered what she'd found under there. Something dirty, no doubt. She was just feeling relieved that she had someone to sit with when a different voice said, 'Mind if I join you?'

Crap. Of course Guy was here. She'd hoped he might get distracted by some handy murder in London, or have to stay with pregnant Tess. Oh God, she wasn't here too, was she? No, no sign of her. Guy was looking irritatingly good, in some expensive navy suit, a red tie. And there was her old enemy, the citrus aftershave. She moved as far away as possible. He was shaking hands with Fiacra. 'The old team back together, eh?'

Paula fixed on a smile. 'Look, Maggie, it's Mr Guy from Mummy's work.' *Your father! Surprise!*

He bent down and as always Paula held her breath, waiting for him to notice. 'Hello, Maggie.'

Maggie peered out from under the seat. 'Who you?'

'Maggie!' Paula scolded. 'Be polite, you know who he is.' *Your father. This is your father.* One day, it would have to be said. So far, Maggie only looked like her namesake, Paula's mother. No sign of Guy had surfaced yet in her features, thank God. 'No Tess?' she said casually.

'She's not allowed to fly, this far along.' He eased himself into the pew. 'So what kind of church is this, then?'

'Presbyterian,' said Fiacra, talking out of the side of his mouth, like Pat had. 'My mammy blessed me in holy water before she let me out of the house.'

There was a general commotion at the front of the church, everyone standing up. Paula saw Gerard all gussied up in his waistcoat and frock coat, his face very red. The brick-shithouse fella beside him must be his brother. At least one of his uncles had a conviction for being in the IRA. Whereas Avril's grandfather had been the head of his Orange lodge. This wedding was a minefield.

It was the moment she always used to love. The bride in the doorway with her father, nervous, fussing at her unfamiliar long skirt. Everyone looking, smiling. In Paula's case she'd been there alone, determined not to be given away. She'd been so nervous she'd almost bolted, even before seeing the police car outside. Someone was singing a high soprano, wobbly. Avril in her dress, a veil over her face. She'd gone for a safe Princess Kate-like style, her arms and chest covered. Paula stored away details to tell Pat. Then she was walking, her overly made-up face hardly visible under the acres of lace, and her father was shuffling, out of time with the music, and Avril was struggling in her heels. But then she reached Gerard and put up her veil, and they smiled at each other, a small moment of *isn't this daft* in the middle of all that pomp, and he took her hand and tucked it under his arm. Paula turned away, a lump in her throat. Aidan should be here with her, at her side, helping to stop Maggie eating dust off the floor or whatever she was doing down there. It wasn't right. Was she going to miss him for the rest of her life?

The wedding went by, as they always did. Ceremony, photos, into the car, hotel, drinks reception, meal (soup, roast beef, pavlova) and speeches. Carefully worded, welcoming Gerard and Avril to the respective families, no mention made of the tension that had preceded the day. Paula saw the strained look gradually fade from Avril's face, and knew she'd been right. It would all be OK. It was always OK – unless you were her, of course, and your wedding turned into a trip to the police station. As they brought pieces of wedding cake around, she heard her phone vibrate. 'Come on, Miss Maggie, Granddad's here to get you.'

'Don't wanna go home!' She arched her body mutinously in her chair. Her place was strewn about with food, as if she'd smeared her hands in it and wiped them everywhere. Which she might well have done.

'Well, tough, you have to. You have to tell Granny and Granddad all about it, don't you? And you can watch *Frozen*.'

'Can I keep my dress on?'

'Yes, OK. Come on.' She saw Guy smile at her indulgently as she cajoled Maggie from the seat and into her cardigan. Probably thinking of the new child he'd have soon. She knew he'd assumed, and she'd let him believe, that Aidan was Maggie's father. Not exactly a lie, but not the truth either. For a moment she let herself picture it – her and Guy together, him helping to wrangle Maggie, knowing she was his daughter . . . but no. That could never happen.

PJ was waiting outside, leaning against the car, bang on time as always. 'Well, pet. Well, Miss Maggie.'

'Grandda, Grandda, Mum says I can watch *Frozen* in my wedding dress.'

'Sorry,' said Paula, passing Maggie's hand to her father. 'Couldn't get her to go otherwise; she'd have danced the night away. Oh, and she's hopped up on sugar too.'

'Never worry, we'll mind her. You'll get a taxi back?' Even though she had lived away from Ballyterrin for years, her father always wanted to know how she was getting home.

'Yeah, or someone can give me a lift.' Paula glanced back towards the hotel, seeing a familiar balding head through the window of the bar. There was at least one person she knew who didn't drink, after all. Suddenly she had an idea. 'Dad . . . will you come in a minute, say hello?'

'Ah, pet, I'm not dressed for it.'

'Just a minute.'

Taking Maggie in again sent mixed messages that might provoke a mutiny, but all the same Paula walked her to the bar, her father following reluctantly. Avril was there in her wedding dress, posing for family snaps. Paula waved to her in a moment of lull. 'Here's my dad, just wanted to say congratulations.'

'You're looking beautiful, pet,' said PJ, shaking her hand and Gerard's.

'And here's Bob,' said Paula seamlessly, spotting him hovering in the background in his ill-fitting grey suit. She held her breath. It was the first time her father and his former partner had met in years. There was a lot of bad blood between them, she knew, though not exactly what.

Luckily, three-year-olds were quite good at smoothing over social tension. 'Mr Bob, Mummy says I have to go home with Grandda,' said Maggie sulkily.

Bob stooped to the child. 'I think your mammy's right, wee pet. You'll be very tired otherwise.'

'I won't be tired.' Then she yawned, negating her argument somewhat.

Paula saw Bob hesitate, then hold out his hand. 'PJ.'

Another hesitation before PJ took it. 'Bob.'

'You've a lovely wee granddaughter there.'

'Aye, she's a handful all right.' He hesitated. 'I was . . . Pat and I were very sorry to hear about Ian.'

Bob looked at his feet. 'Thanks, PJ. It was hard enough, so it was. Linda's here somewhere too.'

'Tell her I said hello.' PJ turned his attention to the child, who was trying to hide under a chair. 'I better get this one home. Take care, Bob.'

'And you.'

It wasn't much, Paula thought, watching her father cart off a protesting Maggie, but it was a start.

Chapter Thirty

'They make a lovely couple, don't they?'

Paula looked up to see Guy had come over, draining the last of his Peroni. His tie was loosened and his shirtsleeves rolled up; he'd been dancing earlier. Of course he had, the perfect wedding guest, shaking hands and kissing cheeks, dandling children, standing rounds. 'Yeah. Always thought they'd end up together.' In a spotlight, Avril and Gerard rocked gently to their song, the Bon Jovi number 'Always'. It was done, no one had come to blows, and they were married. Avril's mascara was smudged and her hair coming down; she looked blissful.

'Do you remember when you caught them in the corridor that time?' Guy shook his head, pulling up a chair beside her. 'That was awkward.'

It certainly had been. Avril had been engaged to someone else at the time, and Fiacra was in love with her too, and things had kicked off. But Paula also remembered Fiacra's comments at the time, shouted to her and Guy. *Am I the only person who can behave around here?* She'd already been pregnant with Maggie, in desperate denial, no idea whether Aidan or Guy was the father. That question had been answered against her will, and it was not what she'd been hoping for. There was no getting away from it – knowing she had a child with him made her feel tied to Guy forever. Maybe he'd never be just a friend, a work colleague. She looked away from him, at the swirling patterns of the lights. The wedding was winding down, the tea and evening buffet already brought out. She needed to leave soon. She had no one's arms to sway in herself, no one to go home to. This was not her home any more. 'How's Tess then?' she asked lightly. 'Must be soon now.'

'Next week, probably. Not sure I'll be up to it again, after all these years!' The Brookings' daughter was off to university already, and their son had been killed when he was ten, before Guy had come to Northern Ireland in an effort to escape it. He had another child, of course, but he didn't know. How could she tell him? He and Tess were salvaging what was left of their marriage, somehow, with this sticking-plaster baby, and she wasn't about to rip that off. She tried to move the conversation back to work, which was marginally safer. 'Did you get a chance to look into that case for me?'

Guy moved closer, lowering his voice. In order to be heard over the music, his lips were almost grazing her ear. 'Ciaran Wallace, right? I did.'

'And?' She kept her eyes firmly fixed on the dance floor, her expression neutral, as if they weren't discussing a brutal killing.

'The victim was an ex-Army officer, former Intelligence. Captain John King was his name. I asked around.'

Guy had been in the Army before joining the Met, she knew, and still maintained certain contacts that could be useful at times like this. 'Ciaran said he was innocent. Any substance to that?'

'It was rushed through – a lot of pressure to prove it wasn't the actual IRA who did it, that the peace process was holding. DNA was found at the scene, but it was a bit scrappy – could have been a familial match.' So that meant Paddy Wallace could have been the killer, pinning it on his brother. 'Ciaran Wallace lived nearby, he had IRA links but not so much it would seem like he was acting on orders, and the evidence stacked up just enough.'

'He mentioned something else – a hoody at the scene?'

'That's right. There was a hoody that belonged to Ciaran – his flatmates testified he wore it all the time, and it had his hairs and DNA on it. The officer I spoke to seemed to think it was a bit stupid, though, leaving such an obvious piece of evidence at the scene.'

'They didn't think it could be a plant?'

'Like I said, it was rushed through. Ciaran was right there, he'd no alibi, it was his jumper . . . He was the ideal fall guy, I suppose, if you were looking for one.'

Ciaran had not even mentioned his brother as the possible killer. Shielding him, maybe. The more she found out about this family, the less she understood them. 'That guy King. If he was Army Intelligence, would he have known . . . Edward?'

It was Guy who'd first found out about Edward, her mother's handler and lover. Guy was always tactful about it, never probing. 'I believe they worked together, yes.'

She pieced it together. Maeve had suggested there was an informer on Paddy's squad. Sean Conlon was dead, Prontias Ryan was dead, Mark O'Hanlon was dead, Fintan McCabe was dead. What if Paddy had known? What if he'd been chasing that informer all this time? Ryan's killer had wanted revenge, Gerard said, or information. Or both. Men like Edward and this John King had infiltrated Paddy's side, paid his friends to inform on him. He would likely want revenge on them as well. 'Edward's dead too,' she said. 'The PI I hired found out for me. A long time ago now, car bomb. Three years after King was killed.'

'Shame. He'd have been easier to find.' Than her mother, he meant. She'd be hiding even more deeply now, if she was still alive.

'Guy . . .' she began. 'You know how I'm meant to be back to work Tuesday?'

He smiled. 'You want longer?'

'It's just, I'm starting to find things out here. This case of Corry's, it's connected. My mother was at that farm, I think. I have leave left over, don't I?'

'You'd have to let HR know. But there's no reason why not.'

Of course there wasn't, her job was hardly essential. Those graphs could be analysed any time. 'Thanks. End of the week, maybe?'

'That's fine with me. As long as you do actually come back.' It was said lightly, but it did make her wonder. If this couldn't be solved in a week, she'd have to go back to her new life, let Davey Corcoran go on chasing dead ends. Maybe she'd never find anything.

The music changed, a faster song, something with an old-time swing rhythm to appease the fifty-somethings in the crowd. Several couples began to waltz in that stately, precise way of older Irish people at weddings. Guy sat back. 'Anyway, enough of the morbid chat. It's Avril and Gerard's day.' He held out a hand to her. 'How about it? Duty dance?'

She stared at his hand. Remembered the feel of his arms around her on the one night they'd spent together, imagined the weight and shift and smell of him. Her body was already moving towards him, without her even realising it. She checked herself. 'Um . . .'

His face changed. 'Just a suggestion. Silly idea, I guess.'

'I just . . .' They worked together now, and it was good. And there was Tess. She wasn't about to throw all that away, even if part of her would always want to shut her eyes and drink him in when he was nearby. There was just no point. She knew that now. Besides, there was always Aidan, and the memory of his pale, strained face in the prison, the feel of his mouth on hers for just a moment. The leap of hope after so long – he was ready to fight, to appeal his conviction.

'Making sure Maguire doesn't stay in Ballyterrin again?' Corry had come over. She was still wearing her heels, unlike almost every other woman there, and even her hair was still neat, not a strand slipping from its chignon.

Guy held up his hands in mock surrender. 'Just making sure you don't poach her back, Helen. How are things?'

'Not bad. We have the Commission all over us, sadly. Thank your lucky stars you don't have a dead weight like that around your neck in London.'

'I can imagine.'

'Mind if I have a wee word with Maguire, while I still have her?' Paula saw Corry had her BlackBerry in her hand, though she spoke easily. *Something has happened.*

'I should head off,' said Guy, getting up. 'I've an early flight. I'll just go and say goodbye to the bride and groom.'

Corry leaned over to Paula as he left. 'Don't say anything now, but there's been a riot in the prison.' She saw Paula's face go white. 'Not Aidan. He's fine. But Ciaran Wallace is in hospital.'

Margaret

Somehow she made it across the field, slipping in the fresh autumn mud, too afraid to look back. He'd have a gun on him, she was sure. What if it was all a trick? What if any minute now she heard the crack of a bullet? One second. Two. Three. And then there was a gate, and a latch, and she was out onto the road, the tarmac solid under her feet, and a car was screeching to a halt beside her. 'Jesus, watch where you're going, missus!' Some old fella in a flat cap. Could be one of them. She had to risk it.

'Please,' she panted. 'I need a phone. Will you take me to a phone?'

Five minutes later she was in his kitchen, which smelled of cows and hadn't been cleaned in years, while he watched her warily, and she was dialling the number she'd promised to never call. Dimly, she hoped this poor old farmer wouldn't pay the price for what she'd done. These people, the Paddy Wallaces of the world, would hurt you for a lot less. Not another life she'd ruined with her madness and her rage. The phone rang and rang. *Please God, let him answer. Please God.* He was her only chance. She had to leave the country right now, tonight. Sean had made that very clear – run, or her family would pay the price. But what if he'd been moved? What if he'd abandoned her, gone back to England already? How could she get out with no money or passport and not even shoes on her feet? She thought of her house, her clothes in the wardrobe, the dishes she'd washed up before they came for her, leaving the kitchen clean and tidy, as if that mattered. She could never go back there again. Her life as she knew it was over.

There was a click, and she heard his voice, the English

tone of it so rare and fine to her ears. 'Margaret? Is that you?'

And that was when she broke down and cried. Her voice squeaked, used up and tired, barely making a noise. 'Come and get me. You need to come and get me away, right now. We have to be on a ferry tonight, or we'll both be dead.'

Chapter Thirty-One

'You didn't need to come with me, Maguire, for God's sake. You can hardly walk.'

Paula huffed along beside Corry as she strode into Ballyterrin Hospital, an unfortunately familiar location to them both, cursing the blisters her high-heeled shoes had left on her feet even after just a few hours' wear. 'I was the one who spoke to him last. He knows more than he's told us, I'm sure of it. Who attacked him?'

'Guards didn't know. There was some kind of incident on the wing, some fella stabbed him with a home-made shiv. No one's talking. But one thing you can be sure of is that Paddy Wallace will have mates in there.'

'You mean he might have got someone to do this? To his own brother?'

'His own brother who was talking to the police. Nothing Paddy hates more than a tout, remember. He ran a punishment squad. If he hears Ciaran was helping us . . .'

Paula fell silent. So this maybe was her fault too. They'd reached A&E now, and there was Saoirse's locum, a tall, impatient man who greeted them perfunctorily. 'We've stabilised him but he's going straight up to surgery. No questions.'

'When can we talk to him?' said Corry.

'I can't say. Tomorrow, maybe, if he pulls through, but

he has a head injury, a perforated liver and two broken ribs.'

Paula had drifted over to the door to the private room, and through the glass plate she could see Ciaran hooked up to machines, his chest bandaged and his face purple with swelling. 'God. Poor guy.'

Corry gave her a sharp glance. 'You feel sorry for him, after what he did?'

'He said he was innocent.'

'They all say that,' Corry said implacably.

'Yeah, but . . . I kind of believed him. He was set up, he said. He'd nothing to do with the IRA.'

'That's not for us to answer now, Maguire. But as soon as he wakes up I'll have several questions for Mr Wallace. Such as where his brother might be hiding, and if he knows where either of his sisters might be.'

Paula kept looking at him, trying to imagine the man she'd met as a killer. 'Was there anything on the tape?' she asked in a low voice.

'I had Gallagher listen to it. Nothing much of use. It confirms Paddy Wallace had your mother at the farm, and that McCabe and Conlon helped.'

'Any mention of Ciaran?'

'Nothing. But it doesn't prove he wasn't involved.'

There was a motion further down the corridor; someone arguing with the officer on duty. 'Please, I need to see him!'

It was Carly Jones, dressed in a grey sweatshirt and jeans, pale and tearful. Once again her make-up had been left off and she looked much younger, very alone and vulnerable.

Corry motioned her past the officer. 'Carly, you should be at the safe house.' They'd moved her to another one now, with an officer always at her door. Paula could see one puffing after her down the corridor.

'Sorry, boss, she ran off,' he said sheepishly to Corry.

'I had to come. He's my uncle! He's been hurt. My mum would want me to be here.'

'But Carly, he's been in prison, you know. He was convicted of murder.' And her other uncle had kidnapped her. Yet it seemed she still craved it, a family around her.

The girl was almost in tears. 'I don't care. Mum said he was OK, she said she never thought he did the murder. Please, will you let me see him?'

'Of course we will,' Corry soothed. 'But he's asleep now, you see. Why don't you sit down here, and we'll send McQuaid to get you a nice cup of tea.' She directed a steely glance at Carly's hapless protection officer, who bumbled off.

Carly sank into a plastic chair, shivering. 'Please. My mum . . . is there anything?'

'We're doing our best,' Corry said gently. 'We've had the helicopter up every day, we've got their pictures out everywhere, and we're looking into everyone who might know your uncle.'

Except most of them were dead, Paula thought. And even Ciaran, his own brother, was lying in a hospital bed.

'It's my fault.' Carly's tears brimmed and overflowed. 'I should've done what she told me but . . . and now she's gone.'

Paula would have liked to say it was OK, they would find Mairead safe, but couldn't. They had no way of knowing that. All they could offer, as so often, was sympathy and platitudes and cups of tea.

Chapter Thirty-Two

It was still a novelty, joining the queue of women at the prison knowing Aidan would actually deign to see her. And there he was, behind the table, and when he saw her he smiled. She couldn't believe the change in him – from crushing guilt and deadening acceptance to hope. Walking towards him, she felt like she had all those years ago, when she was seventeen and he was eighteen and suddenly he'd looked at her properly and everything was different, and he went from being Aidan, the aloof son of her mother's best friend, to *Aidan*. Everything.

'Maguire.'

His thin arms went around her, and she was so grateful to hear her name in his mouth again that tears sprang to her eyes. She pressed her face into his shoulder to hide them, breathing in his smell, that was somehow still him under the unfamiliar prison washing powder and the staleness of cooped-up bodies. 'You're not hurt?'

They sat down, reluctantly torn apart, but he held her hand across the table and she felt his rough knuckles, the callouses on his fingers from years of scribbling down notes at press conferences, then surviving in prison. 'Ah no, it all kicked off in the other wing. We were on lock-down for hours, mind you.'

'What happened? Do you know?'

He looked around him warily, and she remembered the time he'd been beaten up too, his eye like squashed fruit. Aidan was not popular in here, after supposedly killing a Republican. 'It was Wallace. Someone jumped him in the stairwell.'

'But why? He seemed so quiet, just keeping his head down.'

'Well, I don't know for sure.' She had to lean forward to catch his voice. 'They're saying it was an outside order. Shut him up for a while, you know.'

Paula bit her lip, pushing the guilt away. Someone didn't want him to tell her something. But what? Was it something he'd already mentioned? Nothing stood out. 'So people outside pull the strings in here?'

'Course. There's a few fellas with long sentences, see, so they don't mind getting extra time if it gives them power. And you'd be amazed at what gets in here. Phones, drugs, you name it.' He leaned even closer. 'Listen . . . I wasn't going to tell you this, but Wallace, me and him talk sometimes. He's always saying he didn't do it, that murder, that he's innocent. And he seemed to have the idea I was in the same boat. So I wondered why he'd be so sure, like. That it wasn't me.'

'Did you ask him?' she whispered.

'Aye, eventually. We got to be friends, I s'pose, till they moved him to another wing. But he wouldn't say much. Just that Conlon's number was up, you know. That someone was out for his blood that night anyway.'

'Who?'

'He wouldn't tell me.' But Paula could guess. The same person who'd framed Ciaran for murder in the first place.

'Aidan. Be careful.' Imagine losing him now, when he'd

finally come back to her. She resisted the urge to kiss his scraped knuckles, which seemed to never properly heal. She didn't want to know what that meant about his life in here.

'How's Mags?' he said, deliberately adopting a cheerful tone, which she tried to match.

'Oh, she's fine. Had a good time at Avril and Gerard's wedding, so much that she's now accosting people asking if they can get married and she can be flower girl.' She hesitated. 'Should I bring her next time?' There were kids who came, and various family programmes to keep them in touch. Even one where the inmates could record bedtime stories for their children. But Aidan had never wanted any of that.

He shook his head. 'I'd rather just wait. Maybe, if we can overturn it, she won't have to see me like this.'

He sounded so hopeful. Once she would have given everything for that, but she felt the pressure of it. No one else was looking into this. The evidence had been there to convict, and the PSNI were happy to let Aidan rot. It was all on her. 'I think I know who did it,' she whispered. 'Killed Conlon. But I can't prove it. That's the trouble.'

'That's always been the trouble, Maguire.' His smile was strained, and she knew he was putting it on for her. 'Here, I have to go. They're giving us less time today. Loss of privileges, after the riot.'

Then it was time, and she had to go, with one last fierce hug – both of them too scared to repeat the kiss from last time – and her last image was of him shuffling back to his cell, his shoulders bowed, his body shrunk, his hair shaved so close you could see the scalp. If she didn't get him back for good soon, there wouldn't be much more left to save.

Chapter Thirty-Three

'Someone to see you in reception.'

Paula looked up from her desk, confused, at the DC who'd approached her. Someone new, whose name she didn't know, filling in for Avril. Jennifer? Julie? God, she was bad with names. 'You're sure, for me?'

'That's what she said.' The DC was already turning back to her own work, the mountain of papers on her desk. Paula got up and went through the alarmed doors, her lanyard swinging. She passed through the turnstiles and into the secure reception area. The desk sergeant nodded towards her visitor.

The woman in reception had her back to the desk. Paula's heart failed for a second – she was so like Mairead Wallace, with the same glossy black hair, same hunched shoulders. She turned. Not Mairead, but someone very like her, younger, in skinny jeans and a black polo neck. 'Hello?'

The woman was staring at Paula now. 'Dr Maguire?'

'Yes. You asked to see me?' And why would someone do that when she didn't even work here?

'I saw you on the news. The press conference. I knew it was you.'

Paula frowned. Had she met this woman before? Was it more than the resemblance to Mairead that was jogging her memory? 'I'm sorry . . .'

'You look just like her. Your mum. I knew you were her daughter, you see, when I saw you.'

Right there in the reception of Ballyterrin police station, with the desk sergeant surreptitiously eating a chip butty under the counter, Paula was sure she was going to pass out. Blood roared in her ears. 'You knew my mother?' Past tense. Safer to keep using it, until she knew otherwise.

The woman – she wasn't that much older than Paula herself, she realised now, late thirties maybe – just smiled, a little sadly. 'I was with her. When they took her to the farm. I helped her get away.'

Get away. Those magic two words. 'I'm sorry, I don't know who you—'

'I'm Aisling Wallace. I think you've been looking for me?'

Corry watched her through the glass of the interview room. Aisling Wallace sat neatly, her legs crossed and arms folded away from the table, as if it was dirty (which it likely was). 'It's really her?'

'I think it must be. No one else would have known . . . the things she knew.'

'Huh. Well, there you go. I'd have put money on her being the one in the morgue, God love her. Question is, who's that if it's not Aisling?'

Paula was watching her too. This woman had seen her mother after she'd disappeared on that day in late October. She might know what had become of her afterwards. The truth was so close she could almost close her fingers over it. 'She asked to see me,' she began, but Corry interrupted.

'You can't interview her. You don't even work here, Paula.'

She sighed. It had been worth a shot. 'I can watch?'

'If you must. It might not be what you want to hear, though. Willis has given the go-ahead to question her about your mother. It's a step closer to re-opening the case.'

Poor Willis. All these crimes he'd thought neatly sealed away, and here was Paula digging them all back up again. No wonder he didn't like her. 'I'll watch, then.'

Corry looked at her keenly. 'Leave if it gets too much. I mean it, Maguire. I can't have you messing this one up for us. I know it's hard, but this is just the way of it. Understand?'

She nodded. It was indeed the way of it in Ballyterrin, where everything was always too close to home. Corry opened the door, took a second to straighten her neat trouser suit, and went in to talk to the woman they'd thought dead until ten minutes ago.

Aisling frowned when Corry went in, shortly followed by the other DC, her smooth, dark hair bent over a laptop. 'I wanted to speak to Dr Maguire. Paula. That's her name, isn't it?'

Corry sat down. 'I'm afraid that's not possible. She doesn't officially work for us any more, and since the anonymous call about her mother's remains, the cases have become linked.'

'They weren't her mother's remains,' said Aisling, a touch impatiently. 'That's what I came to say. She got away. I helped her, I untied her.'

Corry kept her cool. 'Just let us set up the tape, Ms Wallace, so we can get all this.' The new officer read the details into the recorder, announcing herself as DC Jennifer Gallagher and explaining Aisling was not under arrest, it was a voluntary interview. 'Now. As you know, we've been trying to find you in relation to the discovery of two bodies on your family's farm. We subsequently received a tip-off that Margaret Maguire was also buried there, but we've found no evidence of that.'

'It was a sheep,' Aisling said. 'It'd died that day. We had to bury something, you see, for Paddy to believe she was dead, she'd been shot trying to get away. I'm not sure he did even then. I'd see him looking at me afterwards – like he knew.' She shivered, drawing her sleeves down over her hands. 'I know he has my sister. I want to help you catch him. Paddy, my brother – he's a psychopath, you see.'

She said it matter-of-factly. Paula could see Corry trying to get the interview back on her preferred tracks. 'Ms Wallace, could you start by taking me through the events of October and November 1993? From when you first became aware of Margaret Maguire, to the date of your leaving Northern Ireland.'

Aisling nodded. Paula had never seen someone so composed in an interview room. There was something about the lighting, the lack of windows, that made even the innocent twitchy. Then she leaned forward, the shadows striping across her pale face, and she started to tell the story Paula had waited twenty years to hear.

They'd been in there for some time when Aisling stopped and said, 'A cup of tea or something would help now, do you not think?'

Corry was leafing through her notes, as if she could scarcely believe her ears. 'Of course, Aisling. Let me just confirm what you've said so far. Your brother Paddy brought Margaret Maguire to the house for interrogation and held her there for four days, during which time you provided food and water.'

'I helped her. I was only young, but I did what I could. I'd never seen a woman out there before and I couldn't believe what they were doing to her. They tied her up, beat her. Paddy cut all her hair off. I was . . . it scared me, that he could act this way. In the past I always thought it was bad people he brought in, people who'd betrayed us, our side. But her . . . she kept talking about her daughter. It made me realise Paddy was off the rails.'

'And at the time you were just seventeen?'

'That's right. And in our family, the girls didn't get much say. Mairead and me were expected to do everything – cook and clean for the boys and their mates. Mammy knew exactly what they were up to in the barn and she didn't care.'

Paula thought of that old woman, sunk into her own decaying flesh. Carrying on her daily life knowing that another woman, someone's mother, was tied up in her barn. It was hard to imagine it now, but they'd been in the middle of a war then. People felt justified, all their rage and hate channelled into the cause. Still. That didn't make it any easier, to think of her mother held there for days, afraid for her life.

Aisling was still talking. 'So one day I decided I'd get her out. I wasn't going to let Paddy kill her. I untied her, told her to run over the fields and escape.'

'And did she?' Corry's voice was calm. Paula was straining, almost touching the video screen in the hot little room she was sitting in, watching. 'What happened?'

'Well. Sean caught her.'

'Sean Conlon?'

Oh, that name again. He'd shot Aidan's father, almost for sure. Aidan had beaten him half to death, if not all the way. The cycle just went on and on.

'Aye. I thought he'd kill her for sure – he was as bad as Paddy, nearly – but he let her go too. He helped me make the plan, afterwards. See, if Paddy came back and just found her gone, he'd know we did it. Sean said he'd kill us. Even me, his wee sister. He was already obsessed with there being some kind of tout in the squad. So we buried the sheep. Paddy never paid any heed to the animals. Ciaran did but he'd gone by then.' It was hard for Paula to get her head round all this. Aisling was not much older than her – she'd have been going through all that while Paula was at home watching *ER* and trying not to think about her mother.

'He'd gone?'

'Yeah. He went to London, I think it was the day before it all kicked off. It was the last straw for him, having a woman there. He didn't like what they were doing, but he'd never have stood up to Paddy.' So Ciaran had not been involved in torturing her mother. But he'd known she was there, and he hadn't done anything to stop it either. He'd lied.

Corry tapped her pen against her pad. 'Sorry, Aisling, I just need to make sure I've got this clear. Sean Conlon and you both helped Margaret Maguire get away?'

'That's what I said. Far as I know she made it. Dunno what happened after, course.' Aisling sat up, her eyes looking round as if for a camera. 'The thing I never understood was why he'd do it. Sean. Why would he save her, after what she did? She'd admitted she was a tout but he let her live. It just didn't make any sense.'

Paula was in the ladies, splashing cold water over her face. She wasn't sure why. It seemed like the kind of thing people did when they'd had a shock. A tiny bit more of her mother's trail uncovered, only to run out again. Where had she gone after escaping the farm? On the ferry to England – Davey had found a record of an official car leaving that night – then to London? Living with Edward, and maybe their child? She wondered had he found anything else in London, the wife and child mentioned in the obituary. He'd have called if so, surely.

'Hiya.'

Turning, she saw Aisling Wallace in the doorway of the ladies, and felt herself flush. What to say to the woman? 'Hello.'

'You were listening?'

Paula nodded.

'It's all true. As far as I know, she got away. I helped her.'

'I know. Thank you for that. I know it wasn't safe for you.'

'It didn't matter. I couldn't let him kill her. But listen.' She took a step closer. 'I helped your mother. Now he has my sister – I want your help to get her back. You don't know what he's like.'

'We're doing all we can, I promise—'

'No, you're not. But I can help. I know him. I want you to do exactly what I say, and I also want to meet my niece.' Her composed face broke into a smile. 'My niece! I saw her on the news too. She looks just like Mairead. I need you to take me to her, and to my other brother, please.'

'But Aisling—'

'Yeah, I know. Take me to see my family and afterwards I'll tell you everything I know about Paddy.'

Margaret

The ferry was freezing, exposed to all the harshness of the Irish Sea, which rocked beneath them like crushed black glass. All the same she wouldn't stay in the car, couldn't be anywhere with closed doors. She'd wrapped his scarf around her head and she could smell him, that tang of coarse wool and aftershave, a whiff of cigarettes. He only smoked when he was on edge, he'd told her. He said he'd been smoking non-stop since she went out of contact, lighting one off another in a frenzy. He said they'd looked everywhere, hauled people in for questioning, leaned on all their other sources. None of the neighbours appeared to have seen her bundled into the car – there was no police report, the RUC were stumbling around in the dark. The farmyard wasn't somewhere they knew about, or they'd have been there in a flash.

She tried to believe him. She wasn't sure she did. But they'd come for her within five minutes of her making the call, roaring up in black Mercedes cars and taking the farmer aside to talk to him in quiet voices. She thought he'd been offered money. He hadn't taken it, pushing them away as if affronted, and when she'd gone, once again bundled into the back of the car with a rug over her head, he'd watched her go with worried eyes. She'd tried to thank him but her mouth felt like it was stopped up with dirt. She didn't even know his name. For a moment, as they were taking her away, she'd wanted to get out and run. Men taking her away, she didn't know where. It wasn't so very different.

Then there was a car journey with her pressed to the floor, two silent men in suits driving, one with an earpiece. Her feet bare and cut, her clothes torn, and her hair hacked off. She didn't know where they were until she heard the screech of birds and the roar of the sea. The ferry terminal, and finally Edward was there in the back of another car, smoking a cigarette down to his ashy fingers, his hat tipped over his face. She'd seen the way he looked at her. She knew she looked awful, and stank too, of the barn and sweat and fear. She'd never realised fear had a smell before.

He'd said nothing to her until they'd driven onto the ferry, clanking over the ramp into its dark innards. Only when she felt it move off did she breathe again. Leaving Ireland. She'd never been out of it in her life before. Whatever documents had been presented were clearly enough to get them through without too many glances at the back seat, where she lay crouched. As soon as they were on and safe, she'd thrown the door open and run to the deck, gulping in the cold night air, drinking it down. Trying to shake off that barn, how close she'd been to being shot in the head. She'd seen it in his eyes, how he'd weighed her up. That man Sean. The one who'd saved her life. She would never know what had tipped it in her favour. Every breath seemed a bonus now. She could have been snuffed out, buried under that boggy soil. She held her trembling hands up to her face, white with cold. Was this real? Had she survived? She felt like a different person, not the same Margaret who'd sat down however many days ago to write a pathetic note to her daughter.

Steps behind her, his light tread. 'Come in now. They have people everywhere, on the boats even . . . it's not safe.'

She turned to him, this stranger with the careworn face that had somehow lodged itself in her heart. 'What will happen now?'

'We'll get you away. Somewhere safe.'

'They think I'm missing? They don't know you found me?' Meaning Paula and PJ. Meaning the family she was running from.

'They can't be told, Margaret. It'll make them targets. At least not until it's all over.' Meaning the peace process, promised for so long, inching closer month by month.

She shivered. 'He said I could never tell them. Or I'd be killed, and them too. I'm supposed to be dead.'

'That might be for the best. If you're dead they can't come after you.'

'But . . .' It meant letting her husband and daughter think she was gone for good, disappeared. It meant no answers. It meant years of looking. Could she do that to them? She looked at him helplessly.

'We just have to get you away for now. Then we can think.' His hand slid up her arm, rubbing it through the borrowed coat. 'You're freezing. Go back in the car.'

'Will you be with me? In the safe place?'

It seemed to her there was a slight hesitation. 'We've both been compromised. We'll have to figure something out. But you'll be safe. I promise it.'

Like he'd promised no one would ever know what she'd done. And yet they'd come to her house, into her kitchen, and taken her away. She'd almost died.

She was shivering miserably. How had it come to this? The day he'd knocked on her door, courteous, with his English accent, asking about the soldier who'd died in her arms, suggesting there were ways she could help to make sure it didn't happen again. It had seemed so harmless – a small thing she could do to fight against the darkness they all drowned in. Copy a letter here, slip a document into her bag there. A way to do some good, not just sit back and watch helplessly as blood fed on blood. But somehow it had ended up with her on the deck of this boat, its heaving making her queasy, running from her life and with his child in her belly. She hadn't told him yet. Would he have come for her faster if he'd known? The thought was treacherous and she pushed it down. He was all she had now. She had to trust him. Her hands slid over her middle. 'Edward . . .'

He flinched at the use of his name. She didn't even know if it was his real one, or just another ghost. 'Let's get inside. It's not safe.' He reached for her, then stepped back, frowning. 'You're hurt.'

'No, I'm OK, just some cuts . . .' She followed his gaze down, down her bare legs and her borrowed too-big shoes, onto the pitching deck of the ferry, where her blood was gleaming black as the sea.

Chapter Thirty-Four

Ciaran's bruising was even worse than the day before, obscuring his features so much he no longer displayed the strong family resemblance all the Wallaces had. But he was conscious at least, although asleep, the swelling in his brain reduced.

Aisling stared at him, her smooth brow furrowed. 'He looks awful.'

'He'll be OK. It's mostly superficial,' said Corry.

'God, I haven't seen him in . . .' She approached the bed, walking slowly. 'Ciaran?' she whispered. 'It's me.'

A flicker around his eyes, a flash of blue. Under the bruising Paula saw the reaction. He wasn't sure who she was at first. Perhaps he thought it was Mairead. Or someone else.

'It's me, Aisling.'

'Jesus Christ,' he croaked. 'Where . . . did you . . .'

'I'm back.' Tears were in her eyes now, turning them jewel-bright. 'What did they do to you?'

'I'll . . . live.'

Aisling turned to Paula and Corry. 'Could you give us a wee minute, please?'

Corry and Paula watched through the window, Corry tapping her fingers impatiently on her folded arms. 'We'll have to question her again soon. They must know something about the girl in the grave.'

Paula sighed. 'What if they do know, and they tell us who killed her? Can we still not arrest anyone, because of the Commission tip-off?'

'I don't know. Tozier's already requested access to the interview tapes. Thorn in my side, that man. I just want a name at this point. Poor girl. It's not right she's lying in there unclaimed.'

Footsteps behind them in the corridor, and there was Carly Jones again, her face twitching with emotion. It was strange – she looked so much like her mother and her aunt, and both of them were so hard to read. They'd been brought up to hide what they felt, maybe. 'Is it true?'

Corry nodded. 'Yes. Your Aunt Aisling has come forward.'

Carly peered through the window. 'Oh! She looks . . . she looks like Mum.'

Corry rubbed her shoulder sympathetically. 'I know this is hard, Carly. But I think your aunt might know something that'll help us find your mum. Why don't you go in and meet her?'

'Can I?'

'Of course. On you go.'

She went in, knocking shyly, and then Aisling was on her feet, and she and the girl stared at each other, and then Aisling strode across the room and took Carly in her arms, murmuring to her as the girl's shoulders heaved.

Corry turned away. 'At least they've some family feeling left, then.'

A while later, the door opened. Aisling was there, her face still composed and with no trace of tears. 'OK. Ciaran and I have talked.'

CLAIRE MCGOWAN

'So . . . you're ready to continue the interview?' Corry
was alert.
'I'm ready.'

Back to the station. Interview room, the same DC accom-
panying, tape in the machine. Everything being done
properly, especially with Declan Tozier hovering. Paula had
seen him pass through the office earlier, closeting himself
with Willis, no doubt to complain about the irregular way
this case was proceeding. But she no longer cared. She'd long
ago crossed a boundary, and now she just wanted answers.

'So you told us Margaret Maguire was being held at your
family farm, and you helped her escape, aided by Sean
Conlon. Prior to this she was held and interrogated by your
brother Paddy, along with Sean Conlon and also Fintan
McCabe. Members of Paddy's punishment squad.' The tape
had indicated the same, but Paula would never confirm that
for herself. She didn't want to know what could be heard on
it.

'That's right.' Aisling still looked composed, although
she must be exhausted.

'And what happened after? If Paddy believed you had
killed and buried Margaret, how did it end up like this?'
Corry swept a hand over the crime scene photos. 'Two
people dead, Ciaran in prison, all of you scattered? You in
hiding?' Aisling had already told them she'd been living in a
cottage in Kerry for years, off-grid for the most part, selling
eggs and vegetables to make a small living, working in the
kind of pubs where you got your pay in a brown envelope.
It was still easy enough to live below the radar, in rural
Ireland. 'We know Fintan is the male body we found, but we
still have no ID for the girl.'

Aisling sighed. There were vague shadows under her piercing eyes. 'Well. It all went wrong, didn't it? It was because of Emer. We should have realised she'd go straight to Paddy and tell him everything. I thought she was too young to notice but that was a mistake.'

'Emer?' Corry's head jerked. 'I'm sorry, Aisling, who is that?'

'You didn't know?' Aisling barked a short laugh. 'That makes sense. I wondered why you were so sure it was me in that grave.'

'You're saying you know who the girl is?'

'Of course. Sure wasn't I there the day she was put in? It's Emer.'

'And Emer is . . .'

'Our sister.' She winced. 'At least, that's what we told everyone.'

'Emer was our little sister,' said Aisling. She was so calm again, telling the story as if she'd recited it a hundred times, although Paula was sure she'd never told anyone. It had been a secret eating away at the heart of the Wallace family. All families had secrets, of course. But not like this.

'I was maybe four or five when she came home from hospital. I don't remember that much, but we were told she was our sister. Mammy's baby. Daddy was dead by then. Mammy hadn't been out of the house much beforehand; I suppose she just wore a lot of clothes or something. Anyway, it happened all the time back then. I was too wee to notice what was going on, but Ciaran did. He said once that Emer was really our niece, not our sister. I asked him what he meant but he wouldn't explain. Mammy heard and she locked him in the barn for two days.'

Paula, listening outside again, shivered. The same barn they'd held her mother in?

'Mammy was like that. She was . . . if you crossed her, she had no problem slapping you, or putting you out of the house in the cold, or giving you no dinner for days. We did what she said. Except for Paddy – she let Paddy run wild. I think she was afraid of him. When Daddy was alive he'd slap Paddy down – I saw him punch him in the face one time – but he died when I was three.'

Corry was taking notes. 'We didn't find any record of a fifth child. Was that why? She wasn't your mother's?'

'I don't know if Mammy ever registered her. Too risky, I suppose, to show it was all a lie. That she wasn't Mammy's at all.'

'And whose was she, Aisling?' Corry's voice was also calm. Both of them discussing this awful thing so calmly and quietly.

'I'm sure you've worked it out by now. Anyway I don't know for sure – nobody would ever tell me, I was only the wee one – but I remember everyone crying, Mairead leaving school, all kinds of shouting and screaming.'

'I see. How old was Mairead when Emer was born?'

'Thirteen or fourteen. It was a massive scandal, all hushed up. Then Mammy said Emer was our sister, and no one ever talked about it again.'

'And the father was . . . ?'

A silence of held breath. Aisling shrugged slightly. 'I never knew for sure.'

'Your best guess, then.'

'I saw how our Paddy was about her. Mairead. No one else could have her. He scared away all her boyfriends – he shut one fella's hand in the car door because he was five minutes late picking her up.'

'You're saying Emer might have been Paddy's child, Aisling,' Corry clarified, her tone never shifting, never hinting at the horror she must feel.

'I don't know. But . . . if you ever saw them together, you'd believe it.'

Paula remembered Ciaran had said something similar. *Our Mairead and Paddy. Maybe it's not what you think.*

There was a brief silence, then Corry moved on. This was a murder inquiry, and that was the main point to keep hold of. 'Tell me what happened the night Emer died. You were there, I take it.'

Again, Aisling just nodded. She was so polished – the opposite of her sister, who'd sat raw and shaking in this same room. Aisling Wallace had somehow laminated herself against the world. 'It was the night we let her go. Margaret.' It was odd to hear this stranger say her mother's name, like she'd known her. 'Ciaran had already gone by then like I said – I don't think he could stand to see what they were doing to Margaret. He doesn't know anything about this. Mairead had gone earlier in the year as well, ran off one day without saying goodbye. I suppose she was pregnant again, with Carly. Margaret had got away, and we buried the sheep so we could say it was her, that she tried to escape and Sean shot her. Sean was so on edge – he thought Paddy would find out we'd lied, then he'd kill us. That he'd ask us to dig up the ground, show us her body. Or figure out the grave was too small to be a person. And Paddy was good at picking up when people were on edge.'

As Aisling spoke, she described that night more than twenty years ago. The house filled with fear and suspicion.

Their mammy stirring Irish stew, watching it all with her unfathomable eyes. Did she believe their lie, or did she know what they'd done? She'd already slapped Aisling across the face for letting Margaret escape. *You're too soft, girl.* These children she'd raised. Ciaran fled, Mairead gone by then too. Sean and Aisling going over and over the story they'd rehearsed, praying they hadn't left a chink in the tale. Margaret tried to run. The ropes broke, she got away. Sean shot her in the back of the head. She knew too much, they couldn't risk it. Knew it was breaking protocol but what could you do. So they buried her.

The noise they made woke Aisling's little sister. Emer in the doorway in her nightie and dressing gown, watching it all. Go away to bed, Mammy kept saying, but she didn't. All of them terrified in case the Army came to the farm and saw the fresh-dug grave. It wasn't legal to bury livestock at home. They'd say a dog, maybe. The family dog had died. And in case Paddy asked questions, which was even more frightening than the Army.

'Your mother knew?' Corry asked.

Aisling shrugged. 'I don't know. She must have known Paddy would kill me if he found out, so . . . maybe she went along with it. Or maybe she did believe us.'

Then Emer, chiming in. 'She loved that,' Aisling said, her eyes darkening as if she was seeing it all again. 'Everyone in the room staring at her, like she was a bomb about to go off. She said she knew the woman wasn't buried there. That she'd got away. Sean and I had let her go. And she would tell Paddy as soon as he got in.'

'And then what?' said Corry, who'd been listening quietly, like a priest taking confession.

Aisling shrugged. 'I suppose we panicked. We had to shut

her up – Paddy would have killed us all. He was . . . I can't describe it. Ever since Mairead got away he'd been mad. Like she'd betrayed him. He used that word all the time. You betrayed me. See, the Army had been all over him that autumn. Everywhere he went they were waiting. He thought there was a tout in the group, he was obsessed by it, and . . . I . . . I didn't want to die. I wasn't even eighteen. I'd never voted or driven a car, even.' Her blue eyes were faraway. 'We were all there in the kitchen. Me, Mammy, Sean. Emer, shooting her mouth off, so happy people were listening to her. So Sean said, Emer can I talk to you. In private. She loved that. Being treated like a big grown-up girl. And he . . .' She looked down at her hands. 'You know what happened.'

'He killed her?'

She nodded, swallowing hard. 'I . . . I didn't see. But yes.'

'Aisling, I realise this must be hard, but I have to ask, you're saying Sean Conlon killed Emer? Can you tell us how?' Corry's voice was gentle.

'He . . . he strangled her, I think. She was only wee.' Aisling briefly touched her own throat, face pale with horror. 'Wouldn't have taken much.'

Corry paused at this, the calm way they were discussing the murder of a child. 'Your mother was there for this?' Paula could hardly take it in, a woman standing back as a grown man strangled a teenage girl, one she'd raised as her own daughter. But this was the same woman who'd known they had her mother imprisoned, who'd have let them kill her. Who knew what she was capable of?

'Sean told her it was a lie, that Margaret really was dead but he couldn't risk Emer going to the police or the Army. I don't know if she believed it, but what could she do, like?

Paddy would have kicked off, probably shot Sean, and me, and then we'd have had the police at the door, she'd have gone to jail too, likely. And Emer . . . she was a liability, you see. She wasn't right in the head. Mammy always kept her at home, so maybe that was why, or maybe she was just born like that. It was just easier to pretend, I suppose. Sean . . . well. He said she didn't suffer.'

'And then what?' Corry was keeping her voice very steady.

'Paddy came back.' She couldn't hide the shudder, even after twenty years. 'He came back and there's Sean and me digging another grave, this one for Emer. Well, you can imagine how that looked. And he doted on Emer. Of course he did, she was just like him. So Sean quickly says: it was Fintan. Fintan let Margaret go this afternoon, but luckily I was on the ball, I saw and shot her before she could run. Fintan's the tout, Paddy, he must be. Look, he killed your Emer because she was going to tell you the truth. He's away off now. He tried to run. We'll get him. We'll get him for doing this to your wee sister.'

She described the hour after that. Paddy on the rampage, inflated with the rage he'd felt since his sister Mairead had run from him. Nothing to play with now Margaret was gone too, supposedly buried in the back field, but really escaped. Already on the ferry to England, probably. Asking Sean to tell him what had happened again and again, as he paced in the kitchen, his gun casually on the side.

Aisling backing him up. She'd seen Fintan do it. She'd helped Sean dig the grave. Look. Holding up her small hands with red marks from the spade, dirt embedded round the nails. 'I kept holding up my hands,' she said. 'Like that would convince him somehow.'

'So then what?' said Corry.

'Well, then doesn't Fintan turn up at the door in a panic; he'd been chased by an Army patrol half a mile away, and maybe he'd drawn the soldiers after him, maybe we'd all be caught now. He was an eejit, to risk throwing stones at them when there was so much else at stake. Poor Fintan,' said Aisling with the ghost of a smile. 'Useless, he was. And of course Sean and I are about ready to bust, knowing Paddy won't believe us. If Fintan was the tout, why would he turn up at the farm like that?'

'But he did believe it?'

'Must have. Or maybe he didn't even care at that point, he was so angry. Paddy lifts up his gun and puts it right to Fintan's head. Take a walk, he says, like he's some kind of gangster or something. And they go outside and I can hear Paddy shouting, and I'm so afraid, my hands are shaking too much to keep stirring the stew. Then Paddy comes back in and he says, that's that dealt with. And he picks up his cup of tea . . . I remember the blood all went on the wall of the house outside, and Mammy was raging. She was up all night cleaning it with bleach. That was all she cared about, the paintwork.'

'So he thought Fintan had betrayed him.'

'Yeah. Paddy was obsessed with touts. Saw them everywhere. Paranoid.' She sighed. 'God love Fintan. He was a bit gormless. I don't think he really knew what he was caught up in.'

Paula's mind was racing. Did that mean Sean Conlon was really the one? The tout?

Aisling had almost finished her terrible story. 'So that was that. Fintan was dead, Emer was dead. So I ran, and Paddy had to run too. If the Army came, and they likely would, he couldn't hide everything he'd done. We all just ran, never looked back. I packed a bag and Mammy drove me to the bus station that night. She never even said good-bye to me. Just drove off and left me there, said she never wanted to see my face again. I think she . . . all she cared about was the cause, you know, and she thought Margaret Maguire deserved to die. She knew something was up – that I'd betrayed them somehow. Their stupid cause. But she wouldn't have Paddy kill me all the same. I suppose that was something. So I got away. No one looked too hard for Fintan. No one knew Emer existed to come looking for her. Until now.'

It was late. So late Paula had lost all track of time. They were in Corry's office, the lights burning her eyes, a tasteless cup of machine tea in front of her. 'You OK?'

'Oh, yeah. It's a lot to take in.'

'Think she's telling the truth?'

Paula nodded. 'The dead girl's a relation, we know that. If we'd known there was another sister we'd have had our answer days ago.'

'Not exactly a sister. The DNA tests on Carly confirm it, by the way. Close familial match with the dead girl.'

Paula shuddered. Aisling's story had been told in calm, factual tones. Her description of how Paddy acted towards his sister Mairead. Possessive. Jealous. 'Like she belonged to him,' she'd said, and Paula remembered that message he'd left for her. *Just you and me.* Emer, hidden from school and society, her whole life a lie. Mairead's child. Not her sister at all. And Paula had sent Mairead right back into his arms.

'And how did Mairead feel about all this?' Corry had

asked. 'The way Paddy was, and her own child being brought up as her sister?'

Aisling shook her head. 'That's what I don't know. In the end, she wanted to run, sure. But it wasn't so simple as that. Why did she hold off going till she was pregnant again? She was in her twenties then, she could have run long before that.'

'Carly. Is she Paddy's child too?'

'I don't know. I don't know anything, really. But there's something between them. That's why she's so afraid to go near him, I think. And now he has her back.'

Chapter Thirty-Five

Paula trailed home so late everyone was in bed. Crawling in beside Maggie, she felt guilty at leaving the child again, but told herself it was only for a few days. They were so close to solving this case, and as for her mother . . . Well. She wasn't going to think about that right now. According to Aisling Wallace, she'd escaped. So she could be alive. In the morning, maybe she would call Davey again, see if he'd found anything. But how could you find one woman in a city of millions, someone who'd stayed hidden for twenty years? Or she might be dead now anyway.

She sighed, stroking a lock of damp hair back from Maggie's head. So much for this little girl to learn about one day, her missing grandmother, her unwitting father. Her thoughts turned to Aidan, in his cell, maybe awake, the noise of the other inmates echoing around him. Was it possible she could get him out? And then could they have some kind of life together again, her and him and Maggie? Go back to pretending, to living a lovely lie?

She closed her eyes and tried to make her breathing match the deep sleep of her child, and wished for oblivion to come. Tried to focus on what was good and pure, her daughter asleep, and block out all thoughts of bullets and graves and the dark heart of the Wallace family.

* * *

The next day Paula was up early, before her father even, and sat in the cold kitchen eating toast spread with margarine – Pat was always on some kind of diet. The sky over town was streaked pink; it would be a nice day, finally. She was unlikely to see much of it, as she'd be in the station all day, making the most of what time she had left. She checked in on Maggie and saw she was still asleep, her fists clutching handfuls of her pillow, so she made sure the stair gate was in place and slipped out. Pat would get her up. Here, at least, she had people to take up the slack.

Her car was parked in the street, and as she went to it, bleary-eyed, something caught her eye. She didn't know what it was at first. She scanned it – bonnet, wing mirrors, the body of the rental covered in mud already from the week of bad weather. Something was written in the dirt on the driver-side door. She looked at the four letters, in neat capitals: TOUT. The hairs on the back of her neck stood up and she stepped back instinctively, looking around her. But of course there was nothing, just the quiet suburban cul-de-sac, the houses still shuttered up from the night. Feeling stupid, she hunkered down and looked under the car. The car bomb was a staple weapon of terrorists, and although she wasn't sure what one would look like, she could see nothing strange. Had it just been some passing kid, knowing she worked for the police and her father had too? Or someone else, tracking her here, making her aware they knew where she lived?

She was holding her breath as she turned the key in the ignition, but nothing was wrong, and as she drove she felt her heart rate gradually settle. It was like the tapes. A warning. But from who? Her mind turned to Paddy Wallace, a man only seen in out-of-date pictures, a voice on a tape, and she shuddered. Remembering Bob's advice: *these fellas, they don't mess around.*

With time to spare before work, and feeling jumpy and afraid, Paula found herself back in the hospital, sitting by Ciaran Wallace's bedside. Something about him inspired pity. His chest rose and fell softly, as if he was unaware in sleep that he was shackled to his bed or that an armed guard waited outside his room. What must it be like, being the younger brother of the Ghost, your two sisters gone, your family shattered?

His bruised eyelids fluttered. 'Hello,' she said awkwardly. Not knowing how he'd react to her, if he'd even want to speak to her.

'Dr Maguire.'

'That's right. How are you, Ciaran?'

He swallowed hard. 'Sure it makes a nice break from prison.'

Paula paused. 'We spoke to Aisling. She told us what happened that night. Everything.'

'Oh.'

'You knew?'

He nodded slowly, wincing as the movement hurt his face. 'Not for sure till yesterday.'

'So when we asked you about the dead girl, you weren't sure who it was?'

'Could have been Aisling. She could have been dead for all I knew. We all just ran, you see. Couldn't stay, couldn't be in touch. Our Paddy—'

'You had my mother there. At the farm.'

He winced. 'I never had nothing to do with that. Didn't think it was right, taking a woman, a mother, but Paddy made us. He thought there was a tout, you see, in the squad, and he thought if we took her it'd flush them out. If her handler came to get her out, see, Paddy would know someone had blabbed. Someone on his squad. Sean let her go, then he killed Emer to shut her up about it.'

'And Sean told Paddy the tout was Fintan.'

'So Aisling says. To save his own skin.'

'Because it was really him.'

Ciaran shrugged, with difficulty. 'Seems that way.'

Sean Conlon had played so many different sides it must have made his head spin. No wonder he'd asked Bob for protection. His old handlers must have turned their backs on him, unwilling to be associated with a terrorist. And there was no doubt Sean Conlon had killed people, many people. Choked the life right out of a young girl, even. Yet had he also saved lives, like he'd saved her mother? Passed information to Army Intelligence or MI6? 'So what's Paddy doing now? Why is he after Mairead?'

Ciaran sighed. His voice was hoarse, used up. 'He wants her to himself. Always did. And he always wanted to know who Carly's da was.'

Not him, then, clearly. 'Do you know, Ciaran?'

He said nothing for a time. 'Conlon, probably. Saw them together once. Always thought it was him. She was stuck on that farm all the time, under Mammy's thumb. It had to be one of Paddy's lot.'

So Carly was maybe Sean Conlon's daughter. Another of his children with a different woman. She'd never know her father now. Maybe that was for the best. Imagine finding out your father had killed so many people, then been stamped to death in a car park. 'Ciaran . . . did Paddy have anything to do with Sean Conlon dying?'

Another pause. 'I don't know. I haven't seen our Paddy in ten years. But he could have done. He had grudges, you see. He was picking off everyone from the old squad. Conlon, O'Hanlon . . .'

'Prontias Ryan?'

'Aye. Most likely.'

Paula thought of the man shackled down in his dank living room, blood running from his severed finger. Was there anyone left to talk to? Then she realised something Ciaran had said. '*Ten* years?'

Ciaran went still. 'Aye.'

'Before you went to prison. Paddy was in London that summer?'

'No one knows that. He asked me to cover for him . . . so I did. Next thing you know I'm being arrested for murder.'

Her mind raced. The DNA – so it could have been Paddy after all, mistaken for his brother.

'There was that evidence,' Ciaran said. 'My hoody and that.'

'How can you explain it?'

He tried to shrug again, but winced at the movement in his shoulder. 'Always thought the peelers set me up.' It had happened before, of course, the Guildford Four sentenced to decades in prison on forced confessions and shaky evidence. But here there was another possibility.

'You never thought Paddy might have done it, if he was in London?'

Ciaran said nothing for a moment. 'Maybe. I never asked what he was up to. I didn't want to know.'

'Had you told him where you were living?'

'Course not. I ran. We all did.'

'But he found you.'

'He's good at finding people. Guess I wasn't as careful as the girls. But he wouldn't have let me take the rap, not for something he did.'

'Wouldn't he?'

She saw Ciaran process this, think it through. 'I'm his brother.'

'Meant you came back to Ireland, didn't it? He knew exactly where you were all this time. Punished you for leaving.'

'He wouldn't.' But there was a wavering there, a loss of certainty. Paula didn't press it. The man was in pain, it wouldn't have been right. She was surprised by how quickly she'd come round to the idea that he was innocent.

'I believe you,' she said. 'I don't think you're a killer, Ciaran.'

'I'm not. I always said I didn't do it. They didn't listen.'

'They'd listen if we could catch the real killer.' She let him think about it. 'He has your sister. You know what he's like – what he's capable of. She must be so frightened – she's been running from him for twenty years and now he has her. Can you help us find her, Ciaran? Is there anywhere they might have gone? Anyone who might know something?'

He jerked his head, beckoning her closer. She leaned over, hoping the guard outside wouldn't see, smelling his skin – bleach and cigarettes, as if he hadn't been outside in months. 'Tom Dunne.'

'Who's that?'

Ciaran was tired now, she could see that. His voice was fading. 'His da . . .'

'His father?' She didn't understand.

'Look him up. Tom'll know something.'

'He needs to rest, you know,' Aisling said from the

doorway. She was holding a paper cup and dressed in black jeans and a grey top. She was different to her sister, elegant somehow, contained.

'I know. I was just going.'

'Since you're here, Dr Maguire, can you give me a lift? I don't have a car. It was always too risky, getting a licence.'

'Where do you want to go?'

'Where d'you think?' Aisling threw back the rest of her drink, her long neck pulsing. 'To see my loving mammy, of course. Will you take me?'

Aisling stood over her mother, making no attempt to approach her. She hadn't sat down or taken off her jacket. 'I didn't think she'd still be alive, after all this time.'

Paula wasn't sure what to say, so she stood by, holding her keys. The place gave her the creeps. Something about the smell, the floral notes of cleaning products overlaying death and rot.

Aisling leaned in. 'Mammy. It's me. Aisling.'

There was no reaction from the old woman. She didn't seem to know anyone was there.

'Mammy. Did you never wonder what happened to us all? All your weans, scattered?'

There was a mutter from Mrs Wallace. Paula held her breath to catch it. 'Ungrateful pack.'

Aisling just nodded. 'Aye, well, we did our best, Mammy. You weren't much help. Anyway, I just came to see if you were alive and show you I'm OK. I managed fine.' She set her shoulders straight, as if determined not to let it get to her.

'I'm sorry,' said Paula. 'I don't think she's very lucid.'

'Oh, she knows who I am all right. It's what I thought

she'd say. She always put her bloody united Ireland ahead of us. Well, it didn't happen, Mammy, did it? What was the point of all that?'

No reaction. Aisling turned away. 'I just had one question. All this happened because the farm was sold, yeah? And they found . . . what we'd buried? How come it happened now?'

'As I understand it, your mother's fees here were being paid privately, but that stopped a few months ago. Since the farm was still in her name, it was put up for sale by the council to pay for her care. They couldn't trace any of you, except for Ciaran, of course.'

'I suppose that makes sense. But who was paying the fees before that? I wasn't, and Ciaran wasn't. I doubt Mairead had the money. Was it Paddy?'

'I don't know.' He'd been her favourite, so it made sense if it was.

'It must have been. So. Don't you think it's a bit strange, this all happening now? The payments stop, the bodies are found? What account was it being paid from, do you know?'

'Er . . . I'll have to check.' Surely they would have looked into that, even with the Commission stalling the investigation. But Aisling had a point. Why had the payments stopped now, just when Paddy was back and picking off members of his squad one by one? Was it just a coincidence, or had someone actually wanted those bodies found?

Chapter Thirty-Six

Dunne. Paula was sure she'd heard that name before somewhere. Back at the office, a quick search reminded her: Patrick Dunne, a leader in the IRA in the eighties, who'd wanted to end the hunger strikes early. He'd been shot in his home in the middle of them, in 1981, sparking off riots in Ballyterrin. People thought he'd been killed by a faction from his own side, who felt that letting the hunger strikes go on for longer would build support for their cause, help get Sinn Fein politicians elected. And it had. The man had been shot in front of his young son, who must be the Tom Dunne Ciaran had mentioned. If he'd been four then, he wasn't much older than Paula. Thirty-six or so now. She wondered if she could ferret out an address for him.

She went over to Corry's office and knocked gently on the door. The office seemed quiet, with Avril and Gerard off on a beach in the Caribbean. She heard a murmur inside, and turned the handle without thinking.

Nothing really happened. It was all perfectly above board, Corry and Tozier in there, leaning over some papers on her desk. There was no reason Paula should have noticed a thing, except that she knew Helen Corry pretty well by now, and caught the way she straightened her spine, edged away from him. 'Sorry,' said Paula. 'I just wanted a quick word.'

'Of course,' said Corry, a fraction too quickly. 'Declan was just updating me on the Red Road search.'

'We'll be wrapping it up tomorrow,' he said, rolling the papers up again. 'Unless we find anything. We feel it's unlikely at this point, though.'

Paula had given up all thoughts of finding remains at the site. Her mind was fixed on something else – the image of her mother getting away, running across those desolate fields around the Wallace farm. 'I'm sorry your time was wasted.'

'Not at all. It's our job. I'll leave you to it.'

He went out, and Paula turned innocently to Corry. 'You know, I take it back. He's not so bad, is he? A bit officious, but maybe he has to be.'

'It's not easy for them, following the law. But it's necessary.' Corry scowled at her, defensive. 'What? I can't talk to a colleague in my office?'

'I didn't say a thing.'

'He's asked me for a drink,' Corry said quickly. 'After this, of course.'

'And?'

'I slagged him off so much, Paula. To everyone.'

'He doesn't know that, does he? Are you going to go?'

Corry stared at the door Tozier had just left through. Out in the main office, he could be seen putting on his sensible North Face coat. 'I'm forty-five and I have two teenage weans, Maguire. It's hardly young love. But as you say, he's not so bad, no. Anyway. Do you have a good reason for coming in here and interrupting me?'

'I do,' said Paula. 'But you're not going to like it.'

Paula waited outside the house until she saw the car pull off, and then she stepped out of hers and walked up the neat

garden path. Past the fishing gnomes again. Were there more
of them this time? Perhaps they were multiplying. She knew
Bob would be in. He was always in, and especially when
Linda popped out to the library he'd make sure to be. He
was like her father, their horizons shrinking to four walls,
pottering about doing small repairs, making tea and washing
up the cup, watching daytime TV. It was hard to believe
they'd been hardened RUC officers, both of them, with
networks of contacts among dodgy low lifes, with dark
secrets and evil men out for their blood. At least her father
had moved out of his old house now.

Corry had of course flat out refused to help her find
Dunne's address, sending her away with another scolding
about doing her own investigations. She'd not told Corry
about the writing on the car, knowing she wouldn't be
allowed anywhere near the case if she was thought to be in
danger. But Paula couldn't stop. This was her chance to get
Aidan out of prison and finally find out what had happened
to her mother, she was sure of it. It was all connected, as
Bob had said.

She waved through the glass of the door, convinced that
Bob's heart must sink every time he heard her coming. More
hard questions, more awkward discoveries, more painful
secrets grubbed up from their graves. 'Me again . . . sorry.'

He stood back to let her in. 'I'm just making tea.'

She followed him into the kitchen, which was still
dominated by Ian's big wheelchair and other equipment. She
wondered why they hadn't got rid of it all yet, when their
son was gone. Maybe it was too hard. There was still a faint
hospital smell to the place. 'Sorry to barge in again, Bob. I
need a bit of advice really.'

'Oh aye?'

'You mentioned the name Patrick Dunne to me a few times. Remember?'

'Oh yeah. Got shot during the hunger strikes.'

That was a lifetime ago – the year after Paula was born. 'Ciaran Wallace said I should ask about a Tom Dunne. I know Patrick Dunne's long dead now, but there was a son, wasn't there, that saw him get shot?' She'd remembered the detail because the child had been four, Maggie's age near enough, and the thought of it stuck in her throat.

Bob reached for the local newspaper, which was sitting on the dining table with his reading glasses on top. The *Ballyterrin Gazette*, under new management since Aidan was in prison. Funny, she never bought it now. Too painful. He leafed through and pushed the paper over the table to her. She scanned it quickly – an interview with a local councillor who was hoping to be elected as an MLA. A rising star, they said. The same one she'd seen on TV that time. His name: Tom Dunne. A good-looking man, late thirties maybe. The right age. 'That's the son?'

'Aye. He doesn't try to hide who his da was – sure half the town had relatives in the IRA or UVF or what have you.'

Paula looked again. He was clean-cut, well dressed, the new face of Republican politics for Northern Ireland. 'I might go to see him,' she said, waiting for Bob to talk her out of it. But he didn't, just tidying the newspaper away. Maybe he wanted answers as much as she did.

'Davey called earlier,' he said casually. 'Said you'd been leaving him messages.'

'Oh yes?' Her heart beat a little faster. When he hadn't called back she'd assumed he had nothing to tell her.

'After your man Edward was killed, the lease on his flat was given up. That's all he knows.'

Her mother, suddenly finding herself stranded in London, her lifeline blown up. Had she grieved for him? She must have done. Had she loved him, or had they been thrown together by the need to survive, to avoid their hunters? Except if Paddy Wallace thought Margaret Maguire was dead, no one would have been hunting her. Dead along with the child she carried. The hairs on Paula's neck stood up every time she thought of it. It felt like a film, a story happening to other people, not her ordinary suburban mother.

'Be careful,' Bob said, in his tired way, as he walked her to the door. She nodded, but in truth she had forgotten what that even meant by now. She was so far past being careful. It was way too late for that.

Margaret

1998

'What was that?'

She was awake in the dark, back arched like a cat. Something outside. Bins clattering. Feet.

Beside her, Edward was awake at once too. Long years of army training meant he could sleep anytime and start out of the deepest dreams to be fully alert. 'I'll check.'

'Be careful.'

At least once a week it happened, noises waking her in the night. Ghosts in her dreams. The red bucket. The hand on her head. The smell of her own skin burning.

Edward was at the window, looking out, in his striped pyjamas. He said nothing for a while.

'Is someone there?' Usually it was foxes getting into the bins.

'I don't know.'

'Is there . . .'

'Maybe.'

'Get down from the window then!' The fear was always there. Gun shots in the night. Bombs under the car. They'd been in this flat in Hampstead for six months now, a good long run. She'd got used to the place, the walk to the grocery shop. She nodded to people in the dry-cleaner's. She'd even been to church a few times, trying to pray again, wanting to forget that feeling she'd had in the barn, of sending her cries up to God and being ignored. Her heart sank now, already picturing taking the boxes down, packing up, moving somewhere else again. Another rented flat with damp and stained lino. Sometimes she would remember her house, her own house with the roses in the garden, and it felt like another life. It was another life. These days she wasn't even Margaret, she was Peggy. Edward's wife, in name at least. Not before God, since she was already married. But that was another person. She could only survive by never thinking of PJ back in their house, or Paula. Peggy had never known those people. Peggy was married to Edward, and if things between them were still stiff and formal sometimes, if she knew he kept secrets, if both of them sometimes woke up at night screaming, well, they were alive. It was something, at least, to be alive, to have a warm body in the bed beside her. So Peggy was cultivating an English accent, and learning to talk about the weather instead of politics. Learning not to turn around when anyone mentioned Ireland. She would never see Ireland again.

Edward sat down hard on the bed. 'I'm sorry. It's too risky.'

She sighed. 'It was a good run.'

In the dark, they were both silent. They'd lived together as man and wife for five years now, thrown together after the sketchiest of meetings. She hadn't even known his surname then. Sometimes, in the dark bleak truths of these nights, he still felt like a stranger. One she'd given up her life for. 'I'll check on her.'

She lumbered into the other bedroom, the small one. Just a single bed and a nightlight. She'd done her best not to transmit her fears to the child, but it was impossible. 'Is it bad men?' came a small voice.

'No, pet. It's the foxes. The bad foxes.'

The little girl looked sceptical. She had her toy cat,

Sebastian, clutched tight in one hand, his missing eye reminding Margaret – *Peggy* – of other things, things she would like to forget. This, too, was something. On that terrible night on the ferry, Margaret had been convinced she was losing the child. When they reached Liverpool she'd been rushed to hospital, where she'd lain on a narrow bed with overhead lights blazing, feeling the blood run out of her. Sure she would lose it, and Edward would leave her, and she'd be alone in this strange country, running for her life. But it hadn't happened this way. She had been allowed to keep her child, like some kind of gift. Forgiveness, maybe.

Peggy smoothed the hair off the child's face. She was like her father, everyone said – the square little face, the determined jaw – but Peggy only saw in her the other daughter, the one who thought she was dead. Her little girl looked so like Paula, and it haunted Peggy every day.

Chapter Thirty-Seven

The house wasn't what she'd expected. She'd been thinking of somewhere like Prontias Ryan's place maybe, squalid and sad, with dirt ingrained in the fraying carpet and ready meal cartons stacking up in the kitchen, but of course a man like Tom Dunne wouldn't live there. Instead, this was a large detached house on an expensive street outside Ballyterrin, with a people carrier parked in the drive. Tom Dunne had money, it seemed – and a family.

In the end, she'd simply gone around Corry and found Tom Dunne with surprising ease. A quick Google told her he worked at a law firm in town, and that he was even in the phone book. A man without much to hide, then. All the same he would hardly welcome some strange woman turning up at his door, but she had to risk it. She put on her best professional smile and walked up their long driveway to the door, which had a sturdy wooden frame and panels of stained glass in it. A little brass plaque proclaimed *Home Sweet Home*. The door was opened by a woman in jeans and a striped top, highlighted blond hair in a ponytail. A small child of about two hung onto her ankles. 'Yes?' She was distracted, the child catching her attention.

'I was wondering if Tom was in. I'm doing some work for the PSNI on historic cases.' She flashed her ID. It was out of date now, and she'd get in trouble for using it, but she didn't even work there any more; they could hardly fire her.

It was the start of the summer holidays, so she'd banked on him being home, and sure enough she saw Tom Dunne coming out of the living room, cup of tea in hand. She explained who she was, rushing it, sure he'd know she was lying. Although, technically, it wasn't a lie. She was indeed looking into some historic cases. He was a tall man, open-faced, dressed in the same kind of things Aidan used to wear about the house, jeans and a polo shirt. Dad clothes. There were at least two other children in the house, judging by the noise. Outside one could be heard loudly demanding why they couldn't go on the trampoline even though there was rain pooled on it. 'But it's summer, Mummy. The trampoline is for summer.'

Tom Dunne ushered her into the relative peace of the living room. 'You want to talk about my father, is that it?'

'Yes – if you wouldn't mind having a few words with me? Really we're just trying to establish some links to a few new cases we have.'

He motioned to her to sit down. 'I'm not sure how I can help, but you can ask, certainly. No one was ever caught for my father's murder, as you probably know.'

'It must have been terrible. You were there, I understand.'

'I can't remember much. But I saw it happen, that's true. There was blood on the wallpaper in the hallway. We had to redo it.' He spoke calmly, like someone who had long grown used to their own sorrow. 'I just wish I'd been old enough to identify the gunman. There was just one, I'm sure of that. I saw him drive up, but I couldn't tell them what he looked like or what make of car or anything. My mother was out the back, hanging up the washing. When she came in Dad was already dead.'

'I'm so sorry.' She felt the urge to tell him her own terrible story of the Troubles, but resisted. Ciaran had given her this man's name for a reason. The lovely house and family didn't mean he wasn't involved. 'Mr Dunne, last week a man called Prontias Ryan was killed in town. Nicknamed "Rambo". Does that mean anything to you?'

He took a gulp from his cup, then realised it was empty. 'I should have offered you a drink. Aine'll kill me, forgetting my manners.'

'I'm fine, thank you. Have you heard that name before? Or Mark O'Hanlon?'

'Well, of course.' He set the cup down slowly, as if he was thinking about his answer. 'My father was in the IRA. I've never disputed that. Different times. But he was moving towards peace – he wanted to end the hunger strikes. Someone ordered his murder to keep him quiet, I'm sure of it. That man, Ryan, he was involved. O'Hanlon too. Gave the orders.'

'Sean Conlon as well?' she tested.

He bowed his head in a brief agreement. 'Conlon was the prime suspect as the gunman. He went to prison, at least, though not for killing my father.'

Paula sat forward. 'That's what we're looking into. We think there's a link between those deaths and another case we have. I came to ask if you know anything about that, anything at all. If someone could have ordered the killings as revenge, for example. Former associates of your father's, maybe.'

He looked surprised. 'I'm not involved in any of that, Dr Maguire.'

'Oh no, I wasn't suggesting that at all. We've just hit a bit of a wall, and I'm looking for anyone I can interview, really. A name, that's all.'

'I'm sorry. I just saw it on the news, like everyone else. I've tried to distance myself from it. You see your father killed as a wee boy and it makes violence a bit less appealing, if you know what I mean. I don't know any names.'

'Paddy Wallace?' she tried. 'That mean anything to you?'

He shook his head. 'Not someone my father knew, I don't think?'

'No. Younger. Him and Conlon were on a punishment squad together.'

'Sorry.' He was already standing up, opening the door. She felt disappointed; another dead end.

Out in the hall, a girl of about eight had her hands on her hips. 'Daddy, it's not fair, Siofra took my biscuit.'

'Did she now? Well, we can't have that.' He was already being subsumed back into family life, the large, noisy family she'd always wanted as a child herself. No chance of that unless she could get Aidan out, and this man didn't know anything, it seemed.

'Thank you,' she called. 'I'll leave you be.' She pulled the door behind her and went back to her car, thinking furiously. Someone must know something. The first rule of police work. Someone always knows something. But what good was that if they wouldn't talk?

Sitting in her car, she rang into the office. Corry's line was busy, and Paula wondered fleetingly was she closeted with Tozier again. 'Me here,' she said into the voicemail. 'Just checking if there's any progress on finding out who was paying the nursing home fees for old Mrs Wallace. Catch you later.'

She gave one last look at the large, pleasant family house, reflecting briefly that some people at least managed to move on from their terrible pasts, and drove off.

Chapter Thirty-Eight

Saoirse was looking after Maggie today, while Pat and PJ went to a funeral in Strabane. This was something they did with increasing frequency, the way Paula had been to a spate of weddings in the last few years, her own included. They'd come back later full of comments on the food, the choice of hymns, the grief of the bereaved spouse, like they were reviewing it for some kind of *Which Funeral* magazine. She sat in traffic in her car, mulling it all over, tempted to draw up some kind of whiteboard map like a crazed detective in a film. *It's all connected*, Bob had said. Her mother had perhaps been taken to draw out a tout, and not rescued because her handlers were protecting someone bigger, that was Maeve's theory. An informer, high up in the IRA. Many of those informers still had to carry out killings in order not to be suspected, Paula knew. The more she thought about it, it all seemed to come back to Sean Conlon. He'd been with Mairead – he was Carly's father, like as not. He'd killed Aidan's father and probably Tom Dunne's father too. He'd helped kidnap her mother but let her go for some reason – his promise to Bob, maybe. He'd gone to Bob for help, given him a list of names including Paddy Wallace's, but died that same night in a piss-soaked pub car park. Aidan was in prison for killing him. Her hands gripped on the steering wheel – she did not mourn Conlon, but if he were still alive, they wouldn't be in this mess. And she would be able to ask him – did Margaret really get away? Or did someone go after her?

Is she still alive?

She drew up at Saoirse and Dave's house, noting that Dave's car wasn't there – he must be working late. A Volvo was parked outside. The neighbour's car, maybe. She rapped on the door, distracted, thinking she'd get Maggie home and to bed and make some notes about all this, maybe quiz her dad some more when he came home, though she could never tell him everything she knew. Saoirse had not come to the door; she leaned on the bell. A figure was approaching – a man. Was Dave home after all? But no, it looked too wiry to be him; Dave was a big, shaggy bear of a man. The door opened, and Paula saw the face, and then she understood.

'Come in,' said Paddy Wallace, all charm. He was still handsome, but twenty years clung to his face, and his hair was cropped, flecked with grey. He wore a black T-shirt and jeans, nothing remarkable. And he had a gun in his hand. What kind, she didn't know. Gun makes weren't something she recognised. It looked big and black and very heavy. Paula was focusing very hard on the details, trying to make sense of it all. Of what was going on. If she could understand it, then she could control it, and everything might be fine.

Saoirse was sitting on the sofa with her hands on her knees, very pale, in jeans and a loose top. Her body was angled so Maggie sat behind her, pressed against the back of the sofa, looking confused and cross, her red hair escaping from its bunches. 'Mummy!'

'Yes, pet, just sit still there for a minute like a good girl.' She flashed a quick look at Saoirse, but what could she even say? She'd put her friend in danger. It was unforgivable. She turned to Wallace, trying to keep her voice steady. 'This has nothing to do with my friend. Let her go – she's pregnant, and I have a child. You wouldn't want to hurt a woman anyway, would you?'

He laughed, softly, in his throat. He held the gun loosely, clearly comfortable with it. 'Your mammy tried to use the same argument, Paula, that she had a wean at home. Didn't work for her.'

Paula saw Saoirse's look of confusion. 'But she's done nothing. And my little girl . . .' Her throat closed over with fear. All these years she'd been in danger herself so many times, reckless and stupid, but she'd protected Maggie from the worst this country had to offer. She'd taken her away to the relative safety of London. 'Please don't hurt them.' She heard the pleading in her own voice and hated it.

'Who said anything about hurting? I'm just here for a chat.' The gun swung lazily. How out of place it looked in Saoirse's neat house, her sisal sofa and framed watercolours and nick-nacks. 'You've been sniffing around, Paula, and I don't like that. I'm just here to make sure you stop. Go back to London. No reason for you to be over here getting in trouble.'

Her hands began to shake. He knew where she lived, where her child was. Had he been following her? The Ghost. He could slip around town, a wanted man, and never even be spotted. How did he do it?

There was a noise outside, the sound of a car, and she jerked instinctively, following the muzzle of the gun as Wallace lifted it up. Trying not to think about all the terrible stories she remembered from the Troubles – women shot at home in front of their children, bullets fired into cots, children dying in bombs. Men like Wallace didn't care. They had their own code. 'Who's that now?' he said to himself, and went out to the hallway. *Not Dave, please not Dave.* Paula caught Saoirse's eye and knew she was thinking the same thing. Dave would be home any minute, and how would Wallace, with a gun in his hand, react if a huge man walked into the house?

As he left the room, Paula rushed to the sofa, desperate to feel Maggie in her arms. The little girl squirmed. 'Mummy, there's a bad man.'

'I know, sweetheart.' She clutched Saoirse's arm. 'Christ, are you OK?'

Saoirse nodded. 'We just have to keep him calm.' She'd likely been in worse situations in A&E, but not when she was pregnant after wanting it so long. A red rage was settling in Paula's stomach, fighting with the fear. Point a gun at her pregnant friend, at a three-year-old? He would pay for this.

Wallace was back. 'Just the neighbour. But we shouldn't linger here. So, Paula – are you going to tell me why you've been poking around in my business?'

She tried to keep her voice steady. 'I just needed some answers. My fiancé's in prison for something he didn't do.'

Wallace crossed over to her, perching on the arm of the sofa beside Maggie. She scowled at him. 'Go away! You're a bad man.'

He reached out and smoothed Maggie's red head. Paula's fists clenched. 'Lovely little girl, isn't she? Looks like her grandma. Same hair. That's her daddy in prison, is it? The one my brother's been whispering away to?'

'You arranged it. The attack in prison.' She'd always known the timing was too coincidental.

'Aye, well, our Ciaran should count himself lucky. If he

wasn't my own blood he'd be in a box by now. He was telling my secrets to your daddy, Maggie, and we can't have that!'

Maggie cocked her head, confused. 'My daddy?'

He was searching the child's face, as if he could see the secret written there, as if he was something more than human, able to read minds and hearts. But he said nothing, just stood up again. 'Paula, you've put yourself in the middle of something. And that's a problem, for me and for you too.'

'You're picking off your old squad.' This was clear. But why now, after so many years?

'Aye. One of them betrayed me, and I won't stand for that. None of them left now.'

'Conlon?' She held his gaze.

He shrugged. 'He brought it on himself. You know that. Your fella nearly did the job for me, it wasn't hard to finish it.' There it was, the confession she needed. Aidan hadn't done it. But would she get out of this and be able to tell anyone?

'So he's innocent. He could go free.'

'Maybe. But you won't be telling anyone what you know, will you now?'

What did that mean? Because she'd keep quiet, or because she wouldn't be able to? Her mind raced ahead, stumbling over itself. She made herself raise her chin. 'I'd like some answers, Paddy.'

'Go on then.' He sounded quite reasonable.

'My mother. Where is she?'

Paddy smoothed some fingerprints off his gun. 'To my knowledge she was dead and buried on the farm, like I told the Commission.' So that was him too. Trying to stall the investigation into the two dead bodies, and maybe also find out the truth himself. Perhaps he had suspected Aisling and Sean were lying, all those years ago.

'But she isn't. Is she?'

'It would seem not. The man she was . . . involved with . . .' He was moderating his language to spare Maggie, she realised. Meaning what? He was going to let Maggie go? 'He was in London. Some associates of mine managed to catch up with him and finish him off. If she's anywhere she's there, your mother.'

'You went after her?' She held her breath, waiting to hear her mother was dead anyway, tracked down and killed.

He shook his head absently. 'Didn't know to look, before this. I was daft enough to believe my wee sister and my best pal, when they told me she was dead. More fool me.'

And now he did know to look, he knew she had escaped. And if her mother was still alive, Paula had sent the Ghost back hunting her. Corry was right. She'd dug up the past and she wasn't ready for the consequences, not at all. Panic rose up her arms and legs, freezing her. She had to keep talking, keep him engaged, and above all calm. Panic was the real killer in these situations. She was aware of Saoirse on the sofa, murmuring to Maggie, who had started to make soft crying noises. She was a sturdy little girl but this would be too much for most adults, let alone a toddler. *Think, Maguire, think.* What could she say, what could she offer a man like this to get him away from her child, her friend? 'Your sister's back,' she risked. 'Aisling.'

'Oh yes. Wee Aisling. Quick to stick a knife in my back, she was, for all the age of her. Her and Conlon. They lied to me, right to my face.'

'I can take you to her. Wouldn't you like to find out what really happened that night? What really happened to Emer?'

Wallace tapped the gun against his chin, casually. He was still attractive, not just his features but a kind of magnetism that came off him. That intense focus, and the sense there was nothing he wouldn't do. 'Maybe. So what do you suggest we do, Paula? You see the problem here. I can't let you carry on what you're doing. I can't just leave you and be on my way.'

'I'll come with you,' she said quickly. 'Somewhere else. I know you have a place. Wherever Mairead is.'

'And let your friend here ring the peelers as soon as we're gone?'

'I won't say anything.' Saoirse's voice was shaking. 'Please. I'm pregnant. *Please.*' Her eyes met Paula's, flicking downwards. With a sickening thump of her stomach, Paula saw it: the red stain spreading out from her jeans. Small still. But scarlet as poppies.

Chapter Thirty-Nine

Saoirse was bleeding. The shock, likely. She had to get her away from this. Maggie had not noticed yet, thank God, but surely would soon.

What could she do? Paula knew nothing had worked for her mother. She'd have pleaded for her life, surely, tried to argue and beg her way out of it. For her daughter's sake. Maybe even for the child she was carrying. Not realising she'd been a pawn sacrificed to protect the king – Sean Conlon. But he'd let her go. And he'd had more to lose than anyone, back then. It was possible. She tried again. 'We could arrange a reunion. All your family together, Paddy. Isn't that what you always wanted? Carly too. Your niece. Mairead's girl.'

He frowned at her. 'You think I want to see those traitors?'

'But we should go somewhere else,' she said. Trying to sound like she was on his side. 'It's too public here – the neighbours will hear something. I'll come with you and we'll see what to do next. You can speak to Aisling, maybe – ask her why they did it, why they lied to you. Fintan likely didn't kill Emer, did he? He didn't have it in him. You must have suspected that. So don't you want to find out who did? Aisling's the only one who knows now.'

He was thinking about it, she could see.

'We can help each other,' she said, in a low voice. Too much? She held her breath.

He gestured with the gun, reminding her who held the power in this room. But then he said, 'All right then. Paula, you'll come with me. You'll drive. Nice and easy. If you don't make trouble, I won't make any for you.'

'You'll leave my friend here, and my little girl?' She saw Saoirse edging a cushion in front of herself, trying to hide the blood.

He nodded assent. She sagged in relief, pushing away the thought that it wasn't over for her. At least the others were safe. She hugged Saoirse fiercely, trying not to look at the bloodstain. 'I'm so, so sorry, Glocko. I never thought this would happen. Get to hospital as soon as we've gone. And look after Maggie?'

'But Paula . . .'

'If anything happens . . . will you tell Aidan, I know it wasn't him? Will you tell him I always did?' She lowered her voice. 'Speak to Bob. He'll know what to do. OK?'

'Paula!'

'It's OK.' She squeezed her friend's hand, then pulled Maggie to her quickly, fiercely, afraid that if she lingered she would break down entirely, and whispered, 'Be a good girl, pet. I love you.'

'Mummy, I don't want you to go!'

'I'm sorry, pet. Stay with Auntie Saoirse, OK?'

Then she was following him out the door, to the anonymous Volvo Paddy must have driven there, the gun concealed under his jacket, and the two of them were getting in, all peaceful and calm, like two friends on a day out. As the house receded in the back mirror, all she could think was *they're safe. Thank God, they're safe.* The rest was now on her.

* * *

They drove out of town, Paula at the wheel, Wallace beside her with the gun held casually against her seat. She could feel the press of it on her leg, as with his other hand he tapped at a Nokia phone. Calling for help, maybe? Where was he taking her? She drove with unnatural care, slowing down so much approaching every traffic light that the impatient drivers of Ballyterrin honked and swore at her. Soon they were heading out into the countryside, the housing estates giving way to fields and trees. Following his directions, she pulled off the motorway onto a side road, then another, and another, until the car drove slowly between high hedgerows and bumped over a line of grass down the middle. They were in deep country now, where no one would see or hear them. She wondered where it was – somewhere he owned, a second home or something like that? He must have help, to do the things he'd done. They rumbled over a cattle grid and stopped outside what looked like a small hut or barn. There were no other buildings around, just fields and the slope of the mountain rising up behind. When she got out, urged on by Paddy's almost friendly gesture, she could hear the birds and the faraway sound of traffic. And there, outside the hut, was another man. He came forward to the car. When she saw it was Tom Dunne, she wasn't even surprised, not really. Wallace had to have someone helping him, giving him money, sorting out a place to stay. Dunne had money and influence, and his father's old IRA contacts. He wouldn't have been on Conlon's list because his father was long dead, and he'd only been a child when Sean shot him. But maybe he wanted revenge all the same.

Tom swung his gaze on her, and the mask of the suburban

dad had slipped. She heard him say to Paddy, 'What the hell are you playing at? Thought you were dealing with her?'

'Never you worry. I have it in hand.' Wallace sounded almost chipper.

'I offered to come,' Paula said, hearing how high and frightened her voice was.

He didn't even seem to hear her, addressing Wallace in a harsh whisper. 'What are we going to do? She's made the link now. She came to my *house*.'

'She can't prove anything. She's not even working with the PSNI, not officially. Isn't that right, Paula?'

She swallowed. He'd responded well before when she'd been bullish, kept her chin up. She had to play this right. 'So Tom paid you to take out his father's killers, was that it?'

Tom's eyes were jumping, crazy, compared to Paddy's professional calm. It was him she had to watch out for. Paula made herself keep looking at the men. She said, 'It wasn't right, was it, Tom? No one was ever convicted of killing your dad. Conlon did it, everyone knew, but he never went down for it, or anything else during the Troubles. And why was that? Was someone protecting him? Army Intelligence maybe?'

Wallace was nodding approval. 'Not bad, Paula.'

'Back then, you were trying to flush out the tout in the squad, weren't you, Paddy? Was it Conlon?'

'It would seem that way. Not poor ould Fintan after all.'

She nodded, pieces falling into place. So Maeve's theory was right. No one from the Army had gone to save her mother, because they couldn't risk exposing Conlon, their spy in the organisation. He must have lived on a knife edge. And yet he'd let her mother go, when a bullet in the head would have solved his problem, saved Emer and Fintan from their graves in the pit, put a stop to this chain of events which had led to a man with a gun pointed at her daughter and her friend and now her, alone at this hut with two dangerous men. 'I understand, Tom,' she said, trying to sound reasonable. 'No one was ever caught for taking my mother either – no one would even tell us what happened to her – and I've been looking all this time. I understand you wanted them dead. There's no one mourning men like that. But you've got children – you wouldn't want to leave my wee girl with no mother, would you?'

She saw guilt bloom in his eyes, but the panic was greater. 'Be quiet,' he said roughly. 'Wallace, I need a way out of this. I have my life here, a family, an election campaign.' If people knew he'd paid to have his father's killers bumped off, that would be the end of his political ambitions, his job, his life. He had a lot to lose.

'We'll sort it,' said Wallace. He nudged Paula. 'Go on.'

She stumbled ahead over the muddy ground, into the hut.

Inside, as her eyes adjusted to the gloom, she saw a chair, and Mairead Wallace tied to it. In the corner was a sleeping bag and the remnants of a scratched meal – the place smelled stuffy and airless, the only light coming in from high windows with reinforced glass. It occurred to Paula that her mother was kept like this. Miles from anywhere. Humiliated, restrained. Tortured, even. She thought of Prontias Ryan, on his back in front of his TV, Mark O'Hanlon. Sean Conlon, kicked to death in the parking lot. Fintan McCabe, dead in the earth. So much death.

Mairead had seen her, and her eyes widened, but she said nothing. Paddy gestured to another chair at a small camping table, and Paula sat. What was he going to do now? Dunne had followed them in, looking about him in a way that told

Paula he hadn't known what Paddy was doing here. 'What the hell?' he said again. 'What is this, Wallace? Who's that?'

'I'm his sister,' said Mairead in a hoarse voice. 'He kidnapped me.'

Paddy tutted, pulling another chair for himself to sit on, leaning across its back. 'Always the drama queen, our Mairead. I just wanted us to talk. Be together as a family. When this is all over we can go back to how things were – you, me, Aisling, Ciaran. Carly, even. Seemed like a nice girl.'

'You put Ciaran in prison,' she said. 'I know it wasn't him killed that man.'

'Well, at least I knew where he was. None of you had any loyalty, sneaking off on me. After everything I did when Da died, keeping the farm for us, and the first chance you get you run out.'

'I had to.'

'Oh yes, for wee Carly. Looks just like Emer, doesn't she? But then she would, wouldn't she? All I wanted to know was who her daddy was, Mairead. Who did you betray me with? Why didn't you tell me you were having another baby?' *Another*. So it was true then, about Emer.

Mairead didn't answer, her head bowed.

Paddy went on. 'No matter, I got it out of old Rambo. Seems everyone knew you were sneaking about with Conlon behind my back. Everyone but me. Shame he'll never know he has a lovely daughter, seeing as he's dead.'

Mairead did not react to this. Had she any feelings for the man now, after twenty years? She was trembling, with fear, maybe, or rage, or both. 'Mammy would have made me give her up. You know that. She wouldn't have had her in the house, not after . . . Emer.'

'Oh yes. How did you feel about that? Your own daughter murdered. Your daughter that you abandoned. *Our* daughter.'

'Shut up!'

He went on. 'But that's what she was. Yours and mine. What kind of mother are you, Mairead?'

Mairead was trembling. 'She was never mine. Mammy took her. I didn't know she was . . . I never even knew she was dead. She was, she was . . . she wasn't right, Paddy. You know that.'

'Was that any reason to abandon her, leave her to be killed in cold blood? She was only a child.'

'I was only a child.' She was shaking so hard her voice faltered. 'I was a child too, Paddy, when it happened.'

'Poor Emer. And our own sister covered it up – lied to me. It must have been Conlon killed her. Your fancy man. Did he have a go at Aisling too? Why stop at one of my sisters?'

Mairead's voice shook. 'You think I don't care? Why do you think I came back to this hellhole in the first place? I wanted to know, was it her or was it our Aisling in that grave? My sister who was dead or my . . .' She tailed off. 'You don't know, Paddy. You don't know how it was for me to leave. But I had to. For Carly.'

Dunne, who had been pacing maniacally, now stopped and slammed his hands on the table. 'Paddy! We have to sort this. What are we going to do? You can't just keep this place forever – my wife's da owns it, he might decide to visit.'

So that was the link. Paula tried not to think what it meant that he'd said this in front of her. There was no obvious link between the two men, so no one would think to look for her here. No one knew where she was, and around them stretched the countryside, miles of fields and bogs and barren ground.

'We'll sort it. It'll be over soon.'

And what did that mean? She met Mairead's eyes, saw the panic there, and tried to speak calmly. 'You don't want to hurt Mairead, Paddy. She's your sister.'

'She was quick to hurt me, taking up with Conlon behind my back then running away from me.'

'Well, she thought she'd lose Carly if she didn't. It was a long time ago. And Conlon's paid for it. You're all together again now. You don't want to keep running all your life, do you?'

He hefted the gun in his hand. 'And what do you suggest as an alternative, Miss Paula? Your mammy used to talk about you, you know. As if we'd change our minds, just because she had a wean.'

What could she suggest? What way was there out of this? 'I couldn't prove anything,' she said. 'Just let us go, and you can vanish again. The Ghost, right?'

'She's seen me,' said Dunne. He didn't seem able to look Paula in the eye. 'Who told you to come to my house? Where did you get my name?'

She hesitated. But Paddy had got there first. 'Our Ciaran, was it? Aye, he's worked it all out. Had a lot of time to think. Can't trust anyone these days.'

It echoed what his mother kept saying: *ungrateful pack. Disloyal.*

'We can't let her go,' Dunne said decisively. 'I won't take the fall for this, Wallace.'

She knew better than to plead Maggie. It hadn't worked for her mother; it wouldn't work for her. But somehow, although he'd tortured her mother and murdered so many people, she did not believe Paddy Wallace would shoot her. Disloyalty, betrayal. Those were his triggers. 'I was just trying to help my family,' she tried. 'My fiancé. My mother – I don't know if she's alive or dead. I just needed to know.'

He looked at her curiously. Weighing it up.

'You'd do anything for your family, Paddy. Wouldn't you? Didn't you do it all to get them back? That's why you let the farm be sold. It was you arranged for the payments, wasn't it, to your mother's nursing home? Watching over her as best you could. But if the farm was sold, and they found what was under it, you knew that was the way to bring you all back together again, get Aisling, find out what really happened to Emer.' She went on, putting it together as she spoke. 'It was Carly's Facebook post, wasn't it? Looking for her family. You didn't know she existed before that, did you? It was all for them.'

'Not that they're grateful.' He prodded Mairead with his gun. Her head was slack, all the fight gone out of her. Another mother trying to protect her child.

There was a noise outside and everyone jumped – Paula watched the gun jerk up. Wallace turned on Dunne. 'Who's that? Your in-laws?'

'No! They're away on a cruise.'

Wallace swung the gun to Paula. 'Did your wee mate call the peelers?'

Paula's heart beat hard. 'She doesn't know where we are. We never mentioned Tom in front of her, did we?'

He squinted at her, then grudgingly nodded: that was true. He motioned to Dunne. 'Open it.'

'Me? You're the one with the gun!'

But as they bickered, the handle was turning and the door

opening, letting in a slab of blank white light. A figure stood there in a beige overcoat, despite the season. There was a gun in his hand too – Paula recognised it as RUC issue, the same one her father had squirrelled away in the gun safe he thought she didn't know about. It was Bob Hamilton.

Her heart sank. She might have been able to talk her way out of this, and help Mairead too – she still didn't think Paddy would hurt his own sister – but now Bob was here, and she couldn't protect him, and his hand was shaking as if he hardly had the strength to hold the gun up. She'd hoped he would make the connection to Dunne, send the police to rescue her. Not come himself.

Paddy seemed to recognise him. 'I know you.'

Bob's voice shook too. 'Let the women go.' He saw Dunne, frowned in recognition, then back to Wallace. 'Come on now. This war's long over. You've no fight with these two.'

'I've plenty of fight with my sister.' Recognition dawned, and Paddy smiled. 'Sergeant Hamilton, isn't it? You arrested me a whole heap of times, back in the day. Nothing could stick, though. That's why they call me the Ghost.'

'It was Conlon your fight was with,' Bob said. 'He was your informer. Came to me for help – he even gave me your name. But he's dead now, so why keep this going?'

'Because, Sergeant, I don't like people who aren't loyal. What about you? Did you keep faith with the RUC – or did you lie? We thought you'd at least come and search the farm when we lifted Margaret Maguire. Wouldn't have taken much to find out where we did the interrogations. Draw out the informer that way. But no one ever came near the place. What does Miss Paula think about that, eh? You couldn't even lift a finger to find her mother?'

Paula breathed. How to get out of this one? 'It's all in the past now. There were reasons. My mother, she's long gone now, whether she's alive or dead.'

'Oh, she's alive, and I know where she is,' said Paddy easily. Paula froze. 'Why do you think I tipped the Commission off? Get them to do the digging for me, no sign of her body, so where is she? Must have got away, so that means she never got her punishment. I've plenty of fellas in London can help me out still. Was planning to pay her a wee visit after all this is wrapped up.'

Paula just stared at him. 'They found her? Already?'

'Oh aye. Do you want her address? I'll give you it if you want. Assuming you make it out of here.'

Alive. She was definitely alive, she was really in London. Paula felt herself give way, and had to brace herself to stay on the chair. Was it true, or more of his games? She could hardly let herself believe it.

'Paddy, stop it,' said Mairead, her voice exhausted. 'Don't torment her. You know what it's like to lose your family. Just leave her be.'

'Aye, I do, don't I? Thanks to you. Your mother was guilty of a very serious crime, Paula. She was sentenced, and that sentence still hasn't been carried out. She's on the run too, in her way. I feel no guilt about it, Miss Paula, sorry to tell you.'

Was this it, then? Was she going to die there, unable to tell anyone what had happened to her mother, unable to send a warning, and then Paddy Wallace would make his way to London, to whatever door her mother lived behind, painted or faded or wood or metal, and deliver the bullet that had been hers twenty years ago? Was this all for nothing? She couldn't bear it.

Bob stepped forward, using his other hand to steady his wrist under the gun. He looked like someone's granddad, a harmless wee man. What could he do against the Ghost? 'Patrick Wallace, I am arresting you for the murders of . . .'

What was he doing? Even Paddy looked surprised for a moment, then he laughed. 'Ah, come on now, Bob.'

'. . . Prontias Ryan, John King, Fintan McCabe, Mark O'Hanlon, Sean Conlon . . .'

Aidan. Aidan could be released, if Wallace went down for killing Conlon. She just had to live through this, that was all.

'. . . do not have to say anything . . .'

'Do something!' Dunne's voice cracked. But Paddy seemed to be amused by the whole scene, the tired and broken-down man holding a gun in shaking hands, reciting his code, as if men like these followed the rules. 'Stop him!'

'. . . may be taken down and used in evidence . . .'

Then Dunne was lunging across the room, trying to tear the gun from Paddy's hand, failing, screaming as Bob put a bullet in his shoulder. Shaking hands or not, he could still aim. A small shriek escaped Mairead, and she began to strain on her ropes, trying to move back out of the line of fire.

'Sir, you must stand down, I repeat, stand down.' Poor Bob. Still relying on the rules, the law, as if that had ever done him any good.

Paddy still had that strange little smile on his face as Bob advanced on him, Dunne now stumbling onto the floor, clutching his arm. 'Stop him, for fuck's sake!'

'Pity,' Wallace said. 'You always seemed a decent enough sort, Sergeant.' And he lifted his gun, and fired at Bob.

Margaret

2006

'Come on, we'll be late. It starts at half seven.' Edward had his coat on and car keys in his hand.

'Sorry, sorry.' She couldn't find her purse. Her daughter had moved it, maybe, taking out money for her school lunch or whatever it was today. She went to the bedroom door and knocked. The flat was so small every room could be reached within ten paces.

'What?' The girl had her headphones on, sprawled on her bed in jeans and a vest top. She was now the age Paula had been when Margaret left Ireland, and she could not shake the sense that she would get no further with this daughter either. That she would somehow lose them both, and it was no more than she deserved.

'Have you seen my purse?'

'Oh yeah, it's in the living room. I took out the money for the school trip. You forgot again.'

'Sorry.' She was forgetting a lot of things of late. Stress, Edward said. Nothing to worry about. He could always fall asleep, a habit from years in the Army, bedding down in war zones. But she hadn't learned the habit, and lay awake most nights, listening for scuffles outside. She gave her daughter the usual spiel. 'Dad and I will be back about eleven – don't open the door to anyone under any circumstances. Don't answer the phone. Keep the windows and all the doors locked.'

'I know, I know.' She wasn't sure their daughter had ever

grasped the seriousness of the rules. She'd been running all of her short life; it was normal to her. She probably thought her parents were terrible fuddy-duddies. Even this trip to the theatre, a small local one, was the first time they'd gone out in months. 'Go on, you'll miss the play.'

'You'll be careful?'

'Mum, I'm not leaving the house, there's nothing to be careful about.' She put her headphones back in again. It was still a shock to Margaret to have a daughter growing up as a London teenager. Sharp English accent. Hanging round the bus stop in Croydon with her friends, girls with pierced noses and long straightened hair and confident voices.

'Bye then. I love you.'

'Love you.' They bandied those phrases around in this house, something she had not said enough to Paula. You just didn't, in Ireland, not in those days. It was always implicit.

She hurried downstairs, finding her purse under a sofa cushion, noting that her daughter had cleaned her out of cash again. She made a few final checks – windows, alarm – and went out, locking the door behind her. Edward was in the car already, impatient. He'd dressed up, put on that shirt she'd bought him for Christmas. They should go out more. It wasn't much of a life, him working in private security from an office outside the M25, her loitering at home, over-cleaning the small flat. It was the tenth one they'd lived in since the last incident.

'Ready?'

'Yes, um . . . Sorry. Did I lock it?'

'You locked it, come on!'

'Let me just check.' She ran quickly up the three steps and took out her key. Behind her, she heard the engine rumble into life. His way of hurrying her.

'Come on, we—'

She didn't see it when it happened. That was something to be grateful for. That it could have been worse. It could always be worse. There was a whoosh and a suck of air, a terrible heat and a noise and then a quietness, and she was thrown back against the door, the skin on the back of her neck seared.

It was a full thirty seconds before she could bring herself to turn around and see what they'd done to him.

Chapter Forty

The blood was pumping out from him. Paula was on her knees, pressing her hand into Bob's chest. But she couldn't stop it. There was so much blood. Bob's eyes were staring at the ceiling, the damp stains on it, the cobwebs in the corners. The last thing he'd see if she didn't get him away from here. 'Please!' she shouted to Paddy Wallace. 'We need help! He's hurt.' Dunne too was still howling, swearing, clutching his shoulder.

She felt something on her shoulder. Wallace's hand. Gentle, almost. 'There's no point, Paula. Look at his eyes.' She saw what he meant, the light leaving them, the hardening of his face into pain and out the other side. But she didn't want to believe it. She kept scrabbling, trying to find a way to stop up the bullet wound, give CPR. But there was so much blood her hands just slipped and slid in it.

'I've seen this a hundred times,' said Wallace. 'It's too late for him.'

Someone was saying, *No, no, no.* It was her.

Wallace's hand tightened on her. Outside, she heard noises. The sound of sirens. Rescue. What her mother must have waited and waited to hear locked in that barn, and never had. She'd be dead if it wasn't for Sean Conlon, the man who'd killed so many others.

'Ah,' said Wallace, very softly.

Dunne was struggling to his feet. 'We have to go! They're coming!'

She tried to think. The last message she'd left for Corry. The connection to Dunne. Had it been enough? Had Bob called the police before setting out himself? Had Saoirse?

'Wallace!' Blood was running down between Dunne's fingers. He needed the hospital too. 'We have to get out of here!'

Feet running up to the door. Shouts. *'Police. Stand down!'*

Wallace gripped his gun. He was the Ghost, after all, wasn't he? He'd got out of worse situations. 'Let them come,' he said.

As the door burst open and the armed support officers flooded in, and bullets flew over her head, shouts and running feet and chaos, Paula bent down to Bob. 'Bob. Bob, please. They're here now. Hang on!'

He lifted his hand to her face, and she saw how much effort it cost to do even that. She could barely hear the words that escaped him: *'Find her.'* Then his hand fell back down, a dead weight, and he was gone.

Chapter Forty-One

They buried Bob on the kind of summer day that feels like winter, a chill breeze blowing off the mountains and through the thin jackets of the mourners in the country churchyard. He would lie beside his son Ian, the other grave softened at the edges already by grass. Paula had murmured some pointless words to Linda Hamilton, who stood by the twin graves, rigid and tearless in a black dress. She knew she would not see the woman much, if ever again. How could she, when she'd always feel responsible for Bob's death? Her instruction to Saoirse had brought him running, piecing together the bits of the puzzle, trying to rescue her. If it wasn't for Corry working out that Mrs Wallace's nursing home fees had been paid from a dummy account set up by Tom Dunne, Paula might not have made it out alive either. She thought of his last words: *Find her*. Already her mind was moving on, thinking of a way to get back to London as soon as possible.

She looked around her at the mourners. Her father and Pat, yet another funeral for them to attend. She was glad he and Bob had the chance to speak at least, before Bob died. It wasn't the forgiveness he deserved, but she sensed he would not have wanted that anyway. That he had never been able to forgive himself either. There was Saoirse holding hands with Dave, safe, thank God, her baby's heart still beating strong. Alive. Paula could not have stood it otherwise.

Maggie she'd left with a babysitter, not knowing how she would explain that Mr Bob was gone. For a moment, when the armed team had stormed the hut, she'd not been sure she'd ever see the child again. That she might die there, in a hail of bullets. As it was, even the Ghost hadn't been able to get out of this one, although he hadn't been captured without seriously injuring several officers. But she had got out, and so had Mairead. No one else had died that day. Only Bob.

She blinked away tears, looking around her again. There were Avril and Gerard, back early from honeymoon, Avril crying softly into a hankie. Fiacra, on his own this time, his curls plastered flat. Corry and Tozier, in sober black suits, a foot of space between them. Guy had sent flowers, but had not been able to make it over – Tess had gone into labour the night before. Paula would send something, when the time was right. A card, a small present of some kind. Linda was stooping now to throw flowers into the grave. It would soon be sealed over, and the process of forgetting Bob would carry on. If she could have spoken to him one last time, she would have said that none of it was his fault. That people do what they think best at the time, and they can't do any more than that. That she knew he'd only ever tried to protect her mother. That her mother, too, had not meant for any of this to happen. That they could not go back, so they had to make the best of what they'd been left with.

As the mourners began to file out of the churchyard, she saw someone standing near the edge of the small group. Black trousers, a trench coat. Aisling Wallace.

'It was good of you to come.'

'I thought one of us should.' Mairead and Carly had gone to ground again, reunited, hiding out somewhere so secret that even Paula didn't know where it was. She wondered would Carly be told in time who her father was, and taken to visit his grave. She wondered if she might go herself, now she knew he'd helped to save her mother.

'How is she?'

Aisling set her shoulders against the breeze. 'I don't know. Not sure I'll ever see her again, to be honest. It's why she came back, you know. To find out what happened to Emer. She was still her daughter, even after everything.'

And Aisling had colluded in Emer's death, helped to bury her. Paula had always been sure that girl must have been placed in the earth by someone who'd cared for her.

'There was one thing I was wondering about, Aisling,' she said, careful not to look at the woman. The wind whipped around them as they stood by the grave; so much for the Irish summer.

Aisling had her hands in the pocket of her trench coat. How did a woman who'd lived on a farm for twenty years dress so well? 'What's that?'

'The night Emer died . . . Sean strangled her, you said.'

'To keep her quiet. She'd have told Paddy, he'd have shot us both.'

'It was just strange about the pendant. It was mine, you know. I wondered how she got it. It was tangled in her hair, as if it had just been put on her.'

Aisling was very still. Looking at Paula through the fall of her own dark hair.

'I just wondered, that was all. If that wouldn't be a good time to strangle someone, when you had your hands on their neck, putting a necklace on them. When they didn't expect it. And she was in her nightie, as if she was going to bed. Would she have let Sean Conlon get that close to her, stand behind her? And that jumper she had on, the socks – someone dressed her in those, maybe. They didn't want her to be cold in the grave.'

There was a long silence. She was aware of the other woman, the strength it had taken to defy her brother, a killer, at just seventeen, and run across the country. The woman who, as a teenager, had saved her mother's life. 'It's hard to explain what she was like,' Aisling said finally. 'She was . . . wild. Even Mammy was scared of her. The way she was. Like an animal.'

'That must have been hard for you. You weren't much older.'

'No.' She gave nothing away. 'It was hard for all of us. Mammy, Mairead – it wasn't easy, living out there. A god-forsaken place.'

Paula shot her a quick side-look then turned her eyes back to the headstone, Bob's name freshly chiselled. 'I suppose we'll never know what happened.'

'Maybe not,' said Aisling neutrally. She hunched her shoulders up against the breeze. 'I'm sorry about him. He seemed a good man. And I hope you find your mother. If you do . . . tell her I was OK. I don't regret it.'

Paula watched her walk away, thinking that Aisling had also been given her family back, her brother and sister and niece, if they could salvage the remains of a family from the wreckage. Maybe that was something they'd been able to do for each other.

Chapter Forty-Two

London, 2014

So this was the place, then. After so many years of wondering where her mother was. In a bog, buried in a lonely field, or bricked into a wall somewhere. Instead she had been here, in this unremarkable terraced house on the outer edges of the Northern Line.

The letter from Paddy Wallace had come a few weeks after Bob's death, while he waited in prison for his trial. Just a formality. He was going to be locked up for the rest of his life. Tom Dunne, too, was going to be in prison for several years. He and Mairead were the only other ones who'd heard Wallace say Paula's mother was still alive, and she didn't think either of them would be talking. She'd managed to keep it from Corry, too, who definitely suspected something. He wouldn't say, she insisted. He wouldn't say if he knew where she was. For now, Margaret Maguire would remain missing, officially declared dead.

A line of buzzers showed the house was divided into several flats – her mother, if she was still here, was not living the high life. Edward was dead, of course. Had she married him, or was she married again even? Could you do that if your husband was still alive? If you'd been declared legally dead? Paula stood on the other side of the road, hiding behind a parked car. The street was suburban, bland, children's bikes propped up outside houses, wheely bins in front gardens, cheap cars lining the road. She watched the door opposite. It was a bland day too, nothing remarkable. Warmish, but overcast. The English schools hadn't broken up yet, had they? Maybe that was what made it so quiet. She'd left Maggie at day care, and slipped out of the office. With Guy still off on paternity leave, no one really cared what she did. His baby boy, Peter Brooking, was doing well. Soon, she would call to see him. She would bring a gift and say the right things and not tell Guy about Maggie once again. Not for another while at least. Maybe ever.

So here she was. The address Paddy Wallace had sent her in his letter. Why? An apology, of sorts? A surrender in the war he'd kept fighting long after everyone else? Or a way to show her – *look, I found her. I'll be watching, even from prison*. There were other men out there, shadowy figures he'd worked with. But she couldn't think about that.

She clutched it tight, the scrap of lined paper frayed and sweaty in her hand. This was ridiculous. She couldn't just march up to the door and ring the bell. *Hi, Mum, it's me. Guess you're not dead after all?* And how would she be able to control the anger, the years of suffering and waiting her mother had put her through? The lines of pain written onto her father's face. Her own failed relationships, the pills she'd swallowed at eighteen, every mistake she'd ever made. Could it all be traced back? If her mother hadn't gone missing on that ordinary October day, would Paula's life have been different? Or did she only have herself to blame for her bad choices?

She forced her feet to cross the street. One, two, three, four steps. Up the path, noting where it was overgrown with weeds. A rental, by the looks of it. There were four doorbells. She stared at the lowest one for some time, before realising that the people inside would likely notice if she stood there much longer. And that wasn't how she wanted to announce herself. She leaned on it. Nothing at first. She felt relief, maybe. If there was nobody home, she wouldn't have to go through with it. Then the sound of feet on stairs, and the door was wrenched open before Paula had time to prepare herself.

A girl stood there, about twenty or so, the same age as Carly Jones, with a sheet of red hair rippling down her back. She wore a checked shirt and skinny jeans, and had head-phones looped around her neck. 'Yeah?' A London accent.

'I . . .' Words died in Paula's throat. She was doing the maths in her head. 'Um . . . who are you?'

It was rude, just blurting it out, and the girl frowned. 'I'm Aisling,' she said. Then she turned and hollered over her shoulder. 'Mummmm. Some woman's here.' And before Paula could move or speak or do anything except stand there, open-mouthed, the girl had gone pounding back up the stairs, and someone else was coming in from the kitchen, wiping their hands on a dish towel, in shadow moving into the light, and then she saw who it was.

Margaret

2014

Aisling was at the door, talking to someone. A hawker of some kind or a Jehovah's Witness, they got them a lot round this way. Or someone worse? Aisling had never learned to be as cautious as Margaret would have liked. For her, the fear had never quite gone away, although things had been quiet since Edward died. The current flat was even further out of London. She wondered why she even clung on there, when she could have moved anywhere. Maybe because it was the last place Edward had been. Maybe because it was Aisling's home, and she didn't want her daughter to have to keep running, looking over her shoulder. It was eight years since Edward had gone and no one had come after them in that time. Maybe they thought she was dead at that farm. Her thoughts turned to it often, the teenage girl who'd given her back her life, who she'd named her daughter after. It was the least she could do when without that other Aisling the child would have died with her in that barn, buried in the claggy soil, a forgotten grave with no name. She hoped the girl had made it away safe. Sometimes she even prayed, though why or who to, she didn't know.

Her own Aisling was still talking. Margaret set the dish she was drying on the rack, feeling the draft sweep in from the road, the air stale and dusty.

'Muuumm,' her daughter was calling. She went out, flicking the dish towel over her shoulder, mouth open to say something about shutting the door, or chase whoever it was away, muttering a warning about not opening the door to strangers. Had she forgotten the rules in the years since her father died?

And then she saw.

The woman in the door was instantly recognisable. How could she not be, when it was like looking at her thirty-something self? She'd been not much older when she'd had to run. The woman wore jeans and brown leather sandals, her nails unpainted, her red hair in a messy braid over one shoulder. Blazer, T-shirt. No make-up. Margaret took her in, and saw the stranger do the same to her. Her motherly clothes, hands reddened from the dishes, hair frizzy in the heat.

'Hi,' said the woman, and the Ballyterrin accent clashed on Margaret's ears. So long since she'd heard it. She was aware of Aisling standing on the stairs, puzzled, and of how alike the two were. Of course they were alike. There was nothing surprising there.

'Oh,' said Margaret. Her hands clenched, rising up despite herself to touch the young woman's face. 'It's you.'

Epilogue

Three months later

'Where the hell are you taking me, Maguire? I thought we'd
be seeing some sights. Tower of London, Buckingham
Palace, that kind of jazz. Not the outer ring road.'

'Shh, will you. She's asleep.' Paula and Aidan both turned
to look at Maggie in the back, passed out in her car seat, the
motion of driving working like a charm. She'd been wild
with excitement at a day trip with Daddy, ice creams and
lunch in a café and a visit to Hamleys, and now she'd crossed
over into exhaustion, thankfully without passing through
tears and tantrums on the way. Paula had been wary ever
since Aidan had come back into their lives, getting out of
prison when Paddy Wallace was convicted for killing Sean
Conlon that night, partly on evidence from Dunne, who was
hoping for a lighter sentence.

Paula's first instinct, of course, had been to run. She
hadn't been sure what kind of Aidan would be coming home
after all that time in prison. The darkness in him had been
fed – could he still be Daddy, who read stories in funny
voices and dressed up to make Maggie laugh? What kind of
damage would it do to the little girl, all the confusion and

upset? So Paula had thought it best to take Maggie back to London and carry on with her job, letting Aidan visit when he felt able. Once again, she'd left Pat and PJ to pick up the pieces. She'd left Saoirse to recover from her ordeal, although the baby was fine, thank God; it was all fine and she was due in four months and the danger time was over. If it ever could be truly over. If there was ever such a thing as safety. Gradually, they'd worked up to visits with Aidan. First in a hotel, then staying with them in the flat. Maggie had taken it in her stride, as if she'd known all along her daddy would come back to her. And now here they were, the three of them in a rented Fiat Punto on the outskirts of the city, a drab and dusty suburb with nothing to distinguish it at all.

'Seriously, though, where are we?' He looked round at the nondescript street she'd parked the car on. 'I don't think much of your tour guiding, Maguire.'

Maguire. The simple joy of hearing him say her name again, in his light, teasing tone. To be back within touching distance, to be able to pick up his hand or swat him when he made a joke or tell him to scoop up Maggie before she wandered into the road looking at a dog or something. Things she'd taken for granted before she'd lost them. She told herself she never would again, but life didn't work like that. Probably soon they'd be back to their daily routine – Aidan had some freelancing lined up for an investigative website – her at work, Maggie going to school soon. Life carrying on. She couldn't wait for it. A normal life. A normal family. Not much to ask for.

She turned to him. 'You love your mammy, right?'

He looked puzzled. 'Yeah, course.'

'If I said there was something that you couldn't tell her, I mean not ever, would you be able to do that?'

'What kind of thing?'

'You have to decide first. You can never say a word about it to your mammy, not a single word. It'd destroy her if you did. And Dad. So think about it before you answer.'

He squinted. 'Is it something important? To you, I mean?'

'Of course it is.'

'And I could never breathe a word about it.'

'Not one word. I'm deadly serious.'

'Well, then, sure I can. There's plenty I've never told my mammy, believe me, Maguire. Starting with what you and I used to get up to in the front room when she was out making the tea.'

She didn't join in his wicked smile. He'd been almost feverishly playful all day, grabbing fun and freedom with both hands. He too might crash like Maggie if it all got too much for him. 'Promise me, Aidan. Before we go any further.'

'I promise. This is all very mysterious, Maguire.'

She thought about it for a moment. Aidan had lied to her before. He was not perfect. But then, she was still lying to Guy Brooking about her daughter's paternity. And perhaps she wouldn't be able to keep this secret forever, maybe it would come out sometime. But she had to at least try.

She turned the engine off. Maggie was still asleep. Maybe she should have left her at home, waited another day for this particular introduction. But it didn't seem fair. Not when everyone had already waited so long. And if she had learned anything from Bob – never to be thought of without a stab to the heart – it was that you couldn't be sure you'd always have more time with the people you loved. She unbuckled her seat belt, glancing across the road to the number 41. 'Come on then,' she said. 'Get Maggie out. There's somebody you both need to meet.'

Acknowledgements

So here it is – the last Paula Maguire. I'd like to thank everyone who has worked on the books with me, including Ali Hope, Vicki Mellor, Toby Jones, Jemima Forrester, Darcy Nicholson, Kitty Stogdon, Kate Stephenson, Emily Griffin, Sara Adams, Oli Munson, Fran Barrie, Caitlin Raynor, Jo Liddiard, Millie Seaward, Veronique Norton, Sarah Bance for top-notch copyediting, and my wonderful agent Diana Beaumont, who's always there with a helping hand or wise suggestion. I'm sorry if I've forgotten anyone.

Thank you also to everyone has read the books, stocked them in shops, and taken the time to review or contact me about them. Special thanks to David Torrans in ace Belfast bookshop No Alibis, who has always championed me.

I'd also like to thank the amazing crime writing community – way too many to list – for their quotes and support, as well as many fun times in the bar. Thanks as well to my friends and family, for reading and asking when the next Paula was going to be ready.

Thank you to the contact at the ICLVR, who took the time to speak to me about their procedures. I have intentionally exaggerated a few things for dramatic purposes, and any mistakes are of course mine.

That's it from Paula for the time being at least – thanks for following along on this six-year journey with me. As always, I would love to hear from you, either via www.inkstains.co.uk, or on Twitter @inkstainsclaire.

Claire xx

'CLAIRE McGOWAN WILL UNDOUBTEDLY
BECOME A MAJOR NAME IN CRIME FICTION'
PETER JAMES

CLAIRE
McGOWAN

The Lost

Not everyone who's missing is lost

When two teenage girls go missing along the Irish border,
forensic psychologist Paula Maguire has to return to the
hometown she left years before. Swirling with rumour
and secrets, the town is gripped by fear of a serial killer.
But the truth could be even darker.

Not everyone who's lost wants to be found

Surrounded by people and places she tried to forget, Paula
digs into the cases as the truth twists further away. What's the
link with two other disappearances from 1985? And why does
everything lead back to the town's dark past – including the
reasons her own mother went missing years before?

Nothing is what it seems

As the shocking truth is revealed, Paula learns that
sometimes, it's better not to find what you've lost.

978 0 7553 8640 6

HEADLINE

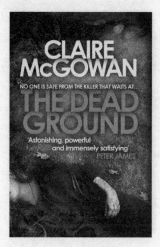

Stolen. Missing. Dead . . .

Forensic psychologist Paula Maguire, already wrestling
with the hardest decision of her life, is forced to put her
own problems on hold when she's asked to help find a baby
taken from a local hospital.

Then the brutal, ritualistic murder of a woman found lying
on a remote stone circle indicates a connection to the
kidnapping and Paula knows that they will have to move
fast if they are to find the person responsible.

When another child is taken and a pregnant woman goes
missing, Paula finds herself caught up in a deadly hunt
for a killer determined to leave no trace, and discovers every
decision she makes really is a matter of life and death . . .

978 1 4722 0439 4

HEADLINE

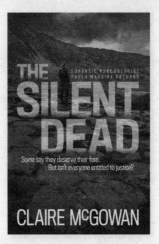

Victim: Male. Mid-thirties. 5'7".
Cause of death: Hanging. Initial impression – murder.
ID: Mickey Doyle. Suspected terrorist and member
of the Mayday Five.

The officers at the crime scene know exactly who the victim is.
Doyle was one of five suspected bombers who caused
the deaths of sixteen people.

The remaining four are also missing and when a second body is
found, decapitated, it's clear they are being killed by the same
methods their victims suffered.

Forensic psychologist Paula Maguire is assigned the case
but she is up against the clock – both personally and
professionally.

With moral boundaries blurred between victim and
perpetrator, will Paula be able to find those responsible?
After all, even killers deserve justice, don't they?

978 1 4722 0442 4

Victim: Female. Twenty-two years of age.
Reason for investigation: Missing person.
ID: Alice Morgan. Student. Last seen at a remote religious shrine in Ballyterrin.

Alice Morgan's disappearance raises immediate questions for forensic psychologist Paula Maguire. Alice, the daughter of a life peer in the Home Office, has vanished along with a holy relic – the bones of a saint – and the only trace is the bloodstains on the altar.

With no body to confirm death, the pressure in this high-profile case is all-consuming, and Paula knows that she will have to put her own life, including her imminent marriage, on hold, if they are to find the truth.

A connection to a decades-old murder immediately indicates that all may not be as it seems; as the summer heat rises and tempers fray, can Alice be found or will they learn that those hungry for vengeance may be the most savage of all?

978 1 4722 2812 3

HEADLINE

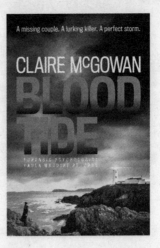

A missing couple. A lurking killer. A perfect storm.

CLAIRE McGOWAN

BLOOD TIDE

Called in to investigate the disappearance of a young couple during a violent storm, Paula Maguire, forensic psychologist, has mixed feelings about going back to Bone Island. Her last family holiday as a child was spent on its beautiful, remote beaches and returning brings back haunting memories of her long-lost mother.

It soon becomes clear that outsiders aren't welcome on the island, and with no choice but to investigate the local community, Paula soon suspects foul play, realising that the islanders are hiding secrets from her, and each other.

With another storm fast approaching, Paula is faced with a choice. Leave alive or risk being trapped with a killer on an inescapable island, as the blood tide rushes in . . .

978 1 4722 2821 5

HEADLINE